5-G IMPACT

DOING LIFE WITH GOD IN THE PICTURE

LARGE GROUP
PROGRAMMING GUIDEBOOK

WILLOW CREEK
RESOURCES®

LARGE GROUP PROGRAMMING:
BIBLE TEACHING,
DRAMA, AND MUSIC

5-G IMPACT
DOING LIFE WITH GOD IN THE PICTURE

LARGE GROUP PROGRAMMING GUIDEBOOK

Copyright © 2001 Willow Creek Community Church

Requests for information should be addressed to:
Willow Creek Association
P.O. Box 3188
Barrington, IL 60011-3188

Executive Director of Promiseland: Sue Miller

Executive Director of Promiseland Publishing: Nancy Raney

Creative Team: Deanna Armentrout, Arnez Bonsol, Pat Cimo, Rodger Kettering, Holly Delich, Sue Miller, Dean Peterson, Aaron Reynolds, Kathy Sanford, Susan Shadid, Tom Swartz, Christy Weygandt

Creative Contributor: Dugan Sherbondy

Editorial Team: Lisanne Kaufmann, Janet Quinn, Nancy Raney

Designer: Diane Doty
Cover Illustrator: Antonio Cangemi
Interior Illustrators: Antonio Cangemi, Dave Cutler, Diane Doty, Roberta Polfus

Many thanks to: the Promiseland staff as a whole who continually contributes, our volunteers who help put supplies together each weekend, and the volunteers who try out, test, and evaluate this curriculum to give us feedback along the way.

Printed in the United States of America.

WILLOW CREEK
RESOURCES®

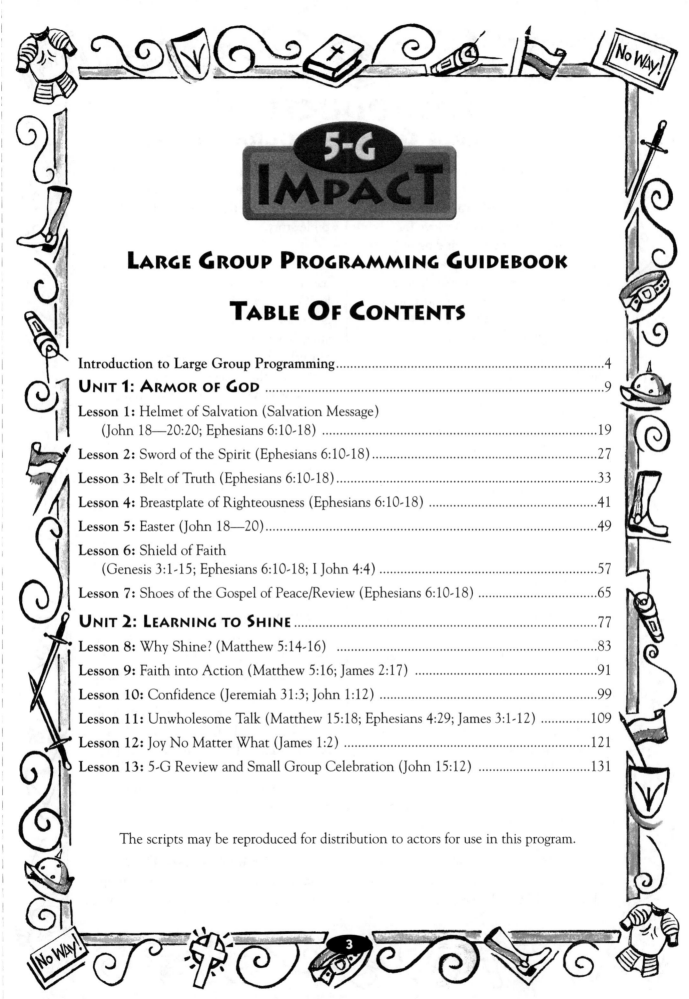

5-G IMPACT

LARGE GROUP PROGRAMMING GUIDEBOOK

TABLE OF CONTENTS

The scripts may be reproduced for distribution to actors for use in this program.

3

INTRODUCTION
TO LARGE GROUP PROGRAMMING

Creating a 5-G children's ministry includes providing a place for kids to experience **Growth** and **Grace.** We want kids to grow in knowledge of God and His love for them, grow in their understanding of His purposes—which include a plan for each of them, and grow in character so they are transformed by the power of Christ. Kids will have the opportunity to experience **Grace** through the presentation of the salvation message, and will be encouraged to extend God's grace to others.

The Large Group Program is designed for children to spend 25-30 minutes of each lesson hour hearing the Bible taught in relevant and creative ways and experiencing contemporary music that reinforces Bible truths. When children step into your Large Group Program, they ought to feel a sense of anticipation. This is a high-energy time that is going to capture the imagination of the children and open their eyes and hearts to Bible truths that will impact their lives in incredible ways. The Promiseland Curriculum values of teaching the Bible creatively, and being child-targeted, relevant, and fun, are all expressed in the Large Group Program.

Prior to the actual teaching of the Bible story is a short introduction called PRE-TEACH. This introduces the children to the Bible truth that is going to be presented in the Bible teaching. Following PRE-TEACH is the actual presentation of the Bible story. This is called the TEACH. After the Bible story has been creatively presented, the teacher wraps up with a POST-TEACH. During this time the teacher summarizes the Key Concept and begins to help children understand the Bible truth that comes out of the Bible story.

Each lesson of the Promiseland Curriculum has three objectives:
KNOW WHAT: This objective is a description of what the children will know after they hear the Bible story.
SO WHAT: This objective introduces the Bible truth that comes out of the Bible story.
NOW WHAT: This objective challenges the children to relevantly apply the Bible truth to their lives.

Usually, the KNOW WHAT and SO WHAT Objectives are achieved during the Large Group Program, and the NOW WHAT is achieved during Small Group time. Below is an example of the objectives for a Promiseland Curriculum 4th/5th Grade lesson:

KNOW WHAT (LG): Children will hear that the Bible originated with God and is useful for guiding our lives.
SO WHAT (LG): Children will learn that the Bible originated with God, was given to us through chosen people, and is the only book that is God's Word.
NOW WHAT (SG): Children will participate in an activity that contrasts the messages popular culture gives us with the wisdom found in the Bible.

LARGE GROUP PROGRAMMING TEAM

What happens during the Large Group Program comes under the direction of the

Large Group Teacher. The Large Group Teacher is a sincere believer to whom God has given the spiritual gifts of leadership, teaching, or creative communication. He or she is comfortable in an up-front role, energetic, and able to lead a large group of children. The Large Group Teacher is the person who will lead PRE-TEACH and POST-TEACH. Depending on the teaching method that is used, the Large Group Teacher may also have a part of the TEACH program.

The Large Group Teacher or Producer develops a team of volunteers who:
• teach the Bible creatively to the children
• present live-action or video-taped dramas
• lead the worship/singing time
• review biblical principles with games and scripts presented in the curriculum
• introduce and teach the key Bible verse for the lesson
• work with the Administrator to acquire materials and teaching props needed each week for the Large Group Program

The majority of the Promiseland Curriculum lessons can be taught with 1-3 people participating in the TEACH segment. These people can rotate from week to week, depending upon how the Bible story is presented. Plan ahead and schedule people in advance to have them help with the Bible story presentations.

LARGE GROUP PROGRAMMING SETS AND ENVIRONMENT

The environment of the Large Group room is important. As kids enter your room, you want them to think, "Something exciting is going to happen here!" "This place is for kids." "I wonder what this is about."

The sets for the teaching area can be as elaborate or as simple as your resources will allow. The value of excellence asks that the best is done to honor God with the resources that are available. Set and prop suggestions are provided for each lesson in the Promiseland Curriculum. Some units use the same set in each lesson of the unit. Other times, there might be some set elements that can be used several times during the 13-week quarter. Look ahead and make plans to acquire and then store the set items that can be used again.

Suggestions for enhancing the Large Group Program:
• Drape fabric from the ceiling to the floor to provide a backdrop.
• Use covered boxes or risers to add some height to sections of the teaching area.
• Build a platform area (about 8" off the floor) that will serve as your teaching stage.
• Use the entire room for teaching. Sometimes the lessons are presented with stations around the room to which the teacher moves. Sometimes both the front and the back of the room are used to present the lesson. Finally, there might be times when the teacher will present the lesson from a stool placed in the middle of the room.
• Use lighting to create teaching moments.

It would be best to have the Large Group Program in a room separate from the Activity Stations. If that is not possible, designate one part of the room as your Large Group Program area and make sure it is separate from the Activity Stations. Or, place the Activity Stations around the walls of the room and use the center of the room as the Large Group Program area.

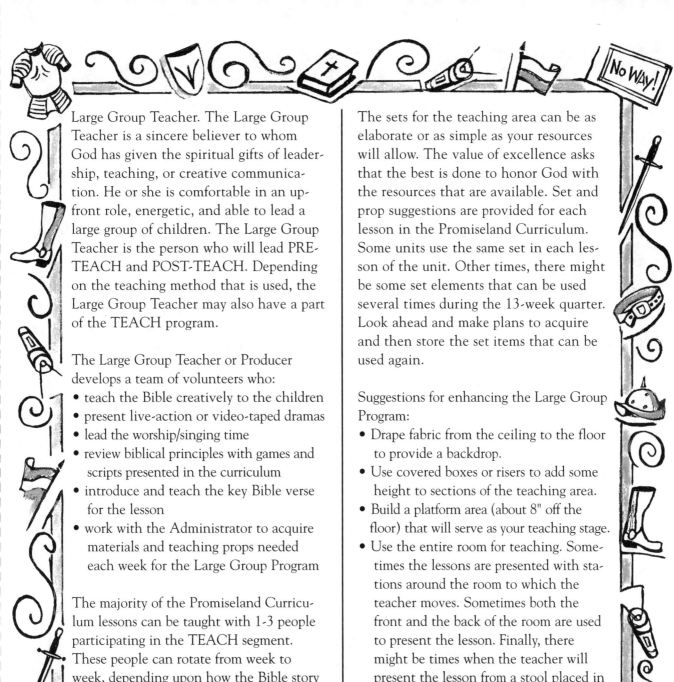

LARGE GROUP PROGRAM

The elements of the Large Group Program are designed to engage a variety of the senses and learning styles of children.

BIBLE TEACHING

The Bible is taught in various creative and relevant ways. Some of the teaching methods used in the Promiseland Curriculum include: drama, video, game shows, interactive discovery, storytelling, interviews, and games. The method and the presentation style will be appropriate for the age level the curriculum is designed to reach.

The Promiseland Curriculum provides a creative approach for teaching the Bible. Optional ideas are given for ways the presentation could be enhanced with some technical features, staging, video, or additional people.

An important key to a successful presentation of the Bible teaching is rehearsal. Memorize the lines and schedule time during the week to meet together and practice the teaching. Children lose interest or don't take things seriously when the presentation is poorly done due to lack of preparation.

Two or three weeks of the 13-week quarter will have the Bible story presented with the video included in the Promiseland Curriculum Kit.

KEY CONCEPT/BIBLE VERSE

Each Promiseland Curriculum lesson has a Key Concept and a Bible Verse. The Key Concept is the "point" of the lesson. It includes the Bible truth and a life application. For example, a Key Concept might be: *God is forgiving, so I can forgive others.* The

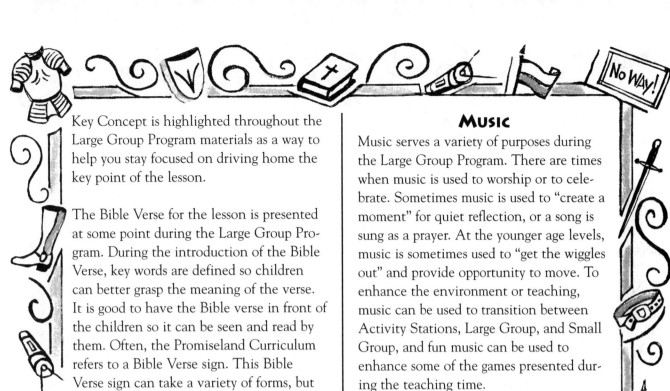

Key Concept is highlighted throughout the Large Group Program materials as a way to help you stay focused on driving home the key point of the lesson.

The Bible Verse for the lesson is presented at some point during the Large Group Program. During the introduction of the Bible Verse, key words are defined so children can better grasp the meaning of the verse. It is good to have the Bible verse in front of the children so it can be seen and read by them. Often, the Promiseland Curriculum refers to a Bible Verse sign. This Bible Verse sign can take a variety of forms, but the goal is to have the Bible Verse in front of the children. Consider some of the following ideas for visually presenting the Bible Verse:

1. Use a PowerPoint® presentation and project the verse onto large screens. This presentation allows you to move words in and out of the verse while it is being taught.

2. Create a large Bible Verse Board. Cover it with felt and stand it on a large easel. Each week put the Bible verse on pieces of paper (one word per piece) and put Velcro® on the back of each piece. This allows you to put the verse on the Bible Verse Board, introducing the words and giving explanation as you go.

3. Have someone who is able to print neatly write the words on a large flip chart or posterboard.

4. Write the Bible verse on an overhead transparency. Use an overhead projector to project the verse onto a screen or wall.

MUSIC

Music serves a variety of purposes during the Large Group Program. There are times when music is used to worship or to celebrate. Sometimes music is used to "create a moment" for quiet reflection, or a song is sung as a prayer. At the younger age levels, music is sometimes used to "get the wiggles out" and provide opportunity to move. To enhance the environment or teaching, music can be used to transition between Activity Stations, Large Group, and Small Group, and fun music can be used to enhance some of the games presented during the teaching time.

Because of the variety of uses for music, music is presented at different times during the Large Group Program. Placing music at different times is one way of keeping the program fresh and unpredictable from week to week.

The songs suggested in the Promiseland Curriculum are included on the Promiseland music CDs. The CD entitled *Doing Life with God in the Picture* has music created especially for this Promiseland Curriculum. Some of the Promiseland songs have music charts available. The CDs can be ordered by calling 1-800-570-9812, filling out the order form on the User Card, or visiting www.PromiselandOnline.com.

SPECIAL FEATURE

Included in your curriculum kit is the *Learning to Shine* video used to creatively assist the Large Group Teacher in teaching Lessons 8-12. The goal of the video is to teach kids to shine their light in a dark world.

LARGE GROUP PRODUCER/ TEACHER'S CHECKLIST

Below is a list of items to consider as you prepare your Large Group Programs:

❍ Decide how you will set up your teaching area for each unit or lesson and acquire the necessary items.

❍ Determine how children will know where to sit. You may wish to place masking tape on the floor, hang an identification banner over each area from the ceiling, or post an identification flag at each Small Group area on the floor.

❍ Decide what music you want to play while kids arrive and exit Large Group.

❍ Refer to the supply list that details all the equipment, props, and materials needed for each lesson presentation. Then, work with the Administrator to obtain each of these items. If equipment is needed, work with the Administrator to decide who will be responsible for running each piece of equipment during the Large Group Program.

❍ Practice! We want to give our very best to God! Be sure the volunteers come prepared. Encourage your actors to act and talk like the people they are portraying. Set up times for rehearsal and encourage them to practice and memorize at home.

❍ Begin to evaluate how technical features such as lighting, sound effects, and video could enhance the Large Group Program. Is there someone in the congregation who might have a vision for this and who could contribute some time and expertise to building this part of the ministry?

❍ Determine who will lead each Large Group Program by welcoming the children, communicating the PRE-TEACH and POST-TEACH materials, introducing the TEACH time, leading the children in music, and closing in prayer.

❍ If the Large Group Program area needs to be cleared during the week, decide how props, sets, and other supplies will be stored.

UNIT 1 OVERVIEW
ARMOR OF GOD

UNIT SUMMARY

This first unit of the Spring Quarter teaches kids that there is a battle between God and Satan. God's mission is to help as many people in this world as possible choose to believe in and follow Him, and grow Christians into the people He wants them to be. Satan's mission is to prevent people from choosing to believe in and follow God, and prevent Christians from growing into the people God wants them to be. Children will have an opportunity in Lesson 1 to choose to become believers and be on God's side in the battle. They will then learn that when they become believers, they have access to the full Armor of God to help them stand firm against the schemes of the devil. Lesson 1 teaches kids to put on the Helmet of Salvation which reminds them that they are in God's family and on His side in the battle. Lesson 2 teaches that the Sword of the Spirit, the Bible, helps children discern right from wrong when they are attacked by Satan. Lesson 3 teaches kids to wear the Belt of Truth which helps them distinguish the difference between God's truth and Satan's lies. Lesson 4 teaches children that putting on the Breastplate of Righteousness—righteous actions—protects their heart and character from Satan's blows. Lesson 5 is the Easter story, telling the amazing lengths God went to make sure nothing would stop His love from being expressed to us. Lesson 6 teaches kids to put on the Shield of Faith to defend themselves against Satan's arrows of attacks on their faith. And finally, Lesson 7 teaches children the importance of putting on the Shoes of the Gospel of Peace so they will be ready to share the good news of Jesus with their lost friends. A review of each piece of the Armor of God is done in this lesson as well.

Armor of God:	How it is used:
Helmet of Salvation	Assures believers of salvation
Sword of the Spirit	Discerns right from wrong
Belt of Truth	Distinguishes between God's truth and Satan's lies
Breastplate of Righteousness	Protects heart and character
Shield of Faith	Defends against Satan's arrows of attacks on faith
Shoes of the Gospel of Peace	Enables good news of Jesus to be delivered

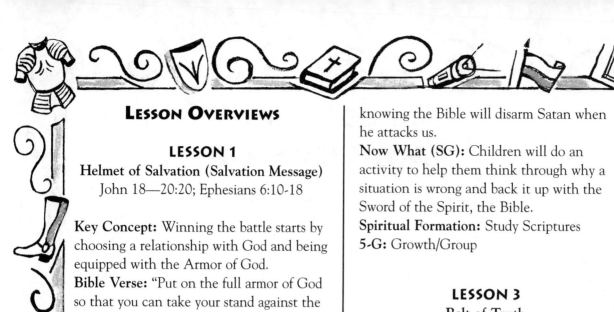

LESSON OVERVIEWS

LESSON 1
Helmet of Salvation (Salvation Message)
John 18—20:20; Ephesians 6:10-18

Key Concept: Winning the battle starts by choosing a relationship with God and being equipped with the Armor of God.
Bible Verse: "Put on the full armor of God so that you can take your stand against the devil's schemes." Ephesians 6:11
Know What (LG): Children will hear how we need to have a relationship with God and put on the full Armor of God.
So What (LG): Children will learn that Jesus died to offer eternal life to everyone who believes. The Helmet of Salvation assures us that our salvation can never be taken away.
Now What (SG): Children will discuss God's plan for salvation and have an opportunity to ask questions about what it means. Children who have already made this decision will have a chance to share their story and review the Bridge Illustration.
Spiritual Formation: Grace
5-G: Grace/Group

LESSON 2
Sword of the Spirit
Ephesians 6:10-18

Key Concept: Winning the battle means knowing our Bible so that we know right from wrong.
Bible Verse: "Put on the full armor of God so that you can take your stand against the devil's schemes." Ephesians 6:11
Know What (LG): Children will hear how the Sword of the Spirit, the Bible, helps us know right from wrong.
So What (LG): Children will learn that knowing the Bible will disarm Satan when he attacks us.
Now What (SG): Children will do an activity to help them think through why a situation is wrong and back it up with the Sword of the Spirit, the Bible.
Spiritual Formation: Study Scriptures
5-G: Growth/Group

LESSON 3
Belt of Truth
Ephesians 6:10-18

Key Concept: Winning the battle means knowing the difference between Satan's lies and God's truth.
Bible Verse: "Put on the full armor of God so that you can take your stand against the devil's schemes." Ephesians 6:11
Know What (LG): Children will hear how the Belt of Truth helps us in the battle by showing us the difference between Satan's lies and God's truth.
So What (LG): Children will learn that God is the source of truth.
Now What (SG): Children will participate in an activity that will help them know the difference between Satan's lies and God's truth.
Spiritual Formation: Study Scripture
5-G: Growth/Grace/Group

LESSON 4
Breastplate of Righteousness
Ephesians 6:10-18

Key Concept: Winning the battle means having strong character by obeying God's Word.
Bible Verse: "Put on the full armor of God so that you can take your stand against the devil's schemes." Ephesians 6:11

10

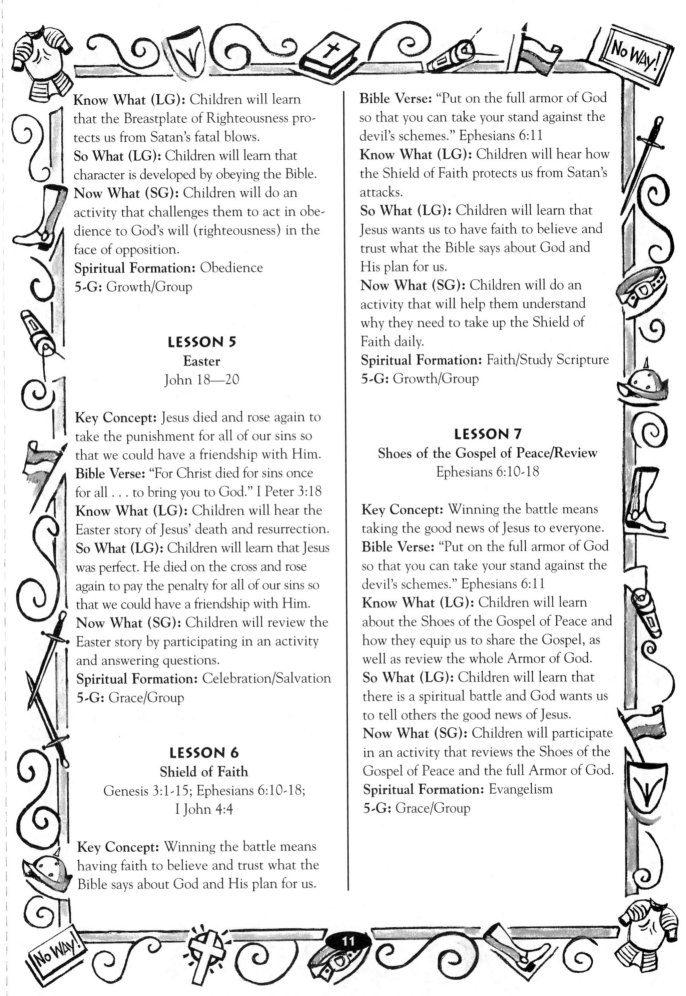

Know What (LG): Children will learn that the Breastplate of Righteousness protects us from Satan's fatal blows.

So What (LG): Children will learn that character is developed by obeying the Bible.

Now What (SG): Children will do an activity that challenges them to act in obedience to God's will (righteousness) in the face of opposition.

Spiritual Formation: Obedience

5-G: Growth/Group

LESSON 5
Easter
John 18—20

Key Concept: Jesus died and rose again to take the punishment for all of our sins so that we could have a friendship with Him.

Bible Verse: "For Christ died for sins once for all . . . to bring you to God." I Peter 3:18

Know What (LG): Children will hear the Easter story of Jesus' death and resurrection.

So What (LG): Children will learn that Jesus was perfect. He died on the cross and rose again to pay the penalty for all of our sins so that we could have a friendship with Him.

Now What (SG): Children will review the Easter story by participating in an activity and answering questions.

Spiritual Formation: Celebration/Salvation

5-G: Grace/Group

LESSON 6
Shield of Faith
Genesis 3:1-15; Ephesians 6:10-18;
I John 4:4

Key Concept: Winning the battle means having faith to believe and trust what the Bible says about God and His plan for us.

Bible Verse: "Put on the full armor of God so that you can take your stand against the devil's schemes." Ephesians 6:11

Know What (LG): Children will hear how the Shield of Faith protects us from Satan's attacks.

So What (LG): Children will learn that Jesus wants us to have faith to believe and trust what the Bible says about God and His plan for us.

Now What (SG): Children will do an activity that will help them understand why they need to take up the Shield of Faith daily.

Spiritual Formation: Faith/Study Scripture

5-G: Growth/Group

LESSON 7
Shoes of the Gospel of Peace/Review
Ephesians 6:10-18

Key Concept: Winning the battle means taking the good news of Jesus to everyone.

Bible Verse: "Put on the full armor of God so that you can take your stand against the devil's schemes." Ephesians 6:11

Know What (LG): Children will learn about the Shoes of the Gospel of Peace and how they equip us to share the Gospel, as well as review the whole Armor of God.

So What (LG): Children will learn that there is a spiritual battle and God wants us to tell others the good news of Jesus.

Now What (SG): Children will participate in an activity that reviews the Shoes of the Gospel of Peace and the full Armor of God.

Spiritual Formation: Evangelism

5-G: Grace/Group

LARGE GROUP PRESENTATION SUMMARY

Each week, the goal of the Large Group Program is to help kids imagine they are in a medieval times setting. The teachers present the teaching in the middle of the room and children sit in a circle along the outer edge of the room. This presentation style helps kids feel like they are in a medieval times arena. The *5-G Impact* video, used three weeks in this unit, illustrates medieval-type armor as well as battle techniques that were used in that period of time. The first week of this Spring Quarter is Salvation Weekend. The salvation message in Lesson 1 is told using banners with words on them that represent each step of the salvation story. After Small Group Time, kids will come back to celebrate with worship and music. They will then watch the *5-G Impact* video which illustrates the importance of wearing a helmet in medieval times and how as believers, we wear the Helmet of Salvation. The *5-G Impact* video in Lesson 2 is used to demonstrate the use of the sword in medieval times as well as how we can use the Sword of the Spirit in our lives. In Lesson 3, an obstacle course challenge, made of tires or inner tubes, shows kids the importance of wearing the Belt of Truth so we don't get tripped up in lies. In Lesson 4, the game Warrior's Challenge, involving six kids, is played to review the past few weeks. The Breastplate of Righteousness is then taught by having one teacher play the role of Satan and the other teacher practice defending. The Easter story in Lesson 5 is told using stations around the room with props at each station that represent part of the story. In Lesson 6, the *5-G Impact* video is used to illustrate the use of the shield in medieval times as well as how we can use the Shield of Faith. Finally, in Lesson 7, kids will divide into two armies where they will role-play a situation to deliver a message. They will learn the importance of the Shoes of the Gospel of Peace as one child runs through an obstacle course of rough terrain. Children will also play Warrior's Challenge II in which they will hear situations and then select the Armor piece that can be used to defend themselves in that situation. This activity will review all of the Armor of God pieces.

LARGE GROUP HELPFUL HINTS

1. In this unit, four medieval-looking banners are used to decorate the Large Group room. They are simply made by cutting various shapes out of different colored pieces of felt, and sewing, gluing, or using Velcro® to stick the pieces of felt onto a larger piece of felt. You may then choose to hang the banners from the ceiling or hang them on the wall. Ideas for designs are included on the following pages. Be sure to store the banners carefully so they can be used each week.

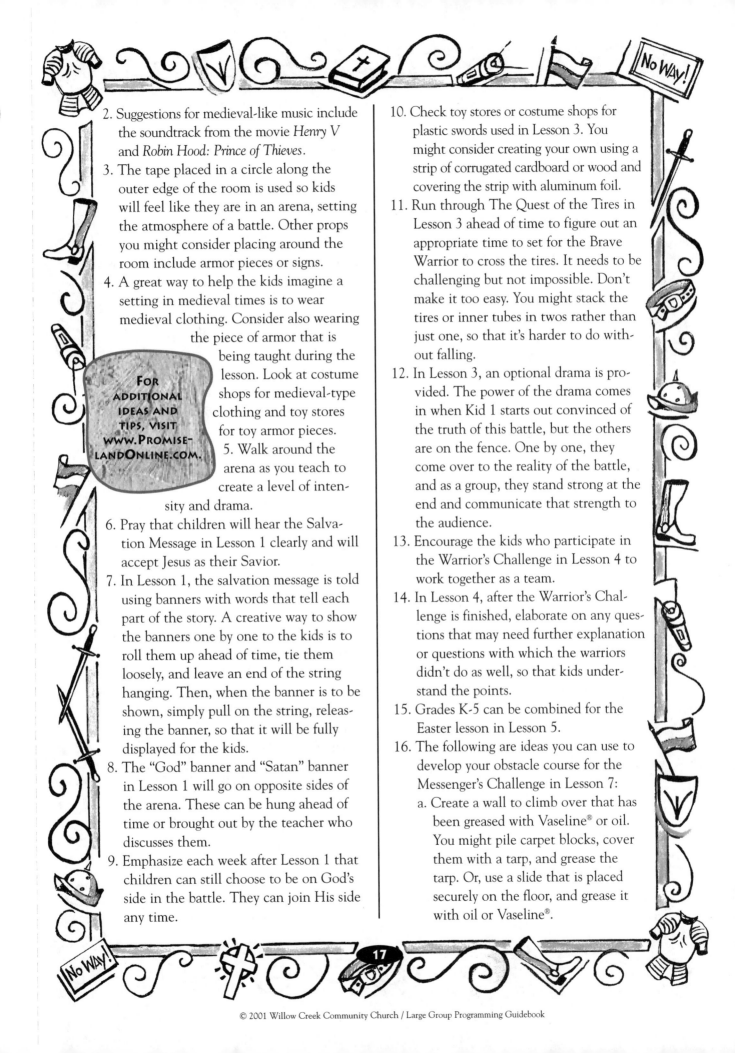

2. Suggestions for medieval-like music include the soundtrack from the movie *Henry V* and *Robin Hood: Prince of Thieves*.

3. The tape placed in a circle along the outer edge of the room is used so kids will feel like they are in an arena, setting the atmosphere of a battle. Other props you might consider placing around the room include armor pieces or signs.

4. A great way to help the kids imagine a setting in medieval times is to wear medieval clothing. Consider also wearing the piece of armor that is being taught during the lesson. Look at costume shops for medieval-type clothing and toy stores for toy armor pieces.

5. Walk around the arena as you teach to create a level of intensity and drama.

FOR ADDITIONAL IDEAS AND TIPS, VISIT WWW.PROMISE-LANDONLINE.COM.

6. Pray that children will hear the Salvation Message in Lesson 1 clearly and will accept Jesus as their Savior.

7. In Lesson 1, the salvation message is told using banners with words that tell each part of the story. A creative way to show the banners one by one to the kids is to roll them up ahead of time, tie them loosely, and leave an end of the string hanging. Then, when the banner is to be shown, simply pull on the string, releasing the banner, so that it will be fully displayed for the kids.

8. The "God" banner and "Satan" banner in Lesson 1 will go on opposite sides of the arena. These can be hung ahead of time or brought out by the teacher who discusses them.

9. Emphasize each week after Lesson 1 that children can still choose to be on God's side in the battle. They can join His side any time.

10. Check toy stores or costume shops for plastic swords used in Lesson 3. You might consider creating your own using a strip of corrugated cardboard or wood and covering the strip with aluminum foil.

11. Run through The Quest of the Tires in Lesson 3 ahead of time to figure out an appropriate time to set for the Brave Warrior to cross the tires. It needs to be challenging but not impossible. Don't make it too easy. You might stack the tires or inner tubes in twos rather than just one, so that it's harder to do without falling.

12. In Lesson 3, an optional drama is provided. The power of the drama comes in when Kid 1 starts out convinced of the truth of this battle, but the others are on the fence. One by one, they come over to the reality of the battle, and as a group, they stand strong at the end and communicate that strength to the audience.

13. Encourage the kids who participate in the Warrior's Challenge in Lesson 4 to work together as a team.

14. In Lesson 4, after the Warrior's Challenge is finished, elaborate on any questions that may need further explanation or questions with which the warriors didn't do as well, so that kids understand the points.

15. Grades K-5 can be combined for the Easter lesson in Lesson 5.

16. The following are ideas you can use to develop your obstacle course for the Messenger's Challenge in Lesson 7:

a. Create a wall to climb over that has been greased with Vaseline® or oil. You might pile carpet blocks, cover them with a tarp, and grease the tarp. Or, use a slide that is placed securely on the floor, and grease it with oil or Vaseline®.

b. Create a rocky path of landscaping rocks.

c. Create a low bridge made by placing a pole on two supports, and grease it with Vaseline®.

SMALL GROUP SUMMARY

For Salvation Weekend Lesson 1, two activities are provided for Small Group time—"Leader's Story" and "Review My Story and Bridge Illustration." The first activity will give children an opportunity to hear their leader's story of how he/she accepted Jesus as his/her Savior. The second activity will give kids who have already accepted Jesus as their Savior a chance to practice telling their story to one another. In Lesson 2, kids will do an activity called "Getting to the Truth!" where they will hear peer pressure and practice getting truth from the Bible. Children will play "Belt of Truth Relay" in Lesson 3 where they will defend against Satan's lies using God's truth and use a tape measure to reel the truth in to their side. In Lesson 4, kids will play "One Righteous Knight" where they will each play roles and learn how to do the obedient thing and be righteous in the midst of many choices. In Lesson 5, children will do an "Easter Story Puzzle" in which they will arrange pictures representing parts of the Easter story into the order in which they happened in the story. In Lesson 6, kids will play "Battlefield Dodge Ball" where they will practice shielding themselves against balls representing Satan's attacks on our faith. Finally, in Lesson 7, children will do an activity in which they will step onto various squares placed on the floor that represent attacks they must defend against or lost people they must try to reach.

SMALL GROUP HELPFUL HINTS

1. For Lesson 1, if kids have already heard your story of when you accepted Jesus as Savior, consider inviting a Christian friend, family member, teenager, or other member of your congregation to share his/her story. Give him/her the audio cassette "Leading Children to Christ." You can order it by calling 800-570-9812. Be prepared yourself as well to lead children to Christ.

2. Write personal notes after Lesson 1 to kids who crossed the line of faith as well as to kids who did not cross the line of faith. Let them know they can ask you questions and that you are there for them.

3. Take some time to discuss the situations in the activity "Getting to the Truth" in Lesson 2 if kids want to share stories or have questions about how to better apply the truth in their lives.

4. Tell children in the activity "Belt of Truth Relay" in Lesson 3 to be careful when they are using the tape measures so they do not get their fingers pinched or hurt their hands.

5. In the Easter Story Puzzle in Lesson 5, you might create a border around the puzzle using string or tape so kids won't go out of the boundary as they move their pieces.

6. If many of your Small Group Leaders will be absent for Lesson 5, consider playing the Easter Story Puzzle as a large group. You could show kids how to play by enlarging the Easter Story Pictures, placing a magnet on the back of each, and using a chalkboard to slide them around. Kids could then do the activity with a partner, as it is written in the lesson.

7. Encourage children in the activity "Battlefield Dodge Ball" in Lesson 6 to have fun as they play, but not play to hurt other children with the balls.

8. Practice the activities with other Small Group Leaders ahead of time so you can easily explain them to the kids.

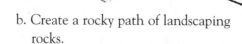

18

UNIT 1: ARMOR OF GOD
HELMET OF SALVATION (SALVATION MESSAGE)

BIBLE SUMMARY

John 18—20:20; Ephesians 6:10-18
The Bible teaches that we live in a world in which there is a battle between God and Satan. The battle is between good and evil, and is a fight for our hearts and souls. We must make a choice of which side we will be on. Kids will hear how they can join God's side by Admitting their sins, Believing Jesus died for their sins, and Choosing to follow Jesus. After kids have an opportunity to respond to the salvation message, they will celebrate with music and worship. Finally, they will learn that the Helmet of Salvation is a reminder to believers that they are in God's family forever.

KEY CONCEPT

WINNING THE BATTLE STARTS BY CHOOSING A RELATIONSHIP WITH GOD AND BEING EQUIPPED WITH THE ARMOR OF GOD.

BIBLE VERSE

"Put on the full armor of God so that you can take your stand against the devil's schemes."
Ephesians 6:11

OBJECTIVES

KNOW WHAT (LG): Children will hear how we need to have a relationship with God and put on the full Armor of God.
SO WHAT (LG): Children will learn that Jesus died to offer eternal life to everyone who believes. The Helmet of Salvation assures us that our salvation can never be taken away.

NOW WHAT (SG): Children will discuss God's plan for salvation and have an opportunity to ask questions about what it means. Children who have already made this decision will have a chance to share their story and review the Bridge Illustration.

SPIRITUAL FORMATION

Grace

5-G

Grace/Group

PEOPLE NEEDED

Two Teachers

SUPPLIES

○ Music for transitions and singing
○ CD player
○ Four colorful medieval-looking felt banners
○ "Satan" banner
○ "God" banner
○ "Sin" banner
○ "A" banner
○ "B" banner
○ "C" banner
○ Large cross
○ Bible Verse sign
○ 5-G *Impact* Spring Quarter video

○ TV/VCR
○ *Optional: Making It Connect CD*
○ *Optional: Doing Life with God in the Picture CD*

IN ADVANCE

- Determine which songs you will use and be prepared to lead or teach them.
- Rehearse the teaching time.
- Create four colorful medieval-looking banners by cutting various shapes out of different colored pieces of felt, and sewing, gluing, or using Velcro® to stick the pieces of felt onto a larger piece of felt. See pages 13-16 for patterns.

- Cut the following words out of felt: Satan, God, Sin, A, B, C. Create six banners out of felt, placing one word on each banner. Hang or place banners in the teaching area.
- Place tape on the floor, creating a large circle or arena, leaving enough room for kids to sit around the outer edge.
- Hang or display the four medieval-looking banners around the room along the outer edge of the arena.
- Prepare Bible Verse sign.
- Cue video to Lesson 1.

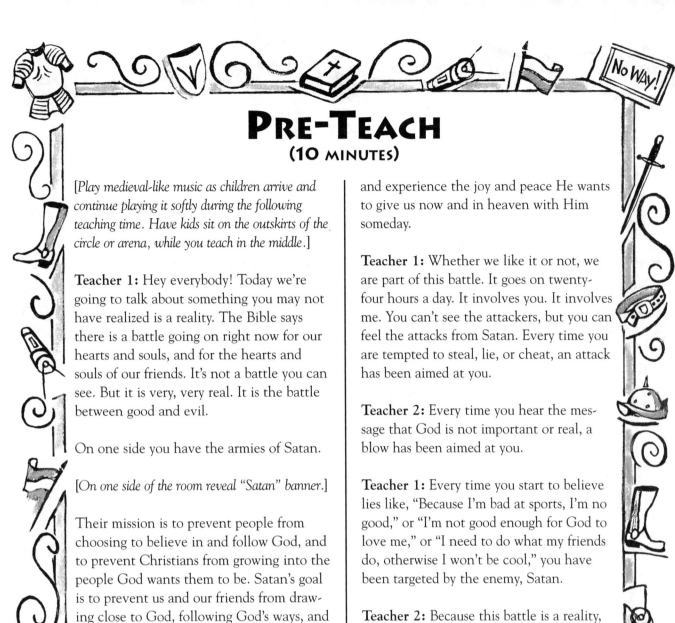

Pre-Teach
(10 minutes)

[*Play medieval-like music as children arrive and continue playing it softly during the following teaching time. Have kids sit on the outskirts of the circle or arena, while you teach in the middle.*]

Teacher 1: Hey everybody! Today we're going to talk about something you may not have realized is a reality. The Bible says there is a battle going on right now for our hearts and souls, and for the hearts and souls of our friends. It's not a battle you can see. But it is very, very real. It is the battle between good and evil.

On one side you have the armies of Satan.

[*On one side of the room reveal "Satan" banner.*]

Their mission is to prevent people from choosing to believe in and follow God, and to prevent Christians from growing into the people God wants them to be. Satan's goal is to prevent us and our friends from drawing close to God, following God's ways, and experiencing the joy and peace God offers.

Teacher 2: On the other side is God and every follower of His.

[*On the opposite side of the room reveal "God" banner.*]

God's mission is to help as many people in this world as possible choose to believe in and follow Him, and grow Christians into the people He wants them to be. His goal is for everyone, including our friends and us, to be in a relationship with Him, love Him, and experience the joy and peace He wants to give us now and in heaven with Him someday.

Teacher 1: Whether we like it or not, we are part of this battle. It goes on twenty-four hours a day. It involves you. It involves me. You can't see the attackers, but you can feel the attacks from Satan. Every time you are tempted to steal, lie, or cheat, an attack has been aimed at you.

Teacher 2: Every time you hear the message that God is not important or real, a blow has been aimed at you.

Teacher 1: Every time you start to believe lies like, "Because I'm bad at sports, I'm no good," or "I'm not good enough for God to love me," or "I need to do what my friends do, otherwise I won't be cool," you have been targeted by the enemy, Satan.

Teacher 2: Because this battle is a reality, every person in this world, including every person in this room, has a choice to make. If you haven't chosen to be on God's side in this battle, you are automatically on the other side. You'll learn why in a minute. There's no staying in the middle on this one. You're automatically over on Satan's side, allowing his attacks to affect you, change you, and shape the person you become. He is preventing you from being and experiencing all that God offers. But you can choose sides and fight. Which side do you want to be on?

TEACH
(15 MINUTES)

Teacher 1: We can fight the enemy. But to fight Satan in this battle, you have to choose to be on God's side and do life with Him in the picture. You have to be in a relationship with Him.

[*Slowly fade music out.*]

That's what we want to talk about today—how you get into a relationship with God. We want to talk about how you choose to be on God's side in this battle. Many of you are already followers of God and you know it. This will be a review for you. Some of you think you are followers of God, but you're not one hundred percent sure. This will clarify it for you. Some of you have never made the choice to be a follower of God. You don't know what I'm going to say. This is for you. This is how you become a follower of God.

Teacher 2: Every one of us in this world has done wrong things—things that separate us from the perfect God. Whether it's a little lie, or a big crime, these wrong things are called sins.

[*Reveal "sin" banner.*]

Sins separate us from God, both from being in a relationship with God now, and from being with God in heaven forever. However, God loves people too much to let things stay that way. Even though we don't deserve it, God wants us on His side. He wants to have a relationship with us. In order for us to be on His side, a price must be paid. Someone must take the punishment for the sins we commit which sepa-rate us from God. God took the punishment for us by sending down His perfect Son, Jesus.

[*Carry cross over and place it between the "sin" banner and "God" banner.*]

God sent Jesus from heaven down here to earth. Jesus went willingly. His job was to show us the right way to live while He was here on earth, then die a horrible death He didn't deserve to take the punishment for you and me. That's how much love God has for us.

Teacher 1: The way has been provided. God provided the way for us to be saved from the separation that exists between God and us.

[*Take cross over to the "sin" banner and throw "sin" banner at the foot of the cross.*]

Even though we sin, God has provided a way for us to be on His side and do life with Him. He has provided a way for sin to be beaten by what Jesus did on the cross. It's a great plan, but we have to sign up. We have to choose. God gives us very clear instructions to follow on how to choose Him. These are instructions showing Him we are choosing to be His followers. Here's what they are, right out of the Bible.

[*Teacher 1 reveals "A" banner.*]

"A" stands for Admit. God says if you want to be in a relationship with Him, in a prayer you need to tell Him you know you are a sinner and need to be saved by Him.

You do this if you're going to do life with Him and be on His side. We call this "ADMIT"—Admit you are a sinner, tell Him you're sorry for your sins, and ask to be forgiven.

[*Teacher 2 reveals "B" banner.*]

Teacher 2: "B" stands for Believe. Let God know that you believe Jesus' death has the power to save you from the separation you and I deserve, once and for all. We call this "BELIEVE."

[*Teacher 1 reveals "C" banner.*]

Teacher 1: "C" stands for Choose. Let God know you choose to accept the forgiveness Jesus provided for you and your sin, so you can be in a relationship with Him, now and forever. We call that "CHOOSE." You're "choosing" God.

[*Teacher 2 displays all three banners.*]

Teacher 2: That's it. Those are the instructions: Admit, Believe, and Choose. Once we have done this, we are in a relationship with God and on His side in the battle. We are doing life with Him. If you've never done these three steps, in a minute we are going to give you an opportunity. You will have a chance to Admit, Believe, and Choose. I'm going to pray, and I want you to take a second and think about what we've said. If you've never done this before, understand what you've heard today, and feel like you're ready to do this, then just echo the things I'm saying in your heart. Let's pray.

PRAYER

Dear God,
Thank You for providing the way for us to be on Your side in this battle. I Admit I am a sinner. I'm sorry for doing wrong things. I Believe Jesus' death has the power to save me from the separation I deserve. I Choose to accept Your forgiveness and follow You, so I can be in a relationship with You, now and forever. Amen.

If you just echoed those words in your heart for the very first time, know that this is a very big deal. God's whole story in the Bible is about that moment happening in the life of every person when they choose to be on His side and do life with Him in the picture. That's what God wants. That's His whole purpose. It's the biggest decision you can ever make.

We want to give you a chance to talk about this with your Small Groups. You're going to head to your groups for about twenty minutes. Then you're going to come back and celebrate this huge decision with music and worship. After that we will spend a few minutes talking about how you equip yourselves for battle against the enemy, now that some of you are on God's side in this battle. If you are on God's side now, Satan will want to attack you with a vengeance. But we are more protected now than ever. Come back and see how.

[*Dismiss to Small Groups. Play medieval-like music as children exit.*]

Music
(after Small Group)

Song suggestions:
"Spin" (*Making It Connect* CD)
"Big House" (*Making It Connect* CD)
"Every Day" (*Doing Life with God in the Picture* CD)

[*Play medieval-like music.*]

[*Show Bible Verse sign.*] "Put on the full armor of God so that you can take your stand against the devil's schemes." Ephesians 6:11

Teacher 1: There is a battle going on. We know that. In fact, we even know how the battle is going to end. The Bible tells us in the end Satan will be defeated by Jesus once and for all, which means we win! But even though we know we will win the battle, there are still lots of little battles we are fighting along the way. We can still be prevented from reaching out to our friends who don't know God. We can still be tempted to do wrong things. We can still be lied to by Satan. We are fighting the battle everyday, trying to become the people God wants us to be while Satan tries to stop that from happening.

Teacher 2: We must equip ourselves for this battle with armor—the Armor of God. You can't see the Armor of God, but it is real. It protects us from the attacks of Satan.

Teacher 1: Over the next few weeks, we enter battle training. We will learn how to do what this verse says: "Put on the full armor of God so that you can take your stand against the devil's schemes." Ephesians 6:11 The apostle Paul says we need the full Armor. So, each week we will learn

about a piece of Armor and how to use it, knowing that we need it all to fight the battle and grow into the people God wants us to be.

Teacher 2: It starts with joining God's side, accepting His salvation, and entering into a relationship with Him. Many of you have already done that. Some of you did it for the first time today. For those of us that have made that choice, the time has come to suit up with the Helmet of Salvation. Watch and see how.

Demonstration Teach

[*Play 5-G Impact video, Lesson 1. The following is provided for you if you would like to read through the script. There may be a slight difference between this script and the video due to video scripting. BE SURE TO SHOW THE OPENING ADVISORY CLIP TO THE KIDS.*]

Teacher: Before we talk about putting on the Helmet of Salvation, we should understand why the Bible tells us to use the Armor of God against Satan. It might be helpful to understand how armor was used, specifically, how a helmet was used in biblical or even medieval times.

Demonstrator 1: In Roman or medieval times, a helmet was a very critical piece of protection. If a soldier took a blow to the head and didn't have a helmet on, he was done for. Allow us to demonstrate.

[*Quarter-staff "no helmet" sequence is performed.*]

Without a helmet to protect him from a blow to the head, the battle would be over for him now. And I, as his enemy, would be

24

free to take him prisoner, or finish him altogether. But if a warrior has a helmet on his head, the story has a much different ending.

[*Quarter-staff "with helmet" sequence is performed.*]

The battle wouldn't be over for me. With a helmet to protect my head, he could give me a knockout blow, but I won't be knocked out. I'll stand strong and be ready to continue the battle.

Teacher: The Helmet of Salvation performs the same job in the battle you and I face. It is a piece of armor we put on in our minds. Instead of being made of metal, it is made of truth from the Bible about our salvation.

How do you put it on? Well, first you have to realize you are being attacked by Satan. You have to identify that Satan is attacking you, trying to prevent you from growing into the person God wants you to be. I call this "ID the Attack." Satan would love to try to get you to believe that when you do wrong things, God doesn't love you anymore, or you're not in a relationship with God anymore because you're too bad. If you are a follower of God, Satan is going to attack you with that lie, to try to "knock you out," and to make you no good at fighting the battle. When you get those feelings, "ID the Attack." Realize the feelings are Satan attacking you.

Then do step two of putting on the Armor. I call this "Unleash the Truth." What is the truth from the Bible that beats this lie from

Satan? Well, if Satan is telling me that I'm not in a relationship with God anymore because I'm too bad, then the truth I can unleash against him is that my relationship with God is FOREVER. There are lots of places the Bible tells me that. Here's just one: "As far as the east is from the west, so far has He removed our transgressions from us." Psalm 103:12.

[*Psalm 103:12 sign is shown.*]

Demonstrator 1: "ID the Attack," "Unleash the Truth," then [*makes forcefield sound effect*] the Helmet comes into place, protecting me from Satan's knockout blow. Sometimes I'll even make that little sound effect in my head when I need to put on the Helmet of Salvation. It's my way of "putting it on." That's how you put on and use the Helmet of Salvation: ID the Attack, Unleash the Truth, and [*makes forcefield sound effect*] the Helmet is on.

[*Stop the video.*]

Teacher 1: Practice that with me. Let's say you do something really bad. You are feeling terrible. You start to convince yourself that God could never love you after this. Is this truth? (*No*) No, who's attacking you? (*Satan*) Exactly! What did you just do? (*ID the Attack*) So, what's the truth? (*God loves me no matter what.*) Exactly! Psalm 103 tells me that, in addition to lots of other places in the Bible. What did you just do? (*Unleash the Truth*). Then, [*do the forcefield sound effect as done in the video*] the Helmet is in place.

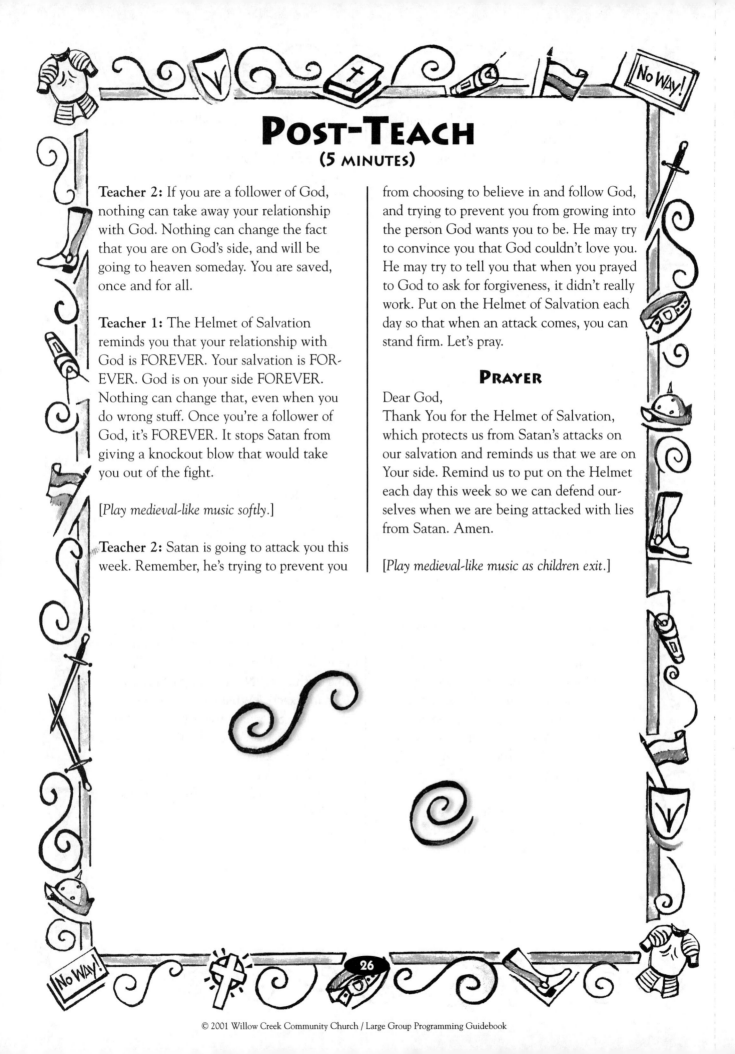

POST-TEACH
(5 MINUTES)

Teacher 2: If you are a follower of God, nothing can take away your relationship with God. Nothing can change the fact that you are on God's side, and will be going to heaven someday. You are saved, once and for all.

Teacher 1: The Helmet of Salvation reminds you that your relationship with God is FOREVER. Your salvation is FOREVER. God is on your side FOREVER. Nothing can change that, even when you do wrong stuff. Once you're a follower of God, it's FOREVER. It stops Satan from giving a knockout blow that would take you out of the fight.

[*Play medieval-like music softly.*]

Teacher 2: Satan is going to attack you this week. Remember, he's trying to prevent you from choosing to believe in and follow God, and trying to prevent you from growing into the person God wants you to be. He may try to convince you that God couldn't love you. He may try to tell you that when you prayed to God to ask for forgiveness, it didn't really work. Put on the Helmet of Salvation each day so that when an attack comes, you can stand firm. Let's pray.

PRAYER

Dear God,
Thank You for the Helmet of Salvation, which protects us from Satan's attacks on our salvation and reminds us that we are on Your side. Remind us to put on the Helmet each day this week so we can defend ourselves when we are being attacked with lies from Satan. Amen.

[*Play medieval-like music as children exit.*]

UNIT 1: ARMOR OF GOD
SWORD OF THE SPIRIT

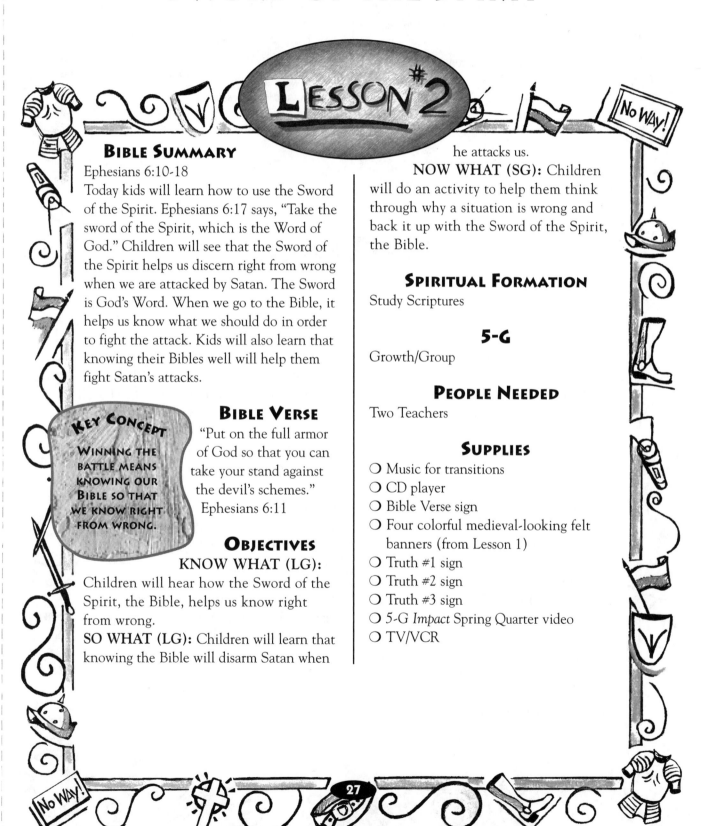

Lesson #2

BIBLE SUMMARY

Ephesians 6:10-18

Today kids will learn how to use the Sword of the Spirit. Ephesians 6:17 says, "Take the sword of the Spirit, which is the Word of God." Children will see that the Sword of the Spirit helps us discern right from wrong when we are attacked by Satan. The Sword is God's Word. When we go to the Bible, it helps us know what we should do in order to fight the attack. Kids will also learn that knowing their Bibles well will help them fight Satan's attacks.

KEY CONCEPT

WINNING THE BATTLE MEANS KNOWING OUR BIBLE SO THAT WE KNOW RIGHT FROM WRONG.

BIBLE VERSE

"Put on the full armor of God so that you can take your stand against the devil's schemes."
Ephesians 6:11

OBJECTIVES

KNOW WHAT (LG): Children will hear how the Sword of the Spirit, the Bible, helps us know right from wrong.

SO WHAT (LG): Children will learn that knowing the Bible will disarm Satan when he attacks us.

NOW WHAT (SG): Children will do an activity to help them think through why a situation is wrong and back it up with the Sword of the Spirit, the Bible.

SPIRITUAL FORMATION

Study Scriptures

5-G

Growth/Group

PEOPLE NEEDED

Two Teachers

SUPPLIES

❍ Music for transitions
❍ CD player
❍ Bible Verse sign
❍ Four colorful medieval-looking felt banners (from Lesson 1)
❍ Truth #1 sign
❍ Truth #2 sign
❍ Truth #3 sign
❍ 5-G *Impact* Spring Quarter video
❍ TV/VCR

27

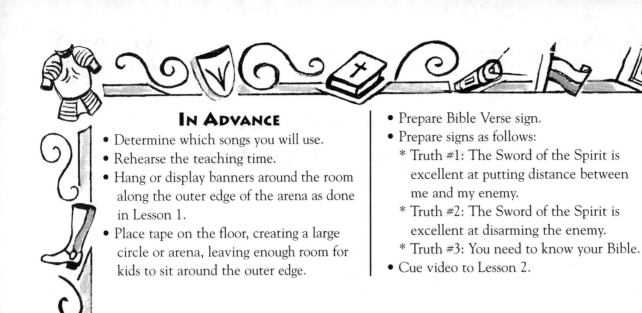

In Advance

- Determine which songs you will use.
- Rehearse the teaching time.
- Hang or display banners around the room along the outer edge of the arena as done in Lesson 1.
- Place tape on the floor, creating a large circle or arena, leaving enough room for kids to sit around the outer edge.
- Prepare Bible Verse sign.
- Prepare signs as follows:
  * Truth #1: The Sword of the Spirit is excellent at putting distance between me and my enemy.
  * Truth #2: The Sword of the Spirit is excellent at disarming the enemy.
  * Truth #3: You need to know your Bible.
- Cue video to Lesson 2.

Pre-Teach
(5 minutes)

[*Play medieval-like music as children arrive and continue playing it softly during the following teaching time. Teach in the middle of the arena.*]

Teacher 1: We face a battle everyday as we go through life. Every time we find ourselves wandering a little further from how God wants us to do life, we are locked in battle with the enemy. Every time we find ourselves tempted to use foul language, to think the worst about someone else, and to selfishly put our own desires above those of other people, we are engaged in hand-to-hand combat with the enemy. It's easy to think these things just happen, that they are just a coincidental part of doing life, but the truth is there is a very real enemy working against us. He wants to prevent people from choosing to believe in and follow God and prevent Christians from growing into the people God wants them to be. Our enemy's name is Satan.

Teacher 2: It's true that you cannot often see his attacks, but does that mean you are helpless? No. For one, if you have chosen to be in a relationship with God, then you are on God's side. He has equipped us for battle. He has given us Armor to use. It is not the kind you can see and touch, but it is very real nonetheless. The apostle Paul calls it the Armor of God. He says:

[*Show Bible Verse sign.*] "Put on the full armor of God so that you can take your stand against the devil's schemes." Ephesians 6:11

We need the full Armor. Each week we will learn about a piece of Armor and how to use it, knowing that we need it all to fight the battle and grow into the people God wants us to be. The Armor of God is made up of several different pieces: A Helmet.

Teacher 1: A Shield.

Teacher 2: A Sword.

Teacher 1: A Belt.

Teacher 2: A Breastplate . . .

Teacher 1: And Shoes. For those of us who are followers of God, who have chosen to fight on God's side in this battle, we must learn how to use this Armor. Every time the enemy attacks you . . .

Teacher 2: When he encourages you to disobey your parents, ignore someone who needs a friend, and makes you think that following the popular crowd is more important than following God . . . you face a choice.

Teacher 1: Take the hit or fight back. When you take the hit, you give in. You do what Satan wants you to do. It's the easier way. But when you fight back, you take up the Armor of God and use it. We learned to put it on in three steps. What are they?

ID the Attack—that's when we recognize that Satan is attacking us. Unleash the Truth—that's when we use truth from the Bible to beat Satan's attack. And immediately [*make forcefield sound effect as done last week*] the Armor goes up to protect us.

[*Fade out music.*]

Teacher 2: When Satan attacks, are you going to take the hit? [*Get kids to say "No!"*] Or, fight back? [*Get kids to say "Yes!"*] Then let the training begin.

Teacher 1: So far we have learned about the Helmet of Salvation. It stops Satan from delivering a knockout blow by reminding us that our relationship with God is FOREVER. Today we equip ourselves with the Sword of the Spirit.

Teacher 2: The Sword of the Spirit, Paul tells us, is the Bible. It is the weapon that tells us right from wrong. It is also the only weapon listed in all of the pieces of Armor. Let's learn how to use it.

TEACH
(20 MINUTES)

Demonstration Teach

[*Play 5-G Impact video, Lesson 2. The following script is provided if you would like to read through the content. There may be a slight difference between this script and the video due to video scripting. BE SURE TO SHOW THE OPENING ADVISORY CLIP TO THE KIDS.*]

Teacher: Before we learn how to use the Sword of the Spirit against our enemy, Satan, it is important to understand how a sword was used by a warrior in the days of Paul.

Demonstrator 1: I'm going to show you how to use a sword in a different way than most of you expect.

When most of us think of a sword, we think of it being used to attack. Certainly the warriors and soldiers of Paul's day used their swords to attack and kill each other. But I think there's a reason why Paul listed the Sword in a list of defensive Armor pieces. Sometimes the warriors in Paul's day faced an enemy they couldn't beat on their own. Certainly Satan is that kind of enemy to us. In those cases, attack is not always the best idea. The best offense is a good defense. Instead of a full-out attack, sometimes a more effective way to use the sword against an enemy was to use it to put some distance between the warriors.

If I was facing an enemy and I knew I couldn't defeat him on my own, it makes more sense for me to put some distance between us—to back away so that I can regroup. But if I just took off and made a run for it, there'd be nothing to stop him from finishing me off as I ran. My sword would give me confidence to back off, dis-tance myself, and regroup.

[*Distancing Sequence is performed.*]

Maybe I would back away to where there were others on my side to help me. Maybe I would be able to move back to where I knew I had other weapons I could use. Maybe backing away would just buy me time. Either way, a warrior's sword gave him confidence to back away from a powerful enemy. That's point number one.

[*Point #1 sign is shown.*] "The sword is excellent at putting distance between me and my enemy."

No enemy wants to get too close to a swinging sword.

Teacher: The Sword of the Spirit, the Bible, is like a swinging sword. Satan cannot fight against the truth of the Bible. It overpowers his attacks.

Our Sword, the Bible, is the Word of God. It has tremendous power in our lives to fight Satan off because it tells us the difference between right and wrong. It is the last thing Satan wants us to know. When we read our Bibles regularly and often, we can use our Swords to back away from Satan and put distance between him and us because it will give us the confidence we need to resist him. In the Bible, James 4:7 says, "Resist the devil, and he will flee from you." When we use the Bible to identify right and wrong, we are resisting Satan. The Bible says that when we do that, then he will flee from us. That's truth number one.

30

[*Truth #1 sign is shown.*] "The Sword of the Spirit is excellent at putting distance between me and my enemy."

The Bible exposes Satan because it shows us right from wrong. When you read and study your Bible, you're swinging a sword.

Demonstrator 1: Another way that a sword is great at helping to defeat a powerful enemy is to attack, not with the purpose of killing your opponent, but with the purpose of disarming your opponent. Let me demonstrate.

Let's say I know I can't beat Dugan. Pretend he's bigger than me, stronger than me, and better than me.

Demonstrator 2: Pretend?

Demonstrator 1: Very funny. I know I can't beat him. But if he attacks me, what choice do I have? I can either take the hit or I can fight back. So, I'll enter battle with him, but with a different goal than he has. He wants to destroy me, but because I know I can't beat him, my goal will be to disarm him.

[*Disarming sequence is performed.*]

By separating him from his weapon, I win this battle. I make him much less of a threat when I disarm him from his weapon. That's point number two.

[*Point #2 sign is shown.*] "The sword is excellent at disarming the enemy."

Teacher: "The sword is excellent at disarming the enemy." The Sword of the Spirit works the same way. This is where the power of the Bible really comes into play. There's not an attack that Satan can throw at you that the Bible can't disarm. When he encourages you to disobey your parents.

[*Kid is shown at the movies.*]

Satan Voiceover: [*attacking*] Who cares if your parents don't let you see rated R movies? They're not here, are they?

Teacher Voiceover: You can either take the hit and do it, or you can fight back.

Kid Voiceover: ID the Attack: This is a no-brainer. I know this is Satan because this is wrong. I'm not supposed to see R movies. My parents said I can't. Unleash the Truth: I know what is right. Ephesians 6:1 says, "Children, obey your parents in the Lord, for this is right. Honor your father and mother—which is the first commandment with a promise—that it may go well with you and that you may enjoy long life on the earth."

Teacher Voiceover: And immediately [*makes forcefield sound effect*] the Sword disarms Satan. Satan disarmed.

Teacher: When Satan tells you to ignore someone who needs a friend.

[*Kid is shown on the playground.*]

Satan Voiceover: [*attacking*] Look at that loser. You don't want to be caught hanging around with him!

Teacher Voiceover: You can either take the hit, or you can fight back.

Kid Voiceover: Yeah, what a loser. Wait a minute. This is Satan. Unleash the Truth: I know what is right. John 13:34 says, "A new command I give you: Love one

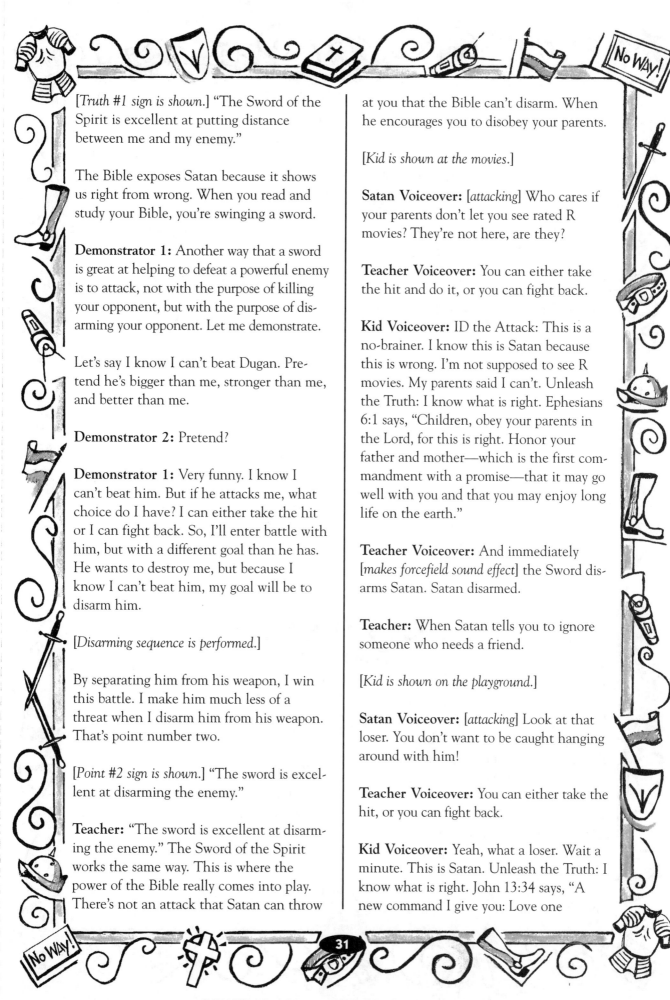

31

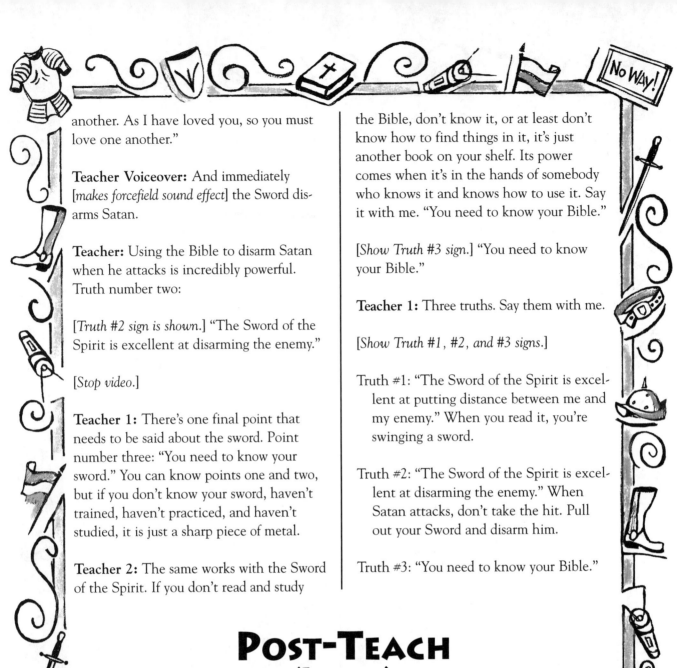

another. As I have loved you, so you must love one another."

Teacher Voiceover: And immediately [*makes forcefield sound effect*] the Sword disarms Satan.

Teacher: Using the Bible to disarm Satan when he attacks is incredibly powerful. Truth number two:

[*Truth #2 sign is shown.*] "The Sword of the Spirit is excellent at disarming the enemy."

[*Stop video.*]

Teacher 1: There's one final point that needs to be said about the sword. Point number three: "You need to know your sword." You can know points one and two, but if you don't know your sword, haven't trained, haven't practiced, and haven't studied, it is just a sharp piece of metal.

Teacher 2: The same works with the Sword of the Spirit. If you don't read and study

the Bible, don't know it, or at least don't know how to find things in it, it's just another book on your shelf. Its power comes when it's in the hands of somebody who knows it and knows how to use it. Say it with me. "You need to know your Bible."

[*Show Truth #3 sign.*] "You need to know your Bible."

Teacher 1: Three truths. Say them with me.

[*Show Truth #1, #2, and #3 signs.*]

Truth #1: "The Sword of the Spirit is excellent at putting distance between me and my enemy." When you read it, you're swinging a sword.

Truth #2: "The Sword of the Spirit is excellent at disarming the enemy." When Satan attacks, don't take the hit. Pull out your Sword and disarm him.

Truth #3: "You need to know your Bible."

Post-Teach
(5 minutes)

[*Play medieval-like music.*]

Teacher 1: Battle Training Challenge: This week commit to practicing with your Sword. Take ten minutes each day to open up your Bible and read it.

Teacher 2: If you don't know where to start, open up the book of John. That's a great place to start. Remember, you're not just reading, you're swinging a sword. You're training yourself to disarm Satan when he attacks this week. He will attack

this week. It's up to us who are fighting the battle to be ready.

Prayer

Dear God,
Thank You for the Bible which is the Sword we can use to disarm Satan. Help us to take a few minutes each day to read the Bible so we can be ready to fight the battle. Amen.

[*Dismiss to Small Groups. Play medieval-like music as children exit.*]

UNIT 1: ARMOR OF GOD
BELT OF TRUTH

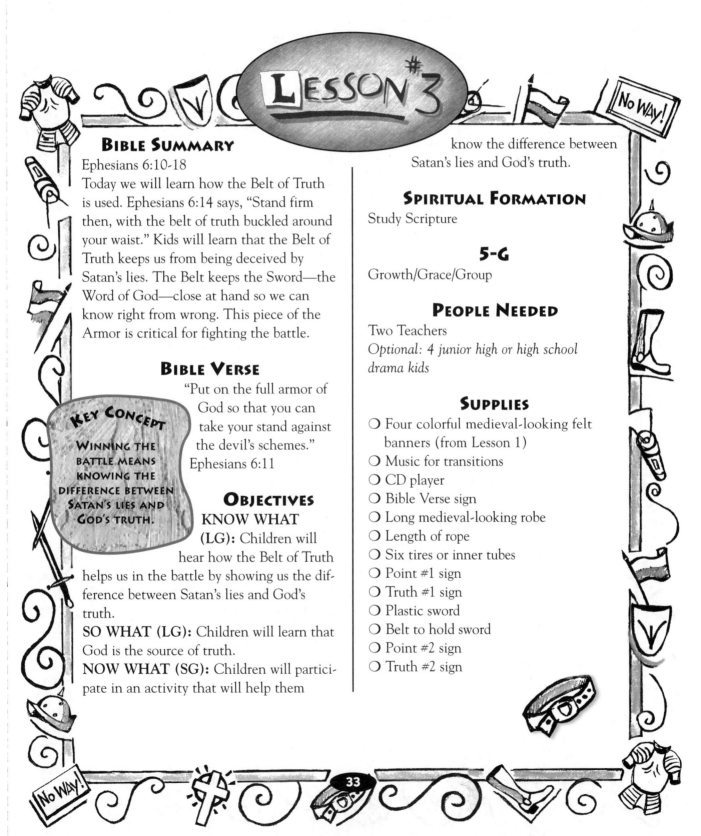

LESSON #3

BIBLE SUMMARY

Ephesians 6:10-18

Today we will learn how the Belt of Truth is used. Ephesians 6:14 says, "Stand firm then, with the belt of truth buckled around your waist." Kids will learn that the Belt of Truth keeps us from being deceived by Satan's lies. The Belt keeps the Sword—the Word of God—close at hand so we can know right from wrong. This piece of the Armor is critical for fighting the battle.

BIBLE VERSE

"Put on the full armor of God so that you can take your stand against the devil's schemes." Ephesians 6:11

KEY CONCEPT

WINNING THE BATTLE MEANS KNOWING THE DIFFERENCE BETWEEN SATAN'S LIES AND GOD'S TRUTH.

OBJECTIVES

KNOW WHAT (LG): Children will hear how the Belt of Truth helps us in the battle by showing us the difference between Satan's lies and God's truth.

SO WHAT (LG): Children will learn that God is the source of truth.

NOW WHAT (SG): Children will participate in an activity that will help them know the difference between Satan's lies and God's truth.

SPIRITUAL FORMATION

Study Scripture

5-G

Growth/Grace/Group

PEOPLE NEEDED

Two Teachers

Optional: 4 junior high or high school drama kids

SUPPLIES

○ Four colorful medieval-looking felt banners (from Lesson 1)
○ Music for transitions
○ CD player
○ Bible Verse sign
○ Long medieval-looking robe
○ Length of rope
○ Six tires or inner tubes
○ Point #1 sign
○ Truth #1 sign
○ Plastic sword
○ Belt to hold sword
○ Point #2 sign
○ Truth #2 sign

In Advance

- Determine which songs you will use.
- Rehearse the teaching time.
- Gather props and set teaching area.
- Hang or display banners as done in Lesson 1.
- Place tape on the floor, creating a large circle or arena.
- Prepare Bible Verse sign.
- Prepare signs as follows:

* Point #1: The belt protects me from getting tangled up.
* Truth #1: The Belt of Truth protects me from getting tangled up.
* Point #2: The belt keeps the sword within easy reach.
* Truth #2: The Belt of Truth keeps the Sword within easy reach.
- *Optional: Recruit four junior high or high school kids for the Battle Drama and rehearse.*

Pre-Teach
(5 minutes)

[*Play medieval-like music as children arrive. Have kids sit on the outskirts of the circle or arena, while you teach in the middle.*]

Optional: Perform the following drama using four junior high or high school kids. If kids need help with their lines, have them place their lines in black folders to read, while still demonstrating emphasis in their words and movement.

Battle Drama

1: We are warriors in a battle.

3: [*whiny*] But I don't want to fight.

1: This battle goes on 24-7.

2: Fight? Why can't we just all be friends?

1: It's not a battle you can see.

4: I don't have time to fight. I have homework to do.

1: But it is very real. It is the battle between good and evil.

2: Evil? So I lied to my parents. I wouldn't call that "evil."

1: On one side are the armies of Satan. Their mission: to tempt us . . .

4: Nobody's home. Let's see what's on TV.

1: To lie to us . . .

3: I don't know if I believe in God anymore. It's just not very cool.

1: To destroy us. On the other side is God. His mission: to love us . . .

2: Like a father should?

1: To show us . . .

2: That we can be friends with Him . . .

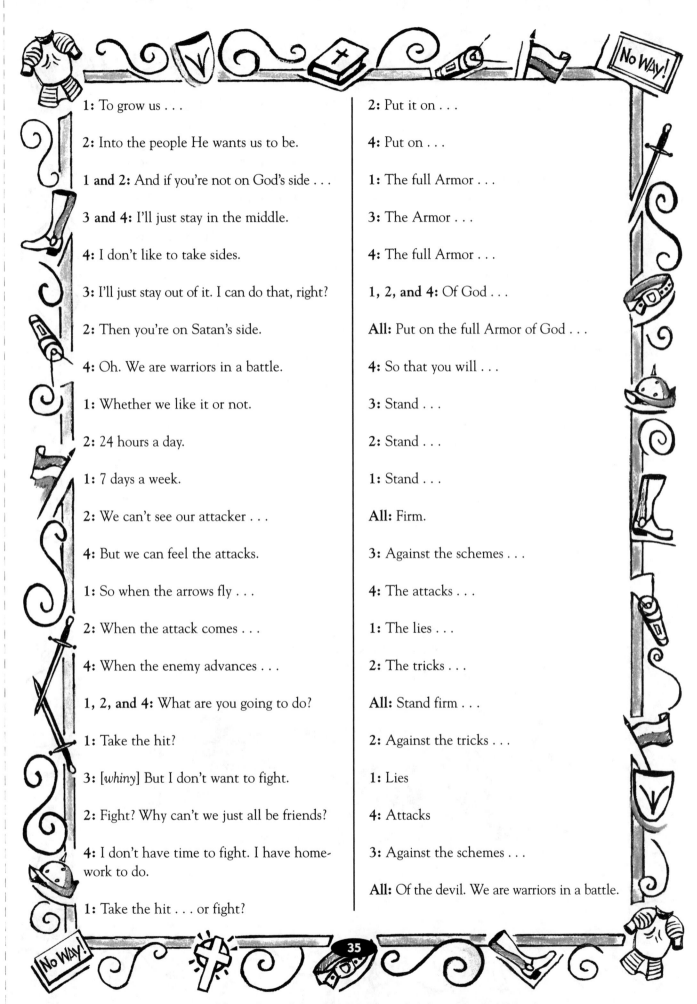

1: To grow us . . .

2: Into the people He wants us to be.

1 and 2: And if you're not on God's side . . .

3 and 4: I'll just stay in the middle.

4: I don't like to take sides.

3: I'll just stay out of it. I can do that, right?

2: Then you're on Satan's side.

4: Oh. We are warriors in a battle.

1: Whether we like it or not.

2: 24 hours a day.

1: 7 days a week.

2: We can't see our attacker . . .

4: But we can feel the attacks.

1: So when the arrows fly . . .

2: When the attack comes . . .

4: When the enemy advances . . .

1, 2, and 4: What are you going to do?

1: Take the hit?

3: [*whiny*] But I don't want to fight.

2: Fight? Why can't we just all be friends?

4: I don't have time to fight. I have homework to do.

1: Take the hit . . . or fight?

2: Put it on . . .

4: Put on . . .

1: The full Armor . . .

3: The Armor . . .

4: The full Armor . . .

1, 2, and 4: Of God . . .

All: Put on the full Armor of God . . .

4: So that you will . . .

3: Stand . . .

2: Stand . . .

1: Stand . . .

All: Firm.

3: Against the schemes . . .

4: The attacks . . .

1: The lies . . .

2: The tricks . . .

All: Stand firm . . .

2: Against the tricks . . .

1: Lies

4: Attacks

3: Against the schemes . . .

All: Of the devil. We are warriors in a battle.

4: It goes on 24-7.

3: It is the battle . . .

2: Against good and evil.

All: Put it on.

[*Have kids return to their seats.*]

[*Play medieval-like music.*]

[*Show Bible Verse sign.*] "Put on the full armor of God so that you can take your stand against the devil's schemes." Ephesians 6:11

Teacher 1: This is what the apostle Paul tells us to do in this battle we are in with Satan. We need the full Armor. We will continue to learn each week in this unit about a piece of Armor and how to use it, knowing that we need it all to fight the battle and grow into the people God wants us to be. Satan wants to prevent people from choosing to believe in and follow God, and to prevent Christians from growing into the people God wants them to be. Paul lists the different pieces of Armor that will protect us from Satan's attacks.

Teacher 2: A Helmet.

Teacher 1: A Shield.

Teacher 2: A Sword.

Teacher 1: A Belt.

Teacher 2: A Breastplate . . .

Teacher 1: And Shoes. We have equipped ourselves with two pieces so far: The Helmet of Salvation and the Sword of the Spirit.

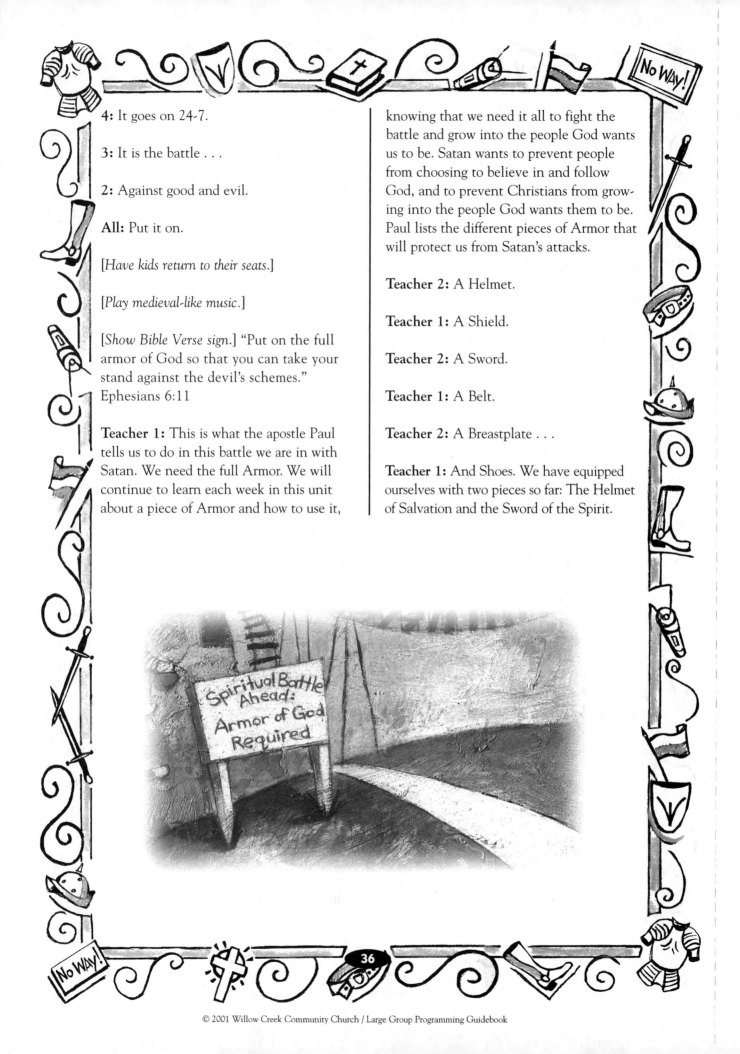

TEACH
(20 MINUTES)

Teacher 1: Today we add the Belt of Truth. Like always, I think it's important for us to understand how this piece of equipment was used by warriors in Roman or medieval times, so we can understand how we should use it. So, let's start there.

[Illustrate the following by putting a robe on and tying a length of rope around your waist.]

Teacher 2: The belt was different in that day than the belts we use today. They didn't have nice little belts like we have that went through the loops in their pants to hold them up. Their belts were lengths of rope or straps of leather that were wrapped around their waist. These belts were wrapped around their waist for two reasons.

First, the belt was wrapped around the waist to keep a warrior's robes from tripping him. Warriors in Paul's day and even in medieval times didn't always wear pants. They instead wore long robes. But in battle, these robes could really get in the way. Let us show you what we mean. We need a warrior from the audience that would like to execute a quest for us: The Quest of the Tires!

THE QUEST OF THE TIRES
[Lay the tires or inner tubes on the ground, setting up an obstacle course. Pick a male volunteer and put the long, flowing robe on him. Pick a female volunteer to be the "Damsel in Distress." Place the male and female volunteers on opposite sides of the obstacle course.]

Teacher 2: Here is your quest, brave one. Over there, you've got your basic DID: "Damsel in Distress." It will be your job to cross our perilous battlefield of tires to reach yonder Damsel in Distress. By reaching her and tagging her, you will rescue her and prove your worth. But you will only have five seconds to reach her before she meets a most unpleasant doom. Since your hands will be busy crossing the battlefield of tires, you may not rig your robes up in any way to ease your crossing. They must dangle and tangle freely. You have five seconds, Brave Warrior. Tarry well!

> ### TEACHING TIP
> A FUN, INTERACTIVE WAY TO LIVEN UP THE QUEST OF THE TIRES IS TO USE A LINE SUCH AS "HELP, SAVE ME!" THAT ALL THE GIRLS IN THE AUDIENCE CAN SAY WITH THE DAMSEL IN DISTRESS AND A LINE SUCH AS "NEVER FEAR!" THAT THE GUYS CAN SAY WITH THE BRAVE WARRIOR. YOU MIGHT GIVE FLOWERS AND A SHAWL TO THE DAMSEL IN DISTRESS TO HOLD. LOTS OF ENERGY AND INTERACTION WITH THE AUDIENCE CAN MAKE THIS A FUN ACTIVITY FOR EVERYONE!

[Play medieval-like music while the volunteer tries to cross the tires course. He may make it to the end, but will stumble along the way.]

Teacher 1: Now we will equip you for your quest. We will belt you around the waist, getting your robes out of the way, and free you to do what you have come to do—rescue yon fair maiden!

[Tie the rope around the volunteer's waist and pull up his robe so it is secured by the rope and does not dangle. Play medieval-like music while the volunteer tries to go through the tires again. Applaud the volunteers as they return to their seats.]

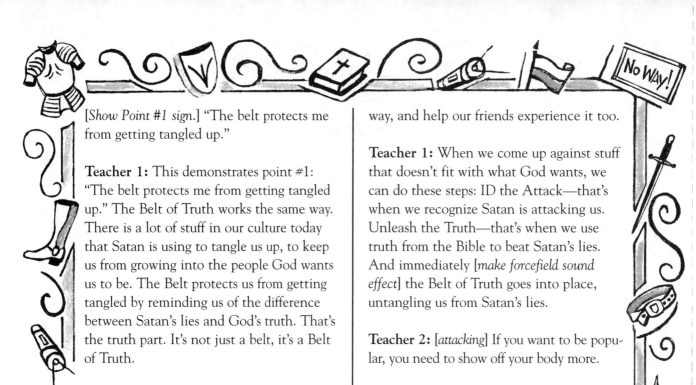

[*Show Point #1 sign.*] "The belt protects me from getting tangled up."

Teacher 1: This demonstrates point #1: "The belt protects me from getting tangled up." The Belt of Truth works the same way. There is a lot of stuff in our culture today that Satan is using to tangle us up, to keep us from growing into the people God wants us to be. The Belt protects us from getting tangled by reminding us of the difference between Satan's lies and God's truth. That's the truth part. It's not just a belt, it's a Belt of Truth.

Pop stars are telling you how to dress which is not always in a way that honors God. Kids at school are telling you that it's okay to try drugs and get involved with sex. Stuff like this will trip you up from being who God wants you to be and helping your friends come to know God. Scientists and teachers are telling you that God is not real and you evolved from monkeys. These are Satan's lies.

Teacher 2: It can get so confusing that you sometimes just want to stop and say, "Would somebody just tell me what the truth is so I can live my life?" It is really easy to get tangled up in the lies that Satan is using these days. These lies tangle us up, making it very hard to be the person God wants us to be and live His way. These lies make it just as hard to walk with God as it was to walk on tires with robes tangling up your feet. But if we're going to beat Satan in battle, then we have to know the difference between his lies and the truth—God's truth. Why do we want to beat Satan and defend ourselves from his lies and attacks? So we can grow into the people God wants us to be. When we do, we experience the peace and joy that comes from living God's

way, and help our friends experience it too.

Teacher 1: When we come up against stuff that doesn't fit with what God wants, we can do these steps: ID the Attack—that's when we recognize Satan is attacking us. Unleash the Truth—that's when we use truth from the Bible to beat Satan's lies. And immediately [*make forcefield sound effect*] the Belt of Truth goes into place, untangling us from Satan's lies.

Teacher 2: [*attacking*] If you want to be popular, you need to show off your body more.

Teacher 1: Well, I want to be popular. I guess I'd better dress like that. Wait a minute. ID the Attack: Showing off my body? Is that what God wants? I bet that's Satan talking. Unleash the Truth: The truth is I don't need to be liked for my body, there's a lot more to me than that and God knows it. That's why the Bible says I should dress modestly. And immediately [*make forcefield sound effect*] the Belt of Truth goes into place, untangling me from Satan's lies. Or how about this?

Teacher 2: Maybe Jesus never even lived. How do you know that He's real?

Teacher 1: Yeah, how do I know for sure? Wait a minute. ID the Attack: Who wants me to believe that? Could it be Satan? Unleash the Truth: The truth is that Jesus is real. The Bible tells me so. But not only that, my life has been changed by Him. And immediately [*make forcefield sound effect*] the Belt of Truth goes into place, untangling me from Satan's lies. That's truth number 1. The Belt of Truth protects me from getting tangled up.

[*Show Truth #1 sign.*] "The Belt of Truth

protects me from getting tangled up."

Teacher 2: [*Put on the belt with your sword in the belt.*] Let's switch back to the belt a Roman soldier or a medieval warrior used to understand another way the belt was used. The belt was good because it kept the sword close. In battle a warrior needs to be able to get to the sword quickly. It can't be like this: En Garde! [*Pull out the sword and face Teacher 1 as if you are ready to fight.*]

Teacher 1: [*In a humorous way, look for a sword but then realize you don't have one handy.*] Oh! I need my weapon. Hold on just a minute. I'll be right with you. I know it's here somewhere.

Teacher 2: I could've finished [*him/her*] off a long time ago. A warrior never knows when the attack is going to come, so it's important to be ready.

Teacher 1: [*Sneak up on Teacher 2.*] En Garde!

[*Teacher 2: Pull out your sword from your belt, showing you are ready for battle.*]

Teacher 1: Just testing.

Teacher 2: See? I was able to enter battle strongly, because my belt keeps my sword close at hand. That's point number 2. The belt keeps the sword within easy reach.

[*Show Point #2 sign.*] "The belt keeps the sword within easy reach."

Teacher 1: The Belt of Truth works the same way. We are in a battle twenty-four hours a day, seven days a week. The lies Satan throws at us sometimes tangle us up really easily. It's confusing sometimes to know how you should dress, what you should watch, or if something is cool to do or not. Satan likes to try to get us to do or believe things that are just on the line. It can be confusing. That's why it's so important to have our Sword close at hand, where we can pull it out often. The Bible is our Sword.

Now, when I say "have it close at hand," do I mean that you have to keep your Bible in your back pocket all the time? No, though

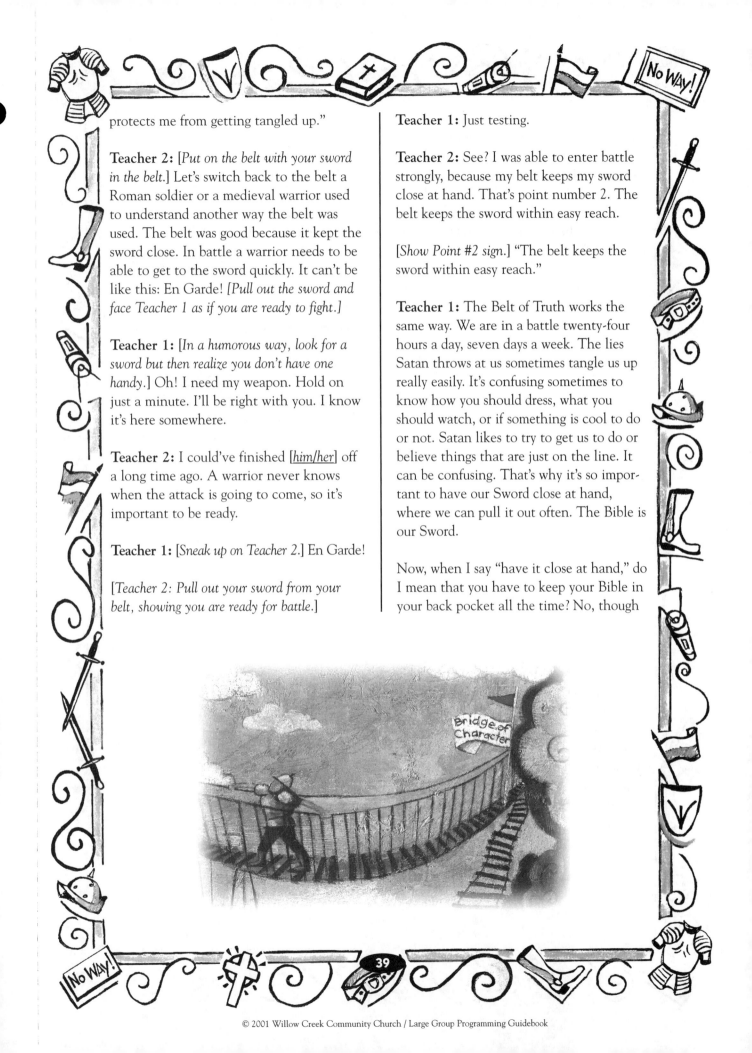

that would not be a bad thing. What I mean is we need to read it often. We need to pull it out often if we're going to avoid getting tangled up in lies and avoid getting surprised by the enemy. It can't be tucked away in that cupboard you never open. It can't be on the bookshelf behind four rows of books. We need to be ready to read it often, so that we can fight Satan off with the truth, and so we can love God, experience the awesome things He wants for us, and share the amazing story of what Jesus has done with our friends. The Belt of Truth reminds us to do that. That's truth number 2. The Belt of Truth keeps the Sword within easy reach.

[*Show Truth #2 sign.*] "The Belt of Truth keeps the Sword within easy reach."

Teacher 2: There are two important points today. Let's say them together.

[*Show Truth signs #1 and #2.*]

1. The Belt of Truth protects me from getting tangled up. By whom? Satan.
2. The Belt of Truth keeps the Sword within easy reach. What's your Sword? The Bible.

Teacher 1: It does these by reminding us there are lies coming at us, so we must know the difference between Satan's lies and God's truth. It's not just a belt. It's a Belt of Truth. Remember, **WINNING THE BATTLE MEANS KNOWING THE DIFFERENCE BETWEEN SATAN'S LIES AND GOD'S TRUTH.**

POST-TEACH
(5 MINUTES)

Teacher 2: Battle Training Challenge: This week Satan's going to come after you in battle. He will try to trip you up. Remember the steps: ID the Attack, Unleash the Truth, and [*make forcefield sound effect*] put on the Belt of Truth. Let the Belt of Truth stop you from getting tangled up. Let it remind you to keep your Sword close so you can take it out often. Let's pray.

PRAYER

Dear God,
Thank You for the Belt of Truth which allows us to keep our Sword, the Bible, close at hand. Help us to put on the Belt of Truth this week so we can defend ourselves against Satan's attacks. Amen.

[*Dismiss to Small Groups. Play medieval-like music as children exit.*]

40

UNIT 1: ARMOR OF GOD
BREASTPLATE OF RIGHTEOUSNESS

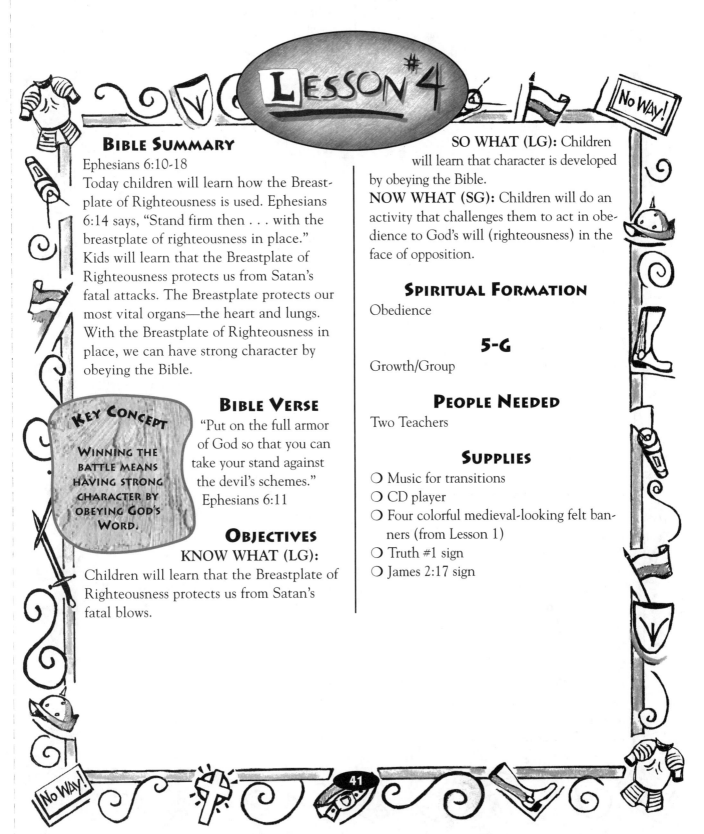

BIBLE SUMMARY

Ephesians 6:10-18

Today children will learn how the Breastplate of Righteousness is used. Ephesians 6:14 says, "Stand firm then . . . with the breastplate of righteousness in place." Kids will learn that the Breastplate of Righteousness protects us from Satan's fatal attacks. The Breastplate protects our most vital organs—the heart and lungs. With the Breastplate of Righteousness in place, we can have strong character by obeying the Bible.

KEY CONCEPT

WINNING THE BATTLE MEANS HAVING STRONG CHARACTER BY OBEYING GOD'S WORD.

BIBLE VERSE

"Put on the full armor of God so that you can take your stand against the devil's schemes." Ephesians 6:11

OBJECTIVES

KNOW WHAT (LG): Children will learn that the Breastplate of Righteousness protects us from Satan's fatal blows.

SO WHAT (LG): Children will learn that character is developed by obeying the Bible.

NOW WHAT (SG): Children will do an activity that challenges them to act in obedience to God's will (righteousness) in the face of opposition.

SPIRITUAL FORMATION

Obedience

5-G

Growth/Group

PEOPLE NEEDED

Two Teachers

SUPPLIES

❍ Music for transitions
❍ CD player
❍ Four colorful medieval-looking felt banners (from Lesson 1)
❍ Truth #1 sign
❍ James 2:17 sign

IN ADVANCE

- Determine which songs you will use.
- Rehearse the teaching time.
- Place tape on the floor, creating a large circle or arena, leaving enough room for kids to sit around the outer edge.
- Hang or display banners around the room along the outer edge of the arena as done in Lesson 1.
- Prepare signs as follows:
  * Truth: The Breastplate of Righteousness protects your heart. But using it requires obedience.
  * "Faith by itself, if it is not accompanied by action, is dead." James 2:17

PRE-TEACH
(10 MINUTES)

[Play medieval-like music as children arrive and continue playing it softly during the following teaching time. Have kids sit on the outskirts of the circle or arena, while you teach in the middle.]

Teacher 1: We have spent the last few weeks training for the battle we are in against the forces of Satan. Satan's armies are fighting to prevent people from choosing to believe in and follow God, and to prevent Christians from growing into the people God wants them to be. There has been a lot of information given, but my hope is that you have really been learning how to defeat Satan in this battle, and this information has been changing the way you go through life and changing the way you respond to the temptations and lies Satan sends your way. Before we add a new piece, I'd like to make sure we know how to use the pieces we have already learned. I want to give us another opportunity to practice what we've learned.

WARRIOR'S CHALLENGE

Teacher 2: Let's enter the arena and give some brave warriors a chance to practice the battle skills they've learned. Let's begin the Warrior's Challenge. Six warriors will enter the arena. They will not battle each other. They are a team, an army, that is in the arena to battle against the influence of Satan in their everyday lives. Questions will be asked, challenges made, and it will be up to this team of six warriors to emerge victoriously. Who would like to enter the arena today and participate in the Warrior's Challenge?

[Select six volunteers and have them enter the center of the arena.]

The rules are simple. All of you will become one army. Your army will be faced with questions you must answer and challenges to which you must respond. After each question or challenge is given, your army will be asked if you will choose to

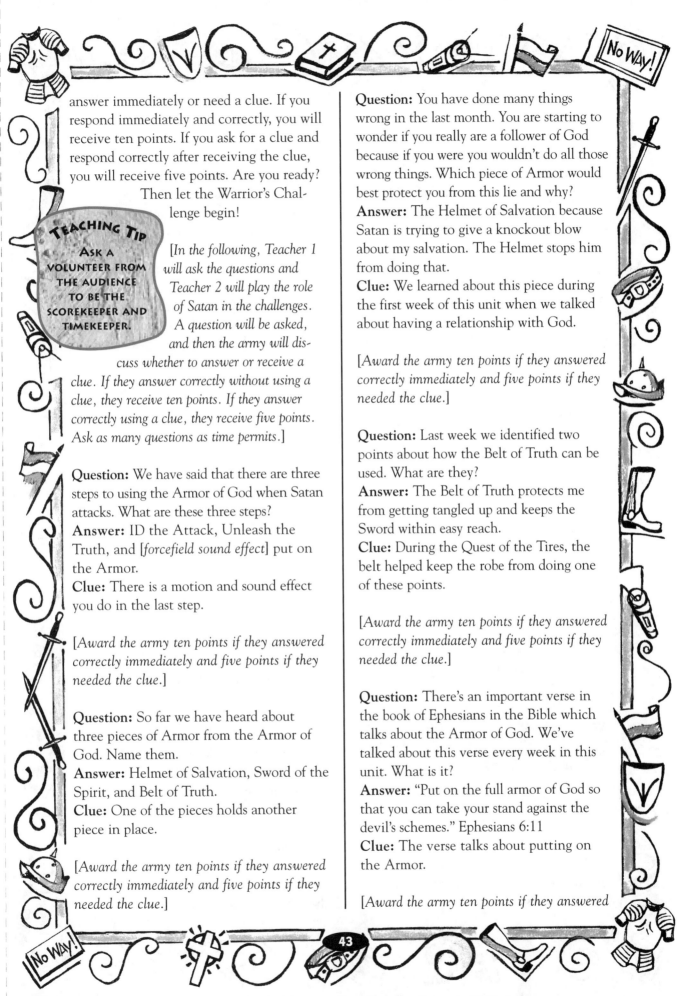

answer immediately or need a clue. If you respond immediately and correctly, you will receive ten points. If you ask for a clue and respond correctly after receiving the clue, you will receive five points. Are you ready? Then let the Warrior's Challenge begin!

[*In the following, Teacher 1 will ask the questions and Teacher 2 will play the role of Satan in the challenges. A question will be asked, and then the army will discuss whether to answer or receive a clue. If they answer correctly without using a clue, they receive ten points. If they answer correctly using a clue, they receive five points. Ask as many questions as time permits.*]

Question: We have said that there are three steps to using the Armor of God when Satan attacks. What are these three steps?
Answer: ID the Attack, Unleash the Truth, and [*forcefield sound effect*] put on the Armor.
Clue: There is a motion and sound effect you do in the last step.

[*Award the army ten points if they answered correctly immediately and five points if they needed the clue.*]

Question: So far we have heard about three pieces of Armor from the Armor of God. Name them.
Answer: Helmet of Salvation, Sword of the Spirit, and Belt of Truth.
Clue: One of the pieces holds another piece in place.

[*Award the army ten points if they answered correctly immediately and five points if they needed the clue.*]

Question: You have done many things wrong in the last month. You are starting to wonder if you really are a follower of God because if you were you wouldn't do all those wrong things. Which piece of Armor would best protect you from this lie and why?
Answer: The Helmet of Salvation because Satan is trying to give a knockout blow about my salvation. The Helmet stops him from doing that.
Clue: We learned about this piece during the first week of this unit when we talked about having a relationship with God.

[*Award the army ten points if they answered correctly immediately and five points if they needed the clue.*]

Question: Last week we identified two points about how the Belt of Truth can be used. What are they?
Answer: The Belt of Truth protects me from getting tangled up and keeps the Sword within easy reach.
Clue: During the Quest of the Tires, the belt helped keep the robe from doing one of these points.

[*Award the army ten points if they answered correctly immediately and five points if they needed the clue.*]

Question: There's an important verse in the book of Ephesians in the Bible which talks about the Armor of God. We've talked about this verse every week in this unit. What is it?
Answer: "Put on the full armor of God so that you can take your stand against the devil's schemes." Ephesians 6:11
Clue: The verse talks about putting on the Armor.

[*Award the army ten points if they answered*

correctly immediately and five points if they needed the clue.]

Challenge: You are going to hear an attack from Satan. You will pick one person, a representative, from your army to defend him or herself against this attack using the three-step defense. This person must talk us through each step, explaining it along the way. If this person can give the correct answer without help from the rest of the army, then the army will receive ten points. If the person needs to get help from the army, then the army will receive five points.

[Have the army choose one representative.]

Satan (played by Teacher 2): "Here's what's true about God. You can't hear Him and can't see Him, so He's not real. He doesn't exist."

Answer: ID the Attack: This isn't true. This is Satan talking. Unleash the Truth: I know this isn't true because the Bible says, "In the beginning God created the heavens and the earth." *[Forcefield sound effect]* the Armor is in place, to defend me against Satan's attack.

> **TEACHING TIP**
> KIDS MAY GIVE A DIFFERENT ANSWER FOR THE BIBLE TRUTH THAN WHAT IS GIVEN IN THESE CHALLENGES. GIVE THE ARMY THE FULL POINTS IF THEY GIVE A BIBLE TRUTH THAT WOULD DEFEND THEMSELVES AGAINST THE LIE SATAN IS USING TO ATTACK.

[Award the army ten points if the representative answered correctly immediately and five points if he/she needed help from the army.]

Challenge: Again, pick one person, a representative, from your army to defend himself or herself against the following attack using the three-step defense. This person must talk us through each step, explaining it along the way. If this person can give the correct answer without help from the rest of the army, then the army will receive ten points. If the person needs to get help from the army, then the army will receive five points.

[Have the army choose one representative.]

Here's the challenge: You tend to go along with your friends, even when you know what they're doing is wrong. It's an area with which you really struggle. You and your friends are hanging out on the playground and they are swearing.

Satan (played by Teacher 2): "Swearing is really no big deal. In fact, it's kind of cool."

Answer: ID the Attack: I know this is wrong. This is Satan talking. Unleash the Truth: The Bible tells me that swearing is wrong. It says, "Do not let any unwholesome talk come out of your mouths." *[Forcefield sound effect]* the Armor is in place to defend me against Satan's attack.

[Award the army ten points if the representative answered correctly immediately and five points if he/she needed help from the army.]

Lightning Truth Challenge: In this challenge, you must send two members forward to enter a truth battle with Satan. Satan will throw out a series of lies and these two people will have to tell what God's truth is that beats that lie. They don't have to quote verses, but they must give a biblical truth that beats the lie. Your army will receive five points for each beaten lie. They can stop once during the lightning truth challenge to discuss with the team for ten seconds, but you will only get two points if you get it right. You will have seventy seconds total. Let's go!

[*Have the army choose two representatives. Teacher 2 will say each of Satan's lies.*]

1. **Satan's lie:** It's okay to disobey your parents as long as you don't get caught.
Answer: The Bible says we must honor our parents.

2. **Satan's lie:** That weird kid at school is a real loser.
Answer: The Bible says we must love one another.

3. **Satan's lie:** Watching violent movies is really no big deal.
Answer: The Bible says that we are to be pure. Putting violence into our heads will hinder us from having pure thoughts.

4. **Satan's lie:** Jesus could never love someone like you.
Answer: The Bible says that Jesus loves us and gave His life for us.

5. **Satan's lie:** Stealing isn't really wrong because everything belongs to God anyway.
Answer: The Bible says that stealing is wrong.

Great job! At the end of this last round, the Warriors had a total of _____ points, making them victorious in our arena!

[*Applaud the warriors as they return to their seats.*]

Bridge of Character

TEACH
(15 MINUTES)

Teacher 2: Today we will learn how to use the Breastplate of Righteousness.

Teacher 1: As always, before we learn how to use the Breastplate of Righteousness, I'd like to talk about how the actual breastplate was used in the days of a warrior, so we can understand better.

The breastplate was a large piece of armor. It was worn over the chest and upper body. In Paul's day, Roman soldiers might have worn lighter weight breastplates made of leather. As weapons and armor advanced, the knights of medieval times much later wore huge breastplates made of heavy plate metal.

The breastplate protected the upper body, but its primary function was to protect the heart. A strong breastplate could stop a sword or a spear tip and protect a warrior from taking a deadly blow to the heart.

But here was the downside. The breastplate was heavy and awkward, and when wearing it, it was hard to move. So, some of the younger knights wouldn't want to wear it in battle. "It's too heavy, it's too awkward," they'd say. But the older, wiser, more experienced knights would always advise them to wear a breastplate into battle. They knew that in a fight, or in a joust, they needed the breastplate to protect their heart. And so the younger knights, if they were smart, would obey the older knights, even if they didn't want to obey. These things apply to the Breastplate of Righteousness as well.

[*Show Truth sign.*] The Breastplate of Righteousness protects your heart. But using it requires obedience.

Teacher 2: Our enemy, Satan, loves to attack us in the heart of who we are and how we act. Satan wants to attack and change the people we become. If he can be successful at affecting our actions, at making us act in ways that don't please God, then he has been successful at attacking us "in the heart." And bit by bit, as he does this, our hearts will change. Our character will change. He will be successful at taking us further and further from being the kind of followers God wants us to be. Satan's attacks on our heart "kill" our character.

If he can get you to be more selfish than generous, he has attacked you at the heart of who you are. If he can get you to be more prideful than humble, he has attacked you at the heart of who you are. If he can get you to be more judgmental than understanding, he has attacked you at the heart of who you are.

It's not just enough to want to be generous, humble, and understanding. If our actions don't demonstrate those things, then we are not living out what we want our relationship with God to be. Satan loves it when we believe one thing and do another.

Teacher 1: But the Bible says this in the book of James:

[*Show James 2:17 sign.*] "Faith by itself, if it is not accompanied by action, is dead." James 2:17

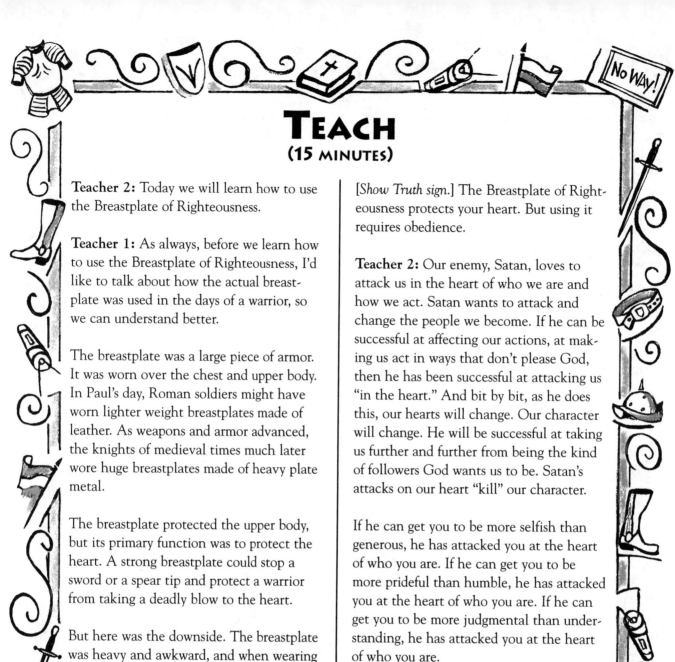

46

In other words, if we say we're followers of God, but our actions don't show it, then we're just talking. That's what Satan wants to make sure is happening and so we have to put on the Breastplate of Righteousness.

Teacher 2: Righteousness is doing right. The Breastplate of Righteousness is our actions and protects our character and hearts. When we live righteous lives obedient to God's Word, then our actions and our beliefs all line up. And our heart, the heart of who we are as followers of God, is protected.

Teacher 1: The Breastplate of Righteousness protects our heart. But using it requires obedience. It means obeying what God wants us to do, even when we don't feel like it. It means obeying the Bible, even when it's hard. When we show that kind of obedience, we stop Satan from attacking us in the heart, and instead we live the righteous lives God wants for us. What does that look like? Let's say I am in a rotten mood. The last thing I feel like doing is being loving.

Teacher 2 (playing the role of Satan): Here comes your little sister. What a brat. Doesn't she know what a bad mood you're in? Give it to her!

Teacher 1: Yeah, little brat . . . wait, ID the Attack: Satan is trying to make me act mean, just because I'm in a bad mood. Unleash the Truth: The truth is God wants me to be loving, even to little sisters. I must obey even if I'm in a bad mood. And [*make forcefield sound effect*] the Breastplate of Righteousness goes into place, protecting my heart and character and keeping them righteous.

It's so easy for us to act out of our bad mood. Even though I know God wants me to be loving to my little sister, it's easy for me to act out of my bad mood, instead of acting out of what is true and what God wants for me.

The steps are the same, but because we're dealing with obeying, we're dealing with action. So, the second step needs to have an "I must obey" part in it to remind us. It's not just enough to know the truth in this case, we need to obey it as well, so that our character and heart are protected. How about this?

Teacher 2 (playing the role of Satan): Everyone else on the bus is swearing. C'mon, don't be such a wimp, just do it.

Teacher 1: ID the Attack: Satan is attacking me, trying to get me to do wrong stuff, just because he knows it will be hard not to do it. Unleash the Truth: The Bible says, "Do not use unwholesome talk." That's it. That's what the Bible says and I need to obey even if my friends think I'm a wimp. And [*make forcefield sound effect*] the Breastplate of Righteousness goes into place, protecting my heart and character.

47

POST-TEACH
(5 MINUTES)

Teacher 2: The people we are and the people we become are not just defined by what we believe. Our walk needs to match our talk. Our actions show everyone around us what kind of character we have. Our actions let everyone know we are followers of God. It takes obedience to have righteous actions.

Teacher 1: Battle Training Challenge: I want to challenge you this week to look for opportunities in your life to obey. We don't like to obey always. But this week I want to challenge you to look for opportunities to obey. When you are in a bad mood this week, or in a really hard situation which makes it hard to obey, remember your steps. ID the Attack, Unleash the Truth— challenging yourself to obey, and [*make forcefield sound effect*] protect your heart with the Breastplate of Righteousness. Let those steps help you to obey.

PRAYER

Dear God,
Thank You for the Breastplate of Righteousness which protects our heart and character. Help us to use the Breastplate this week to help us obey. Amen.

[*Dismiss to Small Groups. Play medieval-like music as children exit.*]

UNIT 1: ARMOR OF GOD
EASTER

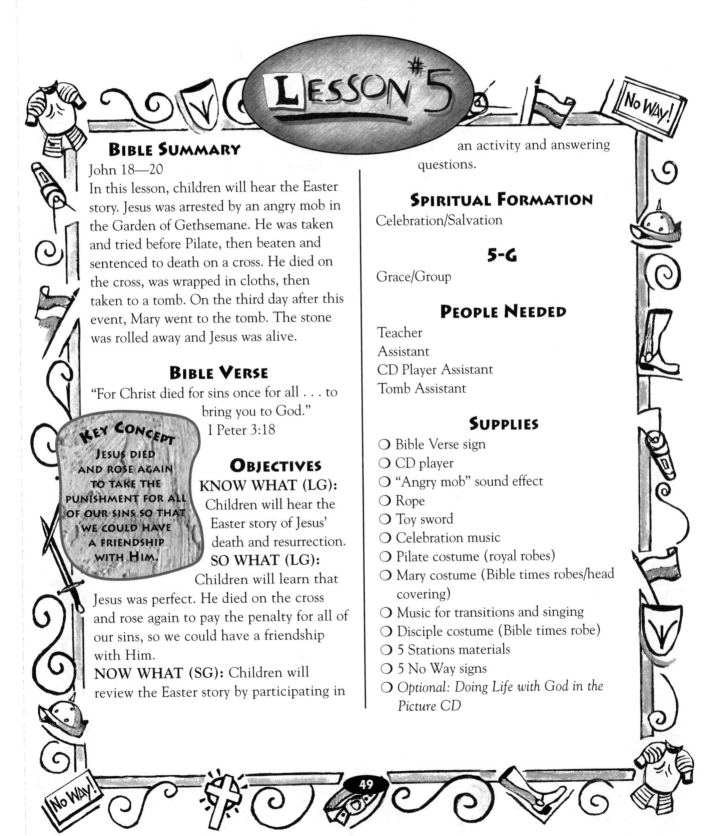

BIBLE SUMMARY

John 18—20

In this lesson, children will hear the Easter story. Jesus was arrested by an angry mob in the Garden of Gethsemane. He was taken and tried before Pilate, then beaten and sentenced to death on a cross. He died on the cross, was wrapped in cloths, then taken to a tomb. On the third day after this event, Mary went to the tomb. The stone was rolled away and Jesus was alive.

BIBLE VERSE

"For Christ died for sins once for all . . . to bring you to God."
I Peter 3:18

KEY CONCEPT

JESUS DIED AND ROSE AGAIN TO TAKE THE PUNISHMENT FOR ALL OF OUR SINS SO THAT WE COULD HAVE A FRIENDSHIP WITH HIM.

OBJECTIVES

KNOW WHAT (LG): Children will hear the Easter story of Jesus' death and resurrection.

SO WHAT (LG): Children will learn that Jesus was perfect. He died on the cross and rose again to pay the penalty for all of our sins, so we could have a friendship with Him.

NOW WHAT (SG): Children will review the Easter story by participating in an activity and answering questions.

SPIRITUAL FORMATION

Celebration/Salvation

5-G

Grace/Group

PEOPLE NEEDED

Teacher
Assistant
CD Player Assistant
Tomb Assistant

SUPPLIES

○ Bible Verse sign
○ CD player
○ "Angry mob" sound effect
○ Rope
○ Toy sword
○ Celebration music
○ Pilate costume (royal robes)
○ Mary costume (Bible times robes/head covering)
○ Music for transitions and singing
○ Disciple costume (Bible times robe)
○ 5 Stations materials
○ 5 No Way signs
○ *Optional: Doing Life with God in the Picture CD*

49

IN ADVANCE

- Determine which songs you will use and be prepared to lead or teach them.
- Gather supplies and set teaching area.
- Photocopy script and rehearse teaching time with Assistant and CD Player Assistant.
- Prepare Bible Verse sign.
- Prepare five No Way signs. Write "NO WAY" in thick black marker on five pieces of cardstock. Depending on how your stations are made, plan to hang, tape, or pin them to the stations.
- Choose celebration music. Use any upbeat, happy-sounding music. For example, you might use Steven Curtis Chapman's "Prologue" off of his *Great Adventure* CD.
- Gather costumes.
- Gather or prepare an "Angry mob" sound effect. You can create one with a group of people if you'd like.
- Gather equipment and prepare the 5 stations. You can make the stations as detailed or as simple as you'd like. Suggestions are as follows:

Station 1: Plants

Station 2: 2 Roman columns with a throne between them; drape purple and gold fabric over a chair to create a throne. (You can purchase Roman columns at craft stores, or create them out of large cardboard rolls.)

Station 3: A cross made from wood or foam board, draped with purple fabric

Station 4: A tomb; drape a dome roofed camping tent with gray and brown fabrics. Zip open the tent door to make an entrance. Place white fabric or sheets inside. Create the stone by cutting foam board in a circle and painting it shades of gray and black. Have Tomb Assistant sit inside the tent, ready to shine two flashlights during the lesson.

Station 5: Make a sun and clouds using foam board or poster board.

- Set up stations around your teaching area as follows:

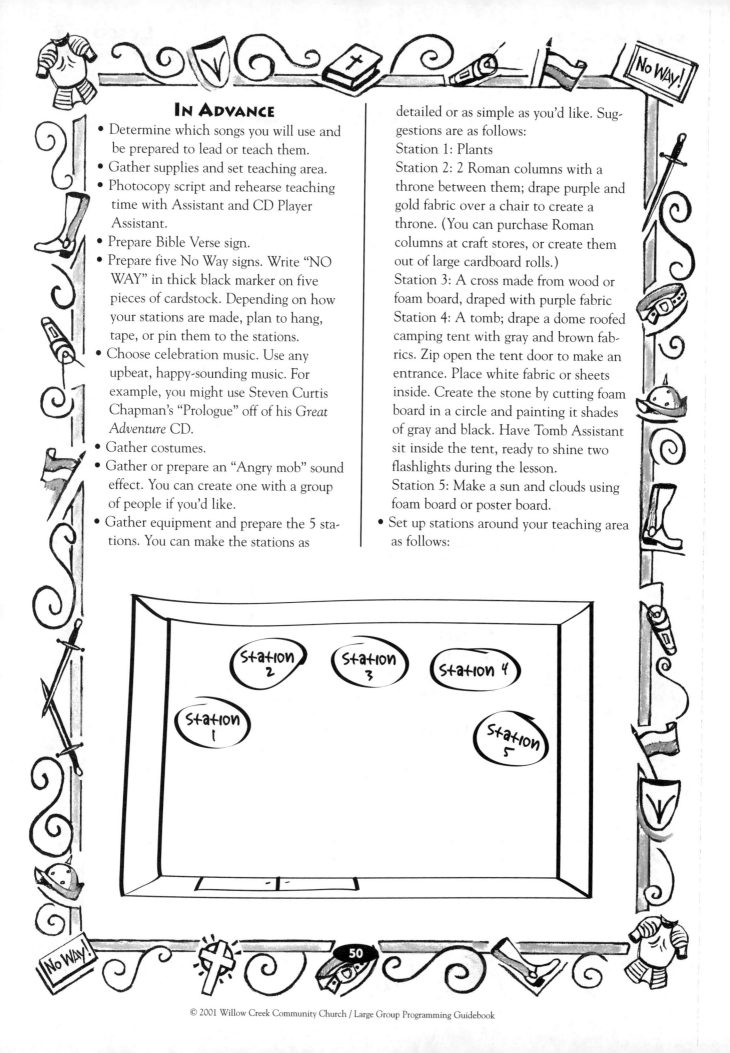

50

Pre-Teach

(5 minutes)

[Play upbeat music as children arrive.]

Teacher: Happy Easter, everybody! Welcome! I'm glad you're here, because Easter is such an awesome time to celebrate God's love for us. At Christmas, we heard about how God's love was unstoppable, and He sent His Son, Jesus, to earth. Today we are going to continue hearing the story of God's unstoppable love. God loves us so much that nothing could stop Him from making a way for us to be with Him forever.

TEACHING TIP
THE PRE-TEACH REFERS TO A CHRISTMAS LESSON FROM THE 5-G IMPACT WINTER QUARTER CURRICULUM. IF YOU DID NOT USE THIS CURRICULUM, SIMPLY TAKE OUT THAT SENTENCE.

God loves the people of the world so much. But because we sin—do things that are wrong—we are separated from God and could not be with Him, and that's a problem. God loves us so much though, that He sent His one and only Son, Jesus, to earth to take care of our sin problem. Jesus died to take the punishment for the sin that separates us from God. On Easter Sunday, we remember what Jesus went through in order to make it possible for us to be Forever Friends with Him and be with God forever. Today, I want to help you understand how God's love was unstoppable. We're going to tell the true story of how Jesus took the punishment for the wrong things we do—our sins.

TEACH

(15 MINUTES)

The following stations are set in a circle around the room:

Station 1: The Garden and the Arrest
Station 2: Pilate's Palace
Station 3: The Cross
Station 4: The Tomb
Station 5: Sun and Clouds

[Teacher walks to Station 1.]

Station 1: The Garden and the Arrest
Teacher: The story gets started in the dark of night. Jesus was with His disciples. The Bible says that Jesus was filled with pain and sadness because He knew the time had come to carry out God's plan. That plan meant Jesus was going to die. Jesus walked with people and talked with people. He was a perfect man who never sinned. He healed people, helped people, and showed people the love of God. Jesus was here on earth because of the amazing, unstoppable love of God, and He would do anything to show people that love. But Jesus knew this meant He would have to do something terribly hard.

Jesus came to earth to carry out God's great plan. God's plan was to provide a way for us to be Forever Friends with Him. That meant that the sin that separates us from God needed to be punished. We're separated from God because we sin, but He has no sin. God is perfect and heaven is perfect, so if He hadn't made a way for us, we couldn't go there to be with Him after we die, because we're not perfect. Because of our sin, we could miss out on being friends with God and being with Him in heaven after we die. But God loves us too much to let us be separated from Him forever. So, He sent Jesus to take the punishment for our sin so that we can be forgiven and be with God forever.

The time had come for Jesus to take our punishment. Jesus sat in a garden, alone in the night, preparing for all He was about to go through. He was going to die for people who didn't understand what He was doing for them. In fact, at that very moment, there were angry people gathering together to look for Jesus. The angry mob wanted Jesus dead. Now, Jesus was a perfect man. He never sinned. Yet this angry mob hated Jesus because He said He was the Son of God, and they didn't believe Him. They thought He was a liar. The angry mob was so stirred up that they wanted to kill Him.

Jesus knew the angry mob was coming. He fell to the ground, praying to God, His Father, in heaven. He asked God to change His plan if it was possible, but Jesus knew it was necessary to take the punishment for our sin. So Jesus obeyed His Father and carried out God's plan because of His unstoppable love for us.

While Jesus was praying in the garden that night, the Bible says His disciples kept falling asleep.

[Assistant enters in disciple costume and falls asleep.]

As they slept and Jesus prayed, the angry mob was looking for Jesus.

52

[*CD Player Assistant plays "angry mob" sound effect. Assistant wakes up, looking terrified.*]

The mob found Jesus in the garden that night. They came after Jesus with swords and torches, and when they found Him, they tied Him up and arrested Him. [*Display rope prop.*] As Jesus was dragged off by the angry mob, His disciples fled! When the angry mob came after Jesus, the disciples probably thought,

Assistant: [*scared*] No way!

[*Assistant runs behind Station 2 and puts on the Pilate costume. Teacher walks to Station 2.*]

Station 2: Pilate's Palace

Teacher: There was so much confusion and chaos that night. The mob dragged Jesus from place to place trying to find a judge or panel of judges who would condemn Jesus to die. They eventually brought Jesus to a government palace to be tried and judged before a leader named Pilate.

[*Assistant enters in Pilate costume looking very pious and concerned.*]

Teacher: Pilate didn't know what to do with Jesus because He knew Jesus hadn't done anything wrong. Jesus was a perfect man. He never sinned. Pilate knew Jesus had committed no crime. There was no reason to have Him killed. But the angry mob kept screaming and waving their swords, asking for Jesus' death.

[*Display sword prop; play sound effect of angry mob.*]

Pilate sent Jesus out to be beaten, but even that didn't satisfy the crowd. When Pilate realized that these people would not be satisfied until Jesus was killed, he shook his head and said—

Assistant: [*in disbelief*] No way.

[*Assistant quickly takes off Pilate costume. Teacher and Assistant walk to Station 3.*]

Station 3: The Cross

Assistant: The angry mob wanted Jesus to be crucified. Crucifying someone means nailing their hands and feet to a wooden cross and leaving them hanging up there until they die. Back in Jesus' day, crucifixion was a way to kill criminals. But Jesus was no criminal. Jesus had spent His entire life loving people, healing people, teaching people, and caring for people. But the angry crowd was so full of hatred that they wouldn't believe He was the Son of God. They couldn't see He had come to love them.

Teacher: This was all part of God's plan. The soldiers laid Jesus' beaten body down on the cross and nailed Him to it. They stood the cross up for everyone to see, and they left Him there to die. Even though Jesus was powerful enough to make it all stop at any second, He hung there and died because He loves us so much and knew that our sin needed to be punished. People shouted to Him saying, "If you are the Son of God, then come down off of that cross and save yourself!" Jesus could have done it. But instead, He said, "No way."

[*Teacher walks behind Station 4 and puts on Mary costume as Assistant continues to teach at the tomb*].

Assistant: Why would Jesus say "no way" to getting down off that cross? Jesus loved us so much that He chose to take the punishment for our sin so we could be Forever Friends with Him and live with God forever. The Bible says the sky grew dark, and there was thunder and lightning. Then, Jesus breathed His last breath. He hung His head and died. Jesus' body was wrapped in cloth, and He was placed in a tomb. A huge stone was placed in front of the entrance to the tomb.

[*Assistant walks to Station 4.*]

Station 4: The Tomb

Assistant: The Bible says that on the first day of that week, a woman named Mary came to visit the tomb where Jesus was buried.

[*Teacher enters in costume as Mary.*]

When she arrived at the tomb, it was opened! The huge stone that had been placed in front of the opening was rolled to the side!

[*Mary takes empty linens from tomb.*]

Assistant: Mary found the cloths in which they had wrapped Jesus when He died. The cloths were empty! Mary was confused. Had someone taken Jesus' body? Mary stood at the empty grave crying. Then, suddenly, two angels appeared in the tomb where Jesus' body had been.

[*Tomb Assistant shines lights out of the tomb. CD Player Assistant starts celebration music softly, and continues to turn up the volume.*]

Assistant: They asked her, "Why are you crying? Jesus isn't here. He is alive!" Then, when Mary turned around, she saw a man standing there!

[*"Mary" turns to look as if Jesus is standing there. CD Player Assistant turns celebration music loud, then begins to fade.*]

Assistant: It was Jesus. He wasn't dead! Jesus was alive! And Mary probably thought—

Teacher: [*excited*] No way!

Assistant: Jesus told Mary to go tell the others that He had risen. Jesus met with His disciples and they could hardly believe it. Jesus wasn't dead! He had risen! When the disciples saw Jesus alive, they all thought,

Assistant and Teacher: [*excited*] No way!

[*Teacher and Assistant walk to Station 5.*]

Station 5: Sun and Clouds

Teacher: This is why we celebrate. Jesus loves us so much that He was willing to suffer and die. I Peter 3:18 says, "For Christ died for sins once for all . . . to bring you to God." This Bible verse says that Jesus died to take the punishment for our sin so we could be with God forever. But when Jesus died, did He stay in that tomb?

Teacher and Assistant: No way!

Assistant: Jesus rose again. That is why we celebrate Easter. By dying for our sins, Jesus showed us how much He loves us. By rising from the dead, Jesus proved He is the Son of God. This sun and these clouds will remind us of the miracle of Easter morning. It reminds us that Jesus rose from the dead, and He is alive!

Post-Teach
(10 minutes)

Teacher: Now let me ask you a few questions.

[*Teacher and Assistant run to Station 1.*]

Teacher: When Jesus was arrested in the garden, did the love of God stop there?

All: No way!

[*Post "No Way" sign on station. Teacher and Assistant run to Station 2.*]

Assistant: When Jesus stood before Pilate, did the love of God stop here?

All: No way!

[*Post "No Way" sign on station. Teacher and Assistant run to Station 3.*]

Teacher: When Jesus hung on the cross that day, He could have stopped the whole thing and climbed down. But did the love of God stop here?

All: No way!

[*Post "No Way" sign on station. Teacher and Assistant run to Station 4.*]

Assistant: When Jesus was buried in a tomb, did the love of God stop here?

All: No way!

[*Post "No Way" sign on station. Teacher and Assistant run to Station 5.*]

Teacher: On the day of Easter, we celebrate the fact that Jesus rose from the dead, and He is alive! Can anything stop the love of God?

All: No way!

[*Post "No Way" sign on station.*]

Teacher: These stations helped us understand why we celebrate Easter. God's love wouldn't let anything get in the way of Jesus dying and rising from the dead. [*Display Bible Verse sign.*] Our Bible verse today says, "For Christ died for sins once for all . . . to bring you to God." I Peter 3:18. Let's say that together. [*Repeat verse together.*] Through His unstoppable love, **JESUS DIED AND ROSE AGAIN TO TAKE THE PUNISHMENT FOR ALL OF OUR SINS.** Jesus died so we can be with God in heaven forever. We are going to sing a few songs to celebrate Easter, but first, let's pray.

Prayer

Dear God,
Thank You for Your unstoppable love. Thank You for loving us so much that You sent Your Son, Jesus, to take the punishment for our sins, and then rise again from the dead. Help us to appreciate this gift. Amen.

Music

Song suggestions:
"24-7-365" (*Doing Life with God in the Picture* CD)
"Joy" (*Doing Life with God in the Picture* CD)

[*Dismiss to Small Groups. Play music as children exit.*]

56

UNIT 1: ARMOR OF GOD
SHIELD OF FAITH

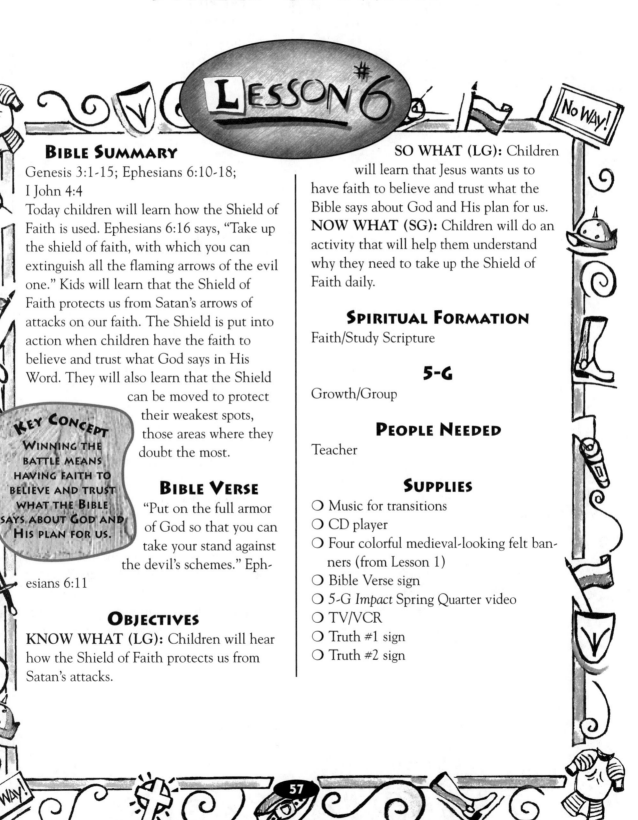

LESSON #6

BIBLE SUMMARY

Genesis 3:1-15; Ephesians 6:10-18;
I John 4:4

Today children will learn how the Shield of Faith is used. Ephesians 6:16 says, "Take up the shield of faith, with which you can extinguish all the flaming arrows of the evil one." Kids will learn that the Shield of Faith protects us from Satan's arrows of attacks on our faith. The Shield is put into action when children have the faith to believe and trust what God says in His Word. They will also learn that the Shield can be moved to protect their weakest spots, those areas where they doubt the most.

KEY CONCEPT
WINNING THE BATTLE MEANS HAVING FAITH TO BELIEVE AND TRUST WHAT THE BIBLE SAYS ABOUT GOD AND HIS PLAN FOR US.

BIBLE VERSE

"Put on the full armor of God so that you can take your stand against the devil's schemes." Ephesians 6:11

OBJECTIVES

KNOW WHAT (LG): Children will hear how the Shield of Faith protects us from Satan's attacks.

SO WHAT (LG): Children will learn that Jesus wants us to have faith to believe and trust what the Bible says about God and His plan for us.

NOW WHAT (SG): Children will do an activity that will help them understand why they need to take up the Shield of Faith daily.

SPIRITUAL FORMATION

Faith/Study Scripture

5-G

Growth/Group

PEOPLE NEEDED

Teacher

SUPPLIES

❍ Music for transitions
❍ CD player
❍ Four colorful medieval-looking felt banners (from Lesson 1)
❍ Bible Verse sign
❍ 5-G *Impact* Spring Quarter video
❍ TV/VCR
❍ Truth #1 sign
❍ Truth #2 sign

57

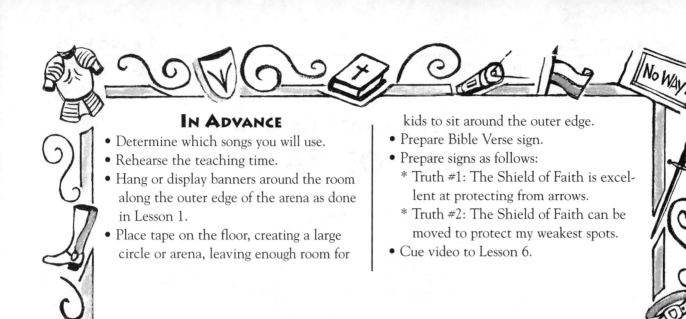

In Advance

- Determine which songs you will use.
- Rehearse the teaching time.
- Hang or display banners around the room along the outer edge of the arena as done in Lesson 1.
- Place tape on the floor, creating a large circle or arena, leaving enough room for kids to sit around the outer edge.
- Prepare Bible Verse sign.
- Prepare signs as follows:
  * Truth #1: The Shield of Faith is excellent at protecting from arrows.
  * Truth #2: The Shield of Faith can be moved to protect my weakest spots.
- Cue video to Lesson 6.

Pre-Teach
(5 minutes)

[Play medieval-like music as children arrive and continue playing it softly during the following teaching time. Have kids sit on the outskirts of the circle or arena, while you teach in the middle.]

Teacher: Over the past several weeks, we have been learning that we are in a battle. The Bible says there is a battle for our hearts and souls and those of our friends. It's not a battle we can see. But it is very, very real. It is the battle between God and Satan.

Satan's mission is to prevent people from choosing to believe in and follow God, and prevent Christians from growing into the people God wants them to be. Satan's goal is to prevent us and our friends from drawing close to God, following God's ways, and experiencing the joy and peace God offers.

God's mission is to help as many people in

this world as possible choose to believe in and follow Him, and grow Christians into the people He wants them to be. His goal is for everyone, including our friends and us, to be in a relationship with Him, love Him, and experience the joy and peace He wants to give us now and in heaven with Him someday. Some of you have made choices to join God's side—to become followers of Him. That is awesome. For those of you who haven't, you can do it at any time. God is just waiting for you to join His side.

We have learned that all of us are under attack by this enemy called Satan. You may not be able to see his attacks and they may not come with the blaring of trumpets, but they are very real attacks. Every time you find yourself tempted to do wrong or believe something about yourself or someone else that isn't true, you're under attack. When you find yourself leaning over to copy an answer on a test or find yourself flipping through channels and lingering on a movie you know you shouldn't watch, you're under attack. When you hear your friends talk about what a joke God and church are, and you start to wonder if they're right, you're under attack.

[*Slowly fade music out.*]

Whether we like it or not, we are part of this battle. It goes on twenty-four hours a day all around us. However, we are not helpless to fight our enemy, Satan. We have learned that we can defend ourselves with the Armor of God. In the Bible, Paul says this:

[*Show Bible Verse sign.*] "Put on the full armor of God so that you can take your stand against the devil's schemes." Ephesians 6:11

We have trained for the past several weeks on how to put on the Armor. We have trained ourselves to recognize Satan's attacks: ID the Attack. We have learned the second step which is to Unleash the Truth—using the Bible to defend against the attack. And finally, we have learned that when we do that, [*make forcefield sound effect*] immediately the Armor goes into place. So far we have learned how to put on the Helmet of Salvation, take up the Sword of the Spirit, put on the Belt of Truth, and put on the Breastplate of Right-eousness. Today we learn to take up the Shield of Faith.

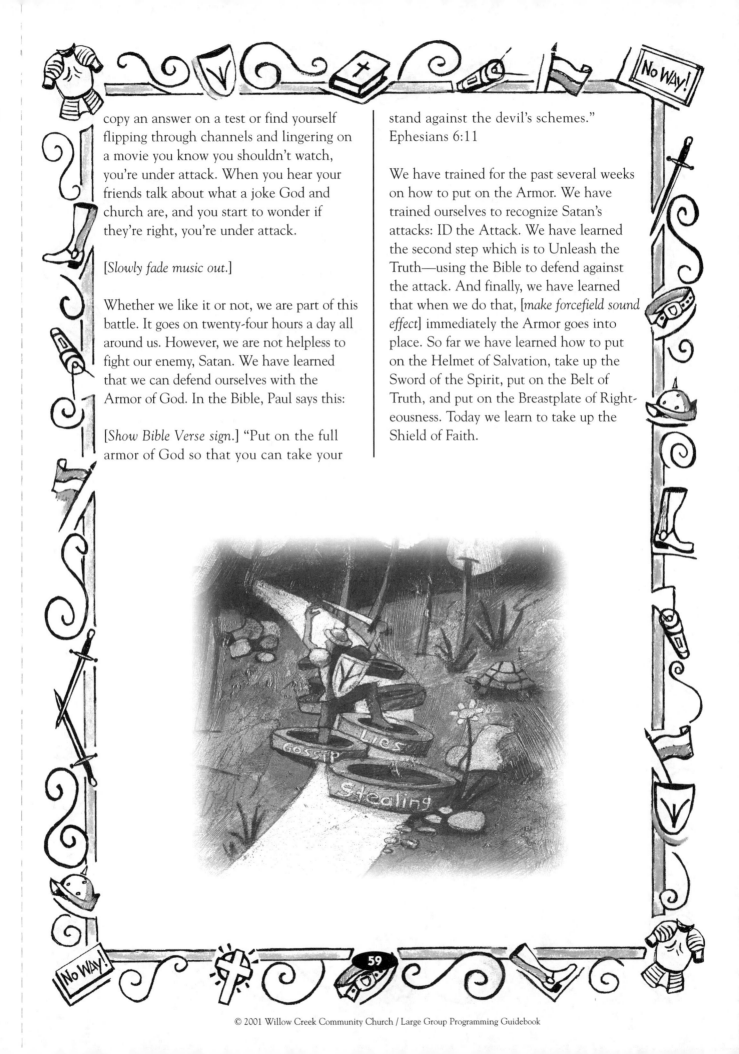

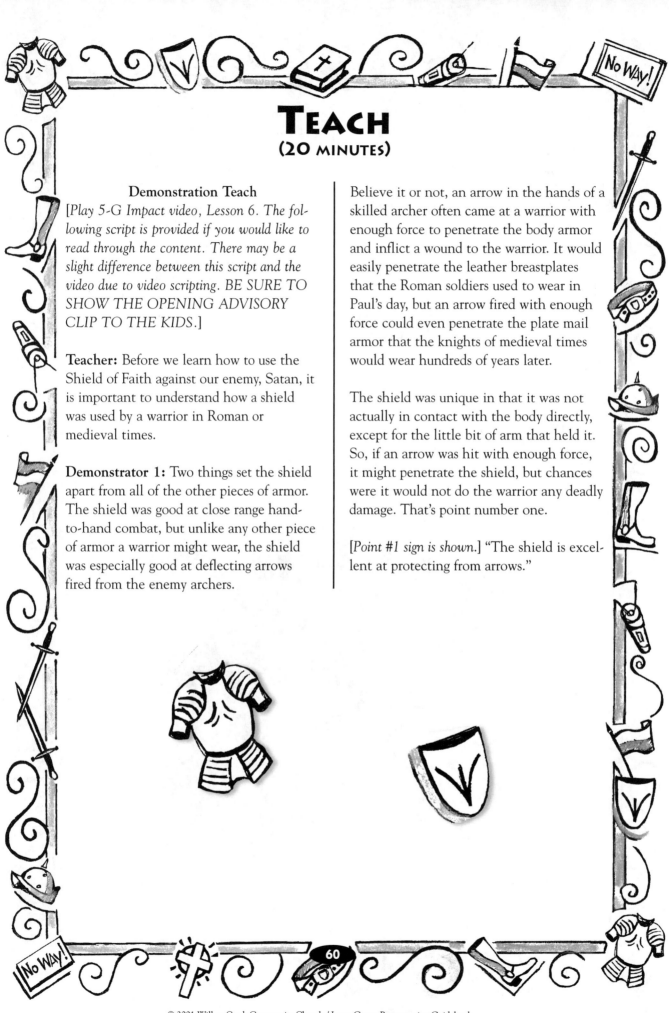

TEACH
(20 MINUTES)

Demonstration Teach

[Play 5-G Impact video, Lesson 6. The following script is provided if you would like to read through the content. There may be a slight difference between this script and the video due to video scripting. BE SURE TO SHOW THE OPENING ADVISORY CLIP TO THE KIDS.]

Teacher: Before we learn how to use the Shield of Faith against our enemy, Satan, it is important to understand how a shield was used by a warrior in Roman or medieval times.

Demonstrator 1: Two things set the shield apart from all of the other pieces of armor. The shield was good at close range hand-to-hand combat, but unlike any other piece of armor a warrior might wear, the shield was especially good at deflecting arrows fired from the enemy archers.

Believe it or not, an arrow in the hands of a skilled archer often came at a warrior with enough force to penetrate the body armor and inflict a wound to the warrior. It would easily penetrate the leather breastplates that the Roman soldiers used to wear in Paul's day, but an arrow fired with enough force could even penetrate the plate mail armor that the knights of medieval times would wear hundreds of years later.

The shield was unique in that it was not actually in contact with the body directly, except for the little bit of arm that held it. So, if an arrow was hit with enough force, it might penetrate the shield, but chances were it would not do the warrior any deadly damage. That's point number one.

[Point #1 sign is shown.] "The shield is excellent at protecting from arrows."

Teacher: The Shield of Faith protects us in the same way.

The Bible talks about Satan shooting flaming arrows at us. But his arrows aren't made of wood and metal. They are made of lies about us and God. These are the arrows Satan shoots at us. The Shield of Faith is excellent at protecting from arrows, because it reminds us to trust and believe what the Bible says about God and His plan for us.

When Satan tries to get you to believe lies about God or yourself, or gets you to doubt what God says in His Word, he's attacking. He's firing arrows at you. So the question becomes, what are you going to do when the arrows fly?

Teacher Voiceover: You could take the hit.

Satan Voiceover: You asked all of your friends to do something today but no one wants to hang out with you. You're a nobody. God wouldn't even want to hang out with you.

Kid Voiceover: [*taking the hit in the chest*] Yeah, I am a nobody.

Teacher Voiceover: Or, you can defend.

Satan Voiceover: You asked all of your friends to do something today but no one wants to hang out with you. You're a nobody. God wouldn't even want to hang out with you.

Kid Voiceover: ID the Attack: That's not true. Satan is trying to get me to believe things about myself and God that aren't true. Unleash the Truth: God loves me and says I am worth a great deal.

Teacher: And [*makes forcefield sound effect*] the Shield [*arrow is fired and deflected*] protects me from Satan's arrow.

Or how about this?

Satan Voiceover: [*attacking*] You are doing lousy at school and your parents haven't stopped fighting. You keep praying that God will make things better but things haven't changed. God doesn't care about you or your situation.

Kid Voiceover: ID the Attack: That's not true. This is an attack from Satan. Unleash the Truth: The Bible says God does care about me, listens to my prayers, and even sent His Son to die for me.

Teacher: And [*makes forcefield sound effect*] the Shield goes into place [*arrow is fired and deflected*] protecting me from Satan's arrow.

Or how about this?

Satan Voiceover: [*attacking*] You thought God was supposed to be powerful and good. Yeah, whatever. He would have prevented your dog from getting hit by that car if He was.

Kid Voiceover: ID the Attack: That's Satan talking, trying to get me to doubt who God is. Unleash the Truth: God is all-powerful and does no wrong. All His ways are good and perfect.

Teacher Voiceover: And [*makes forcefield sound effect*] the Shield goes into place [*arrow is fired and deflected*] protecting me

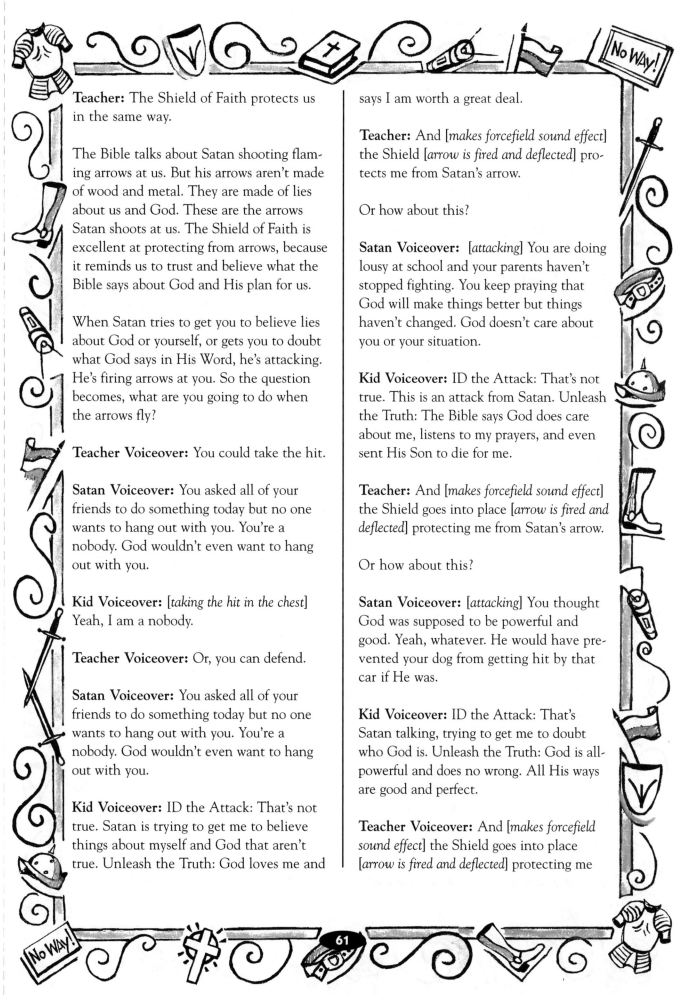

from Satan's arrow.

Teacher: Truth number one:

[*Truth #1 sign is shown.*] "The Shield of Faith is excellent at protecting from arrows."

The Shield of Faith is excellent at protecting from arrows, because it reminds us to trust and believe what the Bible says about God and His plans for us. That's why it's the Shield of Faith. It reminds us to believe the Bible, not Satan.

Let's switch back to the shields of Roman and medieval times and look at another way they were used.

Demonstrator 1: Another way that makes the shield different from the other pieces of armor is that a warrior could move it around to protect his weak spots so he can keep going. Let me explain.

As you look at the armor we wear, where would you say our weak spots are? Hands, face, and maybe the back of the legs. So, if we are engaged in battle, one of the things I'm going to do is go for his weak spot.

["*No-shield*" sequence is performed.]

If I get a shot through like this, and he was unable to protect his face, he's done for. He's out of the battle. But, when you add a shield into the equipment I'm using, and he goes for my weak spot . . .

["*With-shield*" sequence is performed.]

I am able to deflect it. I know my enemy is likely to go for my weakest spots, so I go into battle with a shield, the only piece of armor that I can move around to protect my weak spots. That's point number two.

[*Point #2 sign is shown.*] "The Shield can be moved to protect my weakest spots."

Teacher: The Shield of Faith works the same way. The Shield of Faith can be moved to protect my weakest spots—the areas where I doubt my worth, or doubt God's care and power. Just like an enemy is going to go for a warrior's weak spots, Satan loves to attack us where we are weakest too. Just like a warrior needs to be very aware of his weak spots so that he can defend them, we must be aware of our weak spots so Satan doesn't score hits where we are weakest. What does that mean? Well, if I struggle with feeling good about myself, Satan's attacks are going to hit me there.

Satan Voiceover: [*attacking*] You are the worst hitter on the whole team. You can never do anything right.

Teacher: Tempting me to feel worthless. If I struggle with believing I can be forgiven, Satan's going to attack me there.

Satan Voiceover: [*attacking*] God could never forgive you after you lied to your parents.

Teacher: Tempting me to believe that God couldn't forgive me. We have a responsibility as warriors in this battle to be aware of our weak spots, the areas we struggle, and defend ourselves when Satan tries to hit us there. Just like the shield a warrior uses, the Shield of Faith can be moved to protect my weakest spot. You either take the hit . . .

Satan Voiceover: [*attacking*] You are the worst hitter on the whole team. You can never do anything right.

Kid Voiceover: [*taking the hit*] Yeah, that's true. I can never do anything right. I'm worthless.

Teacher Voiceover: Or, you defend.

Satan Voiceover: [*attacking*] You are the worst hitter on the whole team. You can never do anything right.

Kid Voiceover: ID the Attack: "Wait a minute. I know I struggle with feeling good about myself. I bet this is Satan again."

Unleash the Truth: "The Bible says God loves me and values me. He thinks I am worth a great deal."

Teacher Voiceover: And [*makes forcefield sound effect*] the Shield of Faith goes into place protecting me from getting nailed by Satan in my weak spot.

Teacher: Truth 2:

[*Truth #2 sign is shown.*] "The Shield of Faith can be moved to protect my weakest spots."

[*Stop video.*]

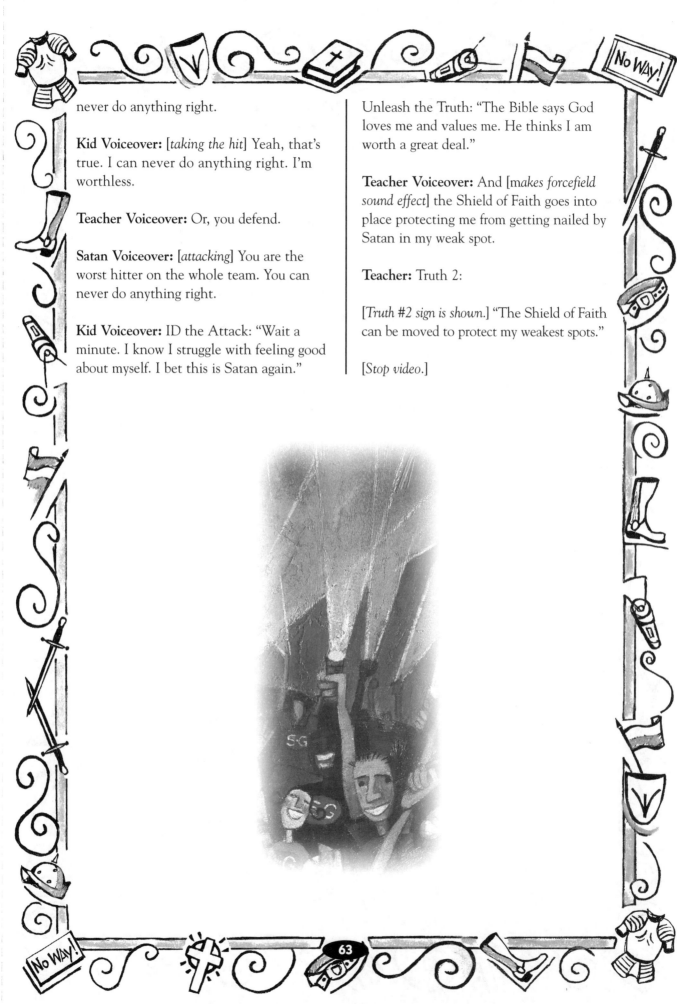

Post-Teach
(5 minutes)

Teacher: There are two ways the Shield of Faith protects you. Say them with me.

[*Show Truth #1 and Truth #2 signs.*]

The Shield of Faith is excellent at protecting from arrows. The Shield of Faith can be moved to protect my weakest spots—the places where I doubt. Whatever I struggle with is my weakest spot. The Shield of Faith reminds me to **TRUST AND BELIEVE WHAT THE BIBLE SAYS ABOUT GOD AND HIS PLAN FOR ME**. I don't just listen to Satan when the arrows fly. I don't just give in to Satan's attack because he's hitting me in my weak spot. The Shield helps me trust that God has plans for me that are different from what Satan wants me to do.

[*Play medieval-like music softly.*]

This week Satan will attack with arrows of lies and attacks on your weak spot. Don't take the hit. ID the Attack, Unleash the Truth, and [*make forcefield sound effect*] defend with the Shield of Faith.

Prayer

Dear God,
Thank You for giving us the Shield of Faith to defend ourselves from Satan's lies and attacks on our faith. Help us to take up the Shield and use it so that we can be protected. Amen.

[*Dismiss to Small Groups. Play medieval-like music as children exit.*]

UNIT 1: ARMOR OF GOD
SHOES OF THE
GOSPEL OF PEACE/REVIEW

BIBLE SUMMARY

Ephesians 6:10-18
Today children will learn how the Shoes of the Gospel of Peace are used. Ephesians 6:14 says, "Stand firm then . . . with your feet fitted with the readiness that comes from the gospel of peace." Kids will learn that the Shoes of the Gospel of Peace remind us that this message must get through, even though the way is tough. We need to be ready to deliver the message at any time. In addition, children will review all six of the Armor of God pieces to help them learn how to win the battle.

KEY CONCEPT

WINNING THE BATTLE MEANS TAKING THE GOOD NEWS OF JESUS TO EVERYONE.

BIBLE VERSE

"Put on the full armor of God so that you can take your stand against the devil's schemes."
Ephesians 6:11

OBJECTIVES

KNOW WHAT (LG): Children will learn about the Shoes of the Gospel of Peace and how they equip us to share the Gospel, as well as review the whole Armor of God.
SO WHAT (LG): Children will learn that there is a spiritual battle and God wants us to tell others the good news of Jesus.

NOW WHAT (SG): Children will participate in an activity that reviews the Shoes of the Gospel of Peace and the full Armor of God.

SPIRITUAL FORMATION

Evangelism

5-G

Grace/Group

PEOPLE NEEDED

Two Teachers
One 4th/5th grade child

SUPPLIES

- ⭘ Music for transitions
- ⭘ CD player
- ⭘ Four colorful medieval-looking felt banners (from Lesson 1)
- ⭘ Two red flags
- ⭘ Two blue flags
- ⭘ Obstacle course (rocks, balance beam, "wall")
- ⭘ Reminder #1 sign
- ⭘ Reminder #2 sign
- ⭘ Ephesians 6:11-17 sign
- ⭘ Six armor signs
- ⭘ *Optional: Six pieces of armor—helmet, sword, belt, breastplate, shield, shoes*

IN ADVANCE

- Determine which songs you will use.
- Select a child ahead of time to be "The Messenger." Explain his/her role, the expectations, and give him/her a chance to see the obstacle course and run through it if possible. Tell him/her that it could be messy and he/she should wear old clothes.
- Rehearse the teaching time.
- Create four large flags out of felt or nylon and set them by the teaching area.
- Prepare signs as follows:
  * The Shoes of the Gospel of Peace remind us that this message must get through, even though the way is tough.
  * The Shoes of the Gospel of Peace remind us to be ready to deliver the message at any time.
  * "Put on the full armor of God so that you can take your stand against the devil's schemes. Stand firm then, with the belt of truth buckled around your waist [*make forcefield sound effect*], with the breastplate of righteousness in place [*make forcefield sound effect*], and with your feet fitted with the readiness that comes from the gospel of peace [*make forcefield sound effect two times*]. In addition to all this, take up the shield of faith [*make forcefield sound effect*], with

which you can extinguish all the flaming arrows of the evil one. Take the helmet of salvation [*make forcefield sound effect*] and the sword of the Spirit [*make forcefield sound effect*], which is the word of God." Ephesians 6:11-17
  * Helmet of Salvation
  * Sword of the Spirit
  * Belt of Truth
  * Breastplate of Righteousness
  * Shield of Faith
  * Shoes of the Gospel of Peace
- Hang or display banners around the room along the outer edge of the arena as done in Lesson 1.
- Place armor signs around the outer edge of the room.
- Set up an obstacle course out of rocks, a balance beam, a created "wall," or other items that are difficult to walk across barefoot (see Unit 1 Overview Large Group Helpful Hints, pages 17-18). Place the start of the course near the back of the room where one half of the blue army will stand and the end of the course near the front where the other half of the blue army will stand.
- *Optional: Gather pieces of armor instead of armor signs and place around the outer edge of the room.*

PRE-TEACH
(5 MINUTES)

[Play medieval-like music as children arrive.]

Teacher 1: Hey everybody! Over the last several weeks we have been training for the battle we are in against Satan and his forces. Satan's goal is to try to prevent people from choosing to believe in and follow God, and to prevent Christians from growing into the people God wants them to be.

We have been training to put on the Armor of God so that we can grow into the people God wants us to be and help God with His mission of helping as many people as possible choose to believe in and follow Him.

Our battle training is close to an end. Today we learn about our final piece of Armor in the Armor of God—the Shoes of the Gospel of Peace.

TEACH
(20 MINUTES)

MESSENGER'S CHALLENGE
[Select two kids in the audience who are in the middle, and give each a red flag. Ask for a group of about six kids to come forward and hold a blue flag up front, representing one half of the blue army. Select another group of kids to stand in the back of the room and hold the other blue flag, representing the second half of the blue army. Make sure "The Messenger" is in this group at the back.]

Teacher 2: Before we talk about the Shoes of the Gospel of Peace, I want you to understand how important a warrior's shoes were to him in battle, so that you can better understand the Shoes that Paul tells us to wear. We're going to need your help to do that. When I point to those of you around the red flags and say "red army," I want the red army to let out a ferocious battle cry. [*Have the red army do their battle cry.*] When I point to those of you at the front and back and say "blue army," I want the blue army to let out a ferocious battle cry. [*Have the blue army do their battle cry.*]

The point of this story is to help you better understand how important a warrior's shoes were to him. I want you to imagine with me that we are in medieval times—in the days of warriors and battles.

[*Play medieval-like music.*]

There is a war going on between two great armies—the red army [*signal the red army to yell their battle cry*] and the blue army [*signal the blue army to yell their battle cry*]. Both armies are strong and mighty, but on this particular day, something different happens. The red army [*signal the red army to yell their battle cry*] fights strongly and courageously, but they are also very cunning. The blue army [*signal the blue army to yell their battle cry*] also fights courageously, but at the end of the day when the red army sits down and makes camp for the night, the blue army discovers something. Somehow in the heat of battle, the red army has managed to separate and divide the blue army.

Half of the blue army [*point to the kids at the front*] is trapped against a sheer cliff face with the red army breathing down their necks. The other half of the blue army [*point to the kids at the back of the room*] is behind the enemy and free from danger. They could make a run for it. In fact, that's what the red army is hoping they will do, so that they can finish off the rest of the blue army. But this half of the blue army [*point to the kids at the back of the room*] chooses not to do that. They have a mission to win this battle and take as many of their friends to the winning side as they can. So they bring in a very special warrior. They bring in "The Messenger."

[*Have the child, pre-selected to be "The Messenger," come forward.*]

This warrior's job is to make [*his/her*] way safely through some very dangerous territory. In fact,

> **TEACHING TIP**
>
> MAKE IT APPEAR THAT YOU ARE RANDOMLY SELECTING SOMEONE TO BE "THE MESSENGER" OUT OF THE BLUE ARMY IN THE BACK.

[*he/she*] must go right through the middle of the enemy, the red army, to get an important message to the other side. This message is critical. It lays out plans for the blue army to defeat the enemy once and for all and means the difference between life and death for those trapped on the other side.

[*Point from back to front.*]

[*Speaking to "The Messenger."*] Your job is to get from here to there with the message. But the way is not easy. Not only do you have to go through enemy territory, the terrain is filled with all kinds of dangers.

[*Point out each specific obstacle in the course.*]

As if things weren't bad enough, "The Messenger" has come unprepared today. [*He/she*] has left [*his/her*] shoes in the camp. So, Messenger, you will have to execute this mission barefoot! [*Have the child remove his/her shoes.*] You will have only thirty seconds. Are you ready? Go!

[*Play upbeat music as "The Messenger" tries to go through the obstacles you have set up. He/she should slip and fall along the way, and not get through the course in time.*]

Okay Messenger, it seems you had a hard time getting there. That may be because you were not properly equipped to take the message from here to there. You had to go through such slippery and rocky terrain and you didn't even have your shoes. Let's try it again, but this time let's equip you. This time we'll have you put on your shoes, and see if that makes you more ready to deliver the message. [*Have "The Messenger" put on his/her shoes.*] You have thirty seconds. Are you ready? Go!

[*Play upbeat music as "The Messenger" goes through the course again. This time he/she should go through it more easily, confidently, and quickly. He/she should make it to the end.*]

Would you say that our messenger was more ready to carry [*his/her*] message through enemy territory when [*he/she*] was equipped with [*his/her*] shoes? [*Have audience clap and cheer.*] Yes, I would agree. Because [*he/she*] was equipped, the blue army gets the message and defeats the red army! The battle is won!

[*Have "The Messenger" return to his/her seat. Encourage everyone to applaud for him/her.*]

Teacher 1: That's how shoes were important to a warrior in Paul's day. This part of the blue army [*point to the back*] could have made a run for it. They were free and clear. But they didn't. They got the message to

their friends, so that all of them could be on the winning side. But getting the message there successfully required being equipped with the shoes.

Teacher 2: In the battle we face with Satan, we are like that half of the blue army [*point to the back*]. Those of us who are followers of God are on the winning side. We could just enjoy that fact and wait around for heaven. But the truth is, we have a mission to get to the end of the battle with as many of our friends as possible.

We have a message we must get to our friends who don't know God [*point to the blue army at the front*]. This message will mean the difference between spending eternity with God and spending eternity apart from God. This message is called the Gospel Message of Jesus. "Gospel" literally means "Good News," and this message is good news to people who haven't heard it. It's the message that Jesus died on the cross so that we can be in a relationship with God. Following Him will change their lives. This is the message we must deliver about Jesus—what He did for us and what He can do for them.

Unlike the blue army who only had one messenger, we are all the messengers in our army. We must take this message, the awesome news about Jesus, to all of our friends who don't know it. They are trapped by the enemy army and they don't know God.

The problem is there are a lot of obstacles that stand between us telling them this message. [*Walk along the obstacles on the*

course, pairing an obstacle with each of the following statements.] We might get made fun of. Maybe we feel we don't know enough to answer questions about God. Or, maybe we just don't feel like we know how to tell our friends about Jesus.

Teacher 1: We need to equip ourselves to deliver this message. We need to put on the Shoes of the Gospel of Peace. When we put on a pair of shoes each morning, we are preparing our feet for walking, running, and playing. They help us get where we are going and what we are doing. The Shoes of the Gospel of Peace are shoes we put on each morning in our mind that remind us to deliver the message of the good news of Jesus to people who don't know the message. When we put them on, they remind us of two specific things.

[*Show Reminder #1 sign.*] The Shoes of the Gospel of Peace remind us that this message must get through, even though the way is tough.

We may get made fun of and people will know we are followers of Jesus when we talk about Him to people. But this message must get through because it means the difference between winning the battle and losing the battle for our friends. Jesus said to go into all the world and tell the good news to everyone. The Bible tells us that Jesus' followers will win the battle, so we can go back in and get our friends. The Shoes of the Gospel of Peace remind us that this message must get through, even though the way is tough.

Teacher 2: Second, the Shoes of the Gospel of Peace remind us to be ready to deliver the message at any time.

[*Show Reminder #2 sign.*]

This involves knowing how to talk about Jesus to your friends. We need to be ready to talk with our friends about God, bring friends to church, and tell them our story and Jesus' story. We spent a whole unit earlier this year about telling our friends about Jesus. Remember the "Lost World" unit? We talked about starting a God talk, bringing friends here, telling them your story—all three parts—and telling them Jesus' story—the bridge across. Being ready to deliver the message at any time means knowing how to do these things. The Shoes remind us to be ready to deliver the message at any time. We need to be on the lookout for opportunities.

This is how the Shoes of the Gospel of Peace equip us in the battle. We wear them as a reminder of the message. But just like

TEACHING TIP

IF YOU DID NOT USE THE FALL QUARTER CURRICULUM CONTAINING THE UNIT "LOST WORLD," SKIP THOSE SENTENCES AND CONTINUE WITH THE TEACH.

you learned each week with the other pieces of Armor, we must remember the three steps of ID the Attack, Unleash the Truth, and equip with the Shoes because Satan will attack and try to prevent us from carrying out the message. We may be on the lookout for opportunities to tell our friends about Jesus, but when we find them, we may back away. We need to ID the Attack because Satan doesn't want you to tell people. He may try to convince you that your popularity or what people will think of you is more important than delivering the message. Then you Unleash the Truth: This is an opportunity to carry out Jesus' command, and you need to get the message through. Instead of backing away from those chances, [*step forward with one foot, making the forcefield sound effect, then do the same with the other foot*] equip yourself with the Shoes of the Gospel of Peace, and step forward to deliver the message.

Teacher 1: We have now equipped ourselves with six pieces of Armor. We have the full Armor of God. Let's take a look at our Bible verse so we can see all of the pieces together. Let's add our sound effect as well after each piece of Armor, just to remind us.

[*Show Ephesians 6:11-17 sign.*] "Put on the

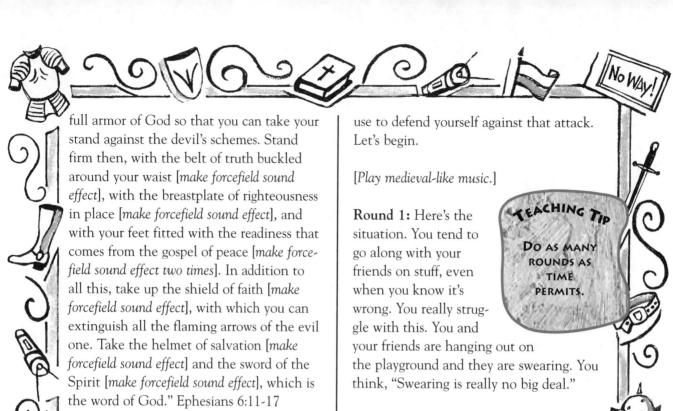

full armor of God so that you can take your stand against the devil's schemes. Stand firm then, with the belt of truth buckled around your waist [*make forcefield sound effect*], with the breastplate of righteousness in place [*make forcefield sound effect*], and with your feet fitted with the readiness that comes from the gospel of peace [*make forcefield sound effect two times*]. In addition to all this, take up the shield of faith [*make forcefield sound effect*], with which you can extinguish all the flaming arrows of the evil one. Take the helmet of salvation [*make forcefield sound effect*] and the sword of the Spirit [*make forcefield sound effect*], which is the word of God." Ephesians 6:11-17

WARRIOR'S CHALLENGE II

Teacher 2: You have been doing a great job with the steps each week of ID the Attack, Unleash the Truth, and [*make forcefield sound effect*] equip yourself with the Armor piece. One thing that may be confusing to you, however, is when to use one piece over another. You might ask yourself, "When should I use the Helmet or when should I use the Belt? Is there a right and wrong piece to use for different situations? Let's clarify that now. Together let's play The Warrior's Challenge II!

Everyone stand to your feet. The rules are simple. I will give you some situations. I will walk you through the steps of ID the Attack, Unleash the Truth, and then you will walk to the piece of Armor you would use to defend yourself against that attack. Let's begin.

[*Play medieval-like music.*]

Round 1: Here's the situation. You tend to go along with your friends on stuff, even when you know it's wrong. You really struggle with this. You and your friends are hanging out on the playground and they are swearing. You think, "Swearing is really no big deal."

ID the Attack: [*take answers*] This is Satan tempting me to do something the Bible says not to do. Unleash the Truth: [*take answers*] The Bible says not to let any unwholesome talk come out of our mouths.

[*Have children go to the armor sign they think defends against the attack. Have someone explain why he or she chose that armor piece.*]

Round 2: You learn about evolution in biology class. Your teacher says we all evolved from monkeys. It even kind of starts to make some sense to you. You begin to think, "Maybe we did evolve from monkeys. Maybe God isn't real."

ID the Attack: [*take answers*] Satan is trying to get you to doubt God. Unleash the Truth: [*take answers*] The Bible says that

God created the heavens and the earth and all living things.

[*Have children go to the armor sign they think defends against the attack. Have someone explain why he or she chose that armor piece.*]

Round 3:
You feel so worthless lately. You feel like you mess up too much, disobey your parents, and don't get good grades in school. You are not even sure that God loves you. You are convinced that you could never tell anyone about Jesus.

ID the Attack: [*take answers*] This is Satan telling me lies about God and myself.
Unleash the Truth: [*take answers*] The Bible says God does love me and sent His Son to die for me.

[*Have children go to the armor sign they think defends against the attack. Have someone explain why he or she chose that armor piece.*]

POST-TEACH
(5 MINUTES)

Teacher 1: There are some real differences between some of the pieces of Armor. The Shield of Faith is really good at protecting our weak spot—the place where we doubt. The Belt of Truth can stop us from getting tangled up in lies. The Breastplate of Righteousness helps our beliefs and actions line up. There are things that make each piece unique.

Teacher 2: The important thing, however, is to wear the full Armor of God all of the time, and use it to fight Satan. If you're stopping Satan's lies, stopping his temptations, and stopping his influence on your life, that's more important than whether or not you used the right piece of Armor. Any piece of Armor is right if it protects you from Satan's influence in your life. That's why Paul says to wear the full Armor of God, so that we are ready for anything.

Remember, when it comes to this battle between God and Satan and his forces, the ending is already clear. God will win in the end. Winning for us means continuing to grow into the people God wants us to be and taking as many of our friends with us along the way. The battle is hard for us. We need to wear the full Armor of God so we are ready for anything.

PRAYER

Dear God,
Thank You for the Armor of God which protects us and helps us defend against Satan's attacks. Help us to put the full Armor of God on each day so we are ready when we need to use it and so we will continue to grow into the Christ-followers You want us to be. Amen.

[Dismiss to Small Groups. Play medieval-like music as children exit.]

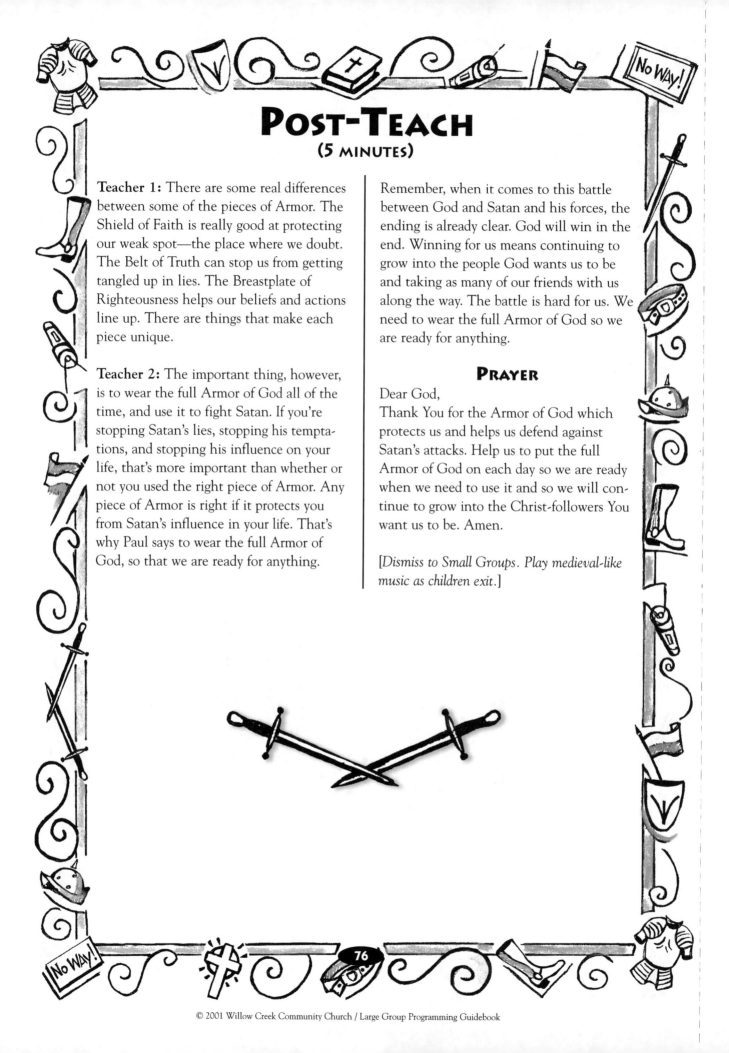

UNIT 2 OVERVIEW
LEARNING TO SHINE

UNIT SUMMARY

This second unit of the Spring Quarter teaches children that believers are the light of the world. If they are following Jesus, they have His light inside of them and need to shine their light in our dark world so others will come to know God. Each week kids will learn that in order to shine, they must overcome obstacles that prevent them from shining. Lesson 8 teaches children to overcome their fears and set an example by living life the way Jesus teaches in the Bible. Lesson 9 teaches kids to match their actions with their faith. Lesson 10 teaches children that as believers, they are children of God, members of God's family, and unconditionally loved. They can build their confidence on God's promises rather than on other things, and have the confidence to shine. Lesson 11 teaches kids to choose to use encouraging words rather than unwholesome talk. Lesson 12 teaches children to be joyful and persevere no matter what they are facing. Finally, Lesson 13 reviews the 5-Gs and teaches kids that these Gs are marks of a fully devoted follower of Christ. Children will spend time in their Small Groups reviewing the 5-Gs and having a Small Group Celebration.

LESSON OVERVIEWS

LESSON 8
Why Shine?
Matthew 5:14-16

Key Concept: Learning to shine means knowing Jesus wants to shine His light through us and set an example for the dark world.

Bible Verse: "Let your light shine before men, that they may see your good deeds and praise your Father in heaven." Matthew 5:16

Know What (LG): Children will learn that believers are the light of the world.

So What (LG): Children will learn that they are to shine their light by living life the way Jesus teaches in the Bible. When they do this, they set an example for the dark world.

Now What (SG): Children will participate in an activity to identify how others have shined and how they could shine in situations they have experienced.

Spiritual Formation: Evangelism/Growth

5-G: Growth/Group

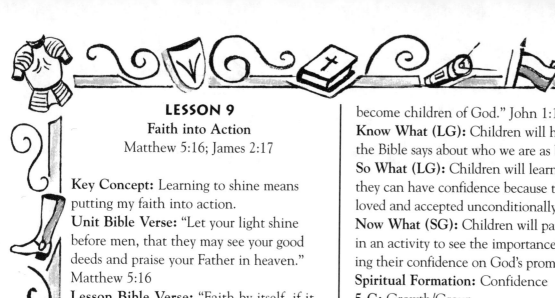

LESSON 9
Faith into Action
Matthew 5:16; James 2:17

Key Concept: Learning to shine means putting my faith into action.
Unit Bible Verse: "Let your light shine before men, that they may see your good deeds and praise your Father in heaven." Matthew 5:16
Lesson Bible Verse: "Faith by itself, if it is not accompanied by action, is dead." James 2:17
Know What (LG): Children will hear that the Bible teaches that our faith in God is shown through our actions.
So What (LG): Children will learn that when believers put their faith into action, they shine and others will be drawn towards God.
Now What (SG): Children will participate in an activity that helps them understand how to put their faith into action.
Spiritual Formation: Faith/Self-discipline (words and actions)
5-G: Growth/Group

LESSON 10
Confidence
Jeremiah 31:3; John 1:12

Key Concept: Learning to shine means being confident in who we are as believers rather than in things around us.
Unit Bible Verse: "Let your light shine before men, that they may see your good deeds and praise your Father in heaven." Matthew 5:16
Lesson Bible Verses: "I have loved you with an everlasting love." Jeremiah 31:3
"Yet to all who received Him, to those who believed in His name, He gave the right to become children of God." John 1:12
Know What (LG): Children will hear what the Bible says about who we are as believers.
So What (LG): Children will learn that they can have confidence because they are loved and accepted unconditionally by God.
Now What (SG): Children will participate in an activity to see the importance of building their confidence on God's promises.
Spiritual Formation: Confidence
5-G: Growth/Group

LESSON 11
Unwholesome Talk
Matthew 15:18; Ephesians 4:29; James 3:1-12

Key Concept: Learning to shine means continuing to control my tongue and speaking words that encourage.
Unit Bible Verse: "Let your light shine before men, that they may see your good deeds and praise your Father in heaven." Matthew 5:16
Lesson Bible Verse: "Do not let any unwholesome talk come out of your mouths, but only what is helpful for building others up according to their needs, that it may benefit those who listen." Ephesians 4:29
Know What (LG): Children will hear that the Bible teaches us we can use our tongue to tear others down or build them up.
So What (LG): Children will learn that God wants us to be careful with our words so that our words may build others up.
Now What (SG): Children will identify situations they may be tempted to use their tongue to hurt others and practice speaking in ways that are encouraging.
Spiritual Formation: Self-discipline
5-G: Growth/Group

LESSON 12
Joy No Matter What
James 1:2

Key Concept: Learning to shine means having joy and perseverance no matter what I'm facing.

Unit Bible Verse: "Let your light shine before men, that they may see your good deeds and praise your Father in heaven." Matthew 5:16

Lesson Bible Verse: "Consider it pure joy, my brothers, whenever you face trials of many kinds, because you know that the testing of your faith develops perseverance." James 1:2

Know What (LG): Children will hear that the Bible teaches that problems can be a test of our faith.

So What (LG): Children will learn that God wants us to have joy no matter what problems we encounter. This will develop perseverance.

Now What (SG): Children will participate in an activity to see how they might persevere and shine through problems.

Spiritual Formation: Perseverance

5-G: Growth/Group

LESSON 13
5-G Review and Small Group Celebration
John 15:12

Key Concept: Doing life with God in the picture means being part of a community of other believers.

Bible Verse: "Love each other." John 15:12

Know What (LG): Children will hear a review of the 5-Gs.

So What (LG): Children will learn that God has an overall plan for us. He wants us to be fully devoted followers of Christ.

Now What (SG): Children will review the 5-Gs and participate in a Small Group celebration where they will celebrate with their Small Groups all that God has done throughout this year.

Spiritual Formation: Celebration

5-G: Grace/Growth/Group/Gifts/Good Stewardship

LARGE GROUP PRESENTATION SUMMARY

The Large Group Programs of Lessons 8-12 use the *Learning to Shine* video. This video shows dramas of kids learning to shine in everyday situations. In Lesson 8, the teacher begins the teaching time in the dark to illustrate that we live in a dark world. The lights are then turned on as the teacher discusses Jesus' light. In Lesson 10, a demonstration using blocks and bricks is used to illustrate the difference between building confidence on God's promises and building confidence on other things. In Lesson 12, the teacher shares an appropriate story about a trial he/she has had and the lessons learned through it. Kids will each receive a small flashlight at the end of Lesson 12. They will turn them on one by one to show what can happen when each person shines. In Lesson 13, stations are set up around the room with props and a 5-G sign at each station to review all that kids have learned this year about the 5-Gs. Much of the material covered in the Large Group Program in Lesson 13 reflects reviews of Fall and Winter Quarter curriculum. If you did not use this curriculum, use the Large Group time for singing and worship only.

LARGE GROUP HELPFUL HINTS

1. The Learning to Shine unit sign will be used each week of Lessons 8-12. Be sure to store it carefully so that it can be used each week.
2. The lyrics on the CD jacket for the song "Learnin' to Shine" are incorrect. Please see www.PromiselandOnline.com for correct lyrics.
3. To set the atmosphere in the room for this unit, consider using fun lights. Set lava lamps, candles, lanterns, flashlights, and other unique lamps around the room.
4. In Lesson 8, you have the option of playing DC Talk's "In the Light" music video or song from their CD. To make the transition to the *Learning to Shine* video as smooth as possible, have an Assistant switch the tapes or turn on the CD while you interact with the kids about their impressions of the drama.

5. In Lesson 8, you will turn off all of the lights after kids are seated. To create a dark room, you may need to place dark shades over windows and black tape on lighted signs. Consider kids or leaders who arrive late and may bring light in as they open the door. Darken the hallway where they would enter or have them wait until the teacher has turned on the lights. The darker the room is, the more effective and cool the lesson will be for the kids.

6. Type out signs to tape on the bricks and blocks in the demonstration in Lesson 10. Create signs in a large size print so that kids can see them.

7. Be aware of seeker kids who have not yet made a choice to accept Jesus as their Savior. Emphasize that they can have Jesus' light inside of them if they choose to accept Him.

8. In Lesson 12, you will tell an appropriate story of a trial you experienced and what God taught you through it. Here are some tips for telling an effective story:
   a. Share the facts of your trial step by step.
   b. Express the feelings you were experiencing during the trial (scared, angry, sad).
   c. Explain how the trial turned out.
   d. Share what God taught you through the trial. (You may still be experiencing the trial. Share what God is teaching you now as you are experiencing it.)

9. There may be someone in your church who has a powerful story about a trial he or she faced that might be willing to share for Lesson 12. Discuss with that person the expectations and the tips for telling an effective story.

10. In Lesson 13, use toys that are popular with 4th and 5th grade kids today.

11. If you do not have easels to use with the stations in Lesson 13, hang the 5-G signs around the room. Place props on small tables near the sign or place the props on the floor next to the sign.

FOR ADDITIONAL IDEAS AND TIPS, VISIT WWW.PROMISE-LANDONLINE.COM.

SMALL GROUP SUMMARY

Each Small Group activity in this lesson gives kids opportunities to practice shining their light. In Lesson 8, kids will hear stories in the Bible. They will then vote by turning on their flashlights if the person or persons shined. Children will also share stories of times when they didn't shine and how they could have shined. In Lesson 9, kids will do an activity in which they guess the action that is being acted out by a child, similar to charades. In Lesson 10, children will build with blocks and see the benefit of building their confidence on God's promises rather than on other things. In Lesson 11, kids will do two activities. In the first activity, children will brainstorm situations where they might be tempted to use unwholesome words. Kids will then give wholesome and encouraging words they could use to change the situation. In the second activity, children will do an activity with their flashlights in which one team will communicate in flashlight code to another team wholesome words to replace unwholesome words. In Lesson 12, children will put sentences together using words and phrases on Word Cards that describe a problem or trial. The group will then brainstorm ways the person in the sentence could have joy and persevere through the problem. In Lesson 13, there is no Kid Connection. Kids will enter

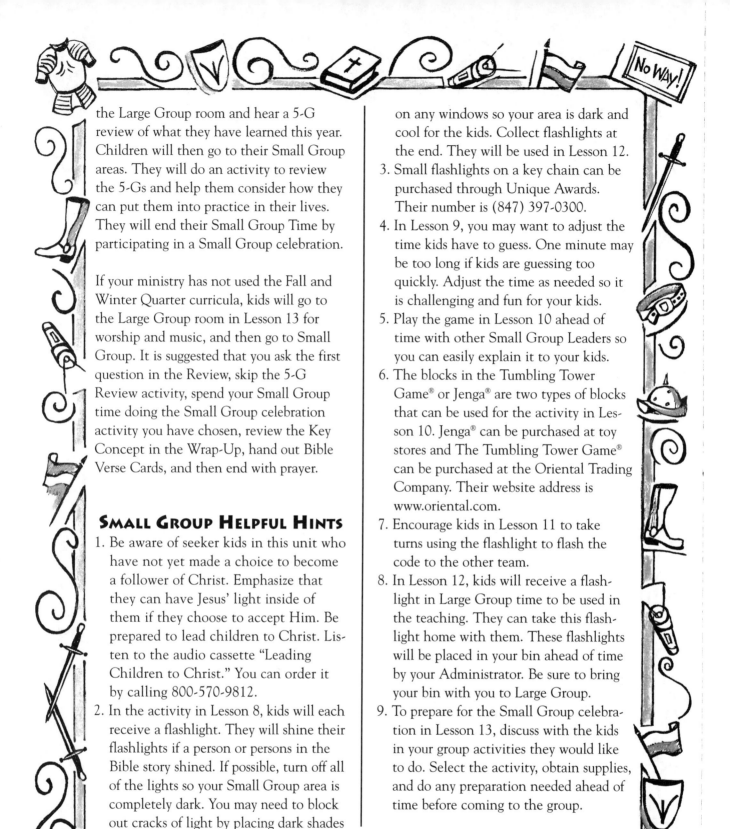

the Large Group room and hear a 5-G review of what they have learned this year. Children will then go to their Small Group areas. They will do an activity to review the 5-Gs and help them consider how they can put them into practice in their lives. They will end their Small Group Time by participating in a Small Group celebration.

If your ministry has not used the Fall and Winter Quarter curricula, kids will go to the Large Group room in Lesson 13 for worship and music, and then go to Small Group. It is suggested that you ask the first question in the Review, skip the 5-G Review activity, spend your Small Group time doing the Small Group celebration activity you have chosen, review the Key Concept in the Wrap-Up, hand out Bible Verse Cards, and then end with prayer.

Small Group Helpful Hints

1. Be aware of seeker kids in this unit who have not yet made a choice to become a follower of Christ. Emphasize that they can have Jesus' light inside of them if they choose to accept Him. Be prepared to lead children to Christ. Listen to the audio cassette "Leading Children to Christ." You can order it by calling 800-570-9812.

2. In the activity in Lesson 8, kids will each receive a flashlight. They will shine their flashlights if a person or persons in the Bible story shined. If possible, turn off all of the lights so your Small Group area is completely dark. You may need to block out cracks of light by placing dark shades on any windows so your area is dark and cool for the kids. Collect flashlights at the end. They will be used in Lesson 12.

3. Small flashlights on a key chain can be purchased through Unique Awards. Their number is (847) 397-0300.

4. In Lesson 9, you may want to adjust the time kids have to guess. One minute may be too long if kids are guessing too quickly. Adjust the time as needed so it is challenging and fun for your kids.

5. Play the game in Lesson 10 ahead of time with other Small Group Leaders so you can easily explain it to your kids.

6. The blocks in the Tumbling Tower Game® or Jenga® are two types of blocks that can be used for the activity in Lesson 10. Jenga® can be purchased at toy stores and The Tumbling Tower Game® can be purchased at the Oriental Trading Company. Their website address is www.oriental.com.

7. Encourage kids in Lesson 11 to take turns using the flashlight to flash the code to the other team.

8. In Lesson 12, kids will receive a flashlight in Large Group time to be used in the teaching. They can take this flashlight home with them. These flashlights will be placed in your bin ahead of time by your Administrator. Be sure to bring your bin with you to Large Group.

9. To prepare for the Small Group celebration in Lesson 13, discuss with the kids in your group activities they would like to do. Select the activity, obtain supplies, and do any preparation needed ahead of time before coming to the group.

82

UNIT 2: LEARNING TO SHINE
WHY SHINE?

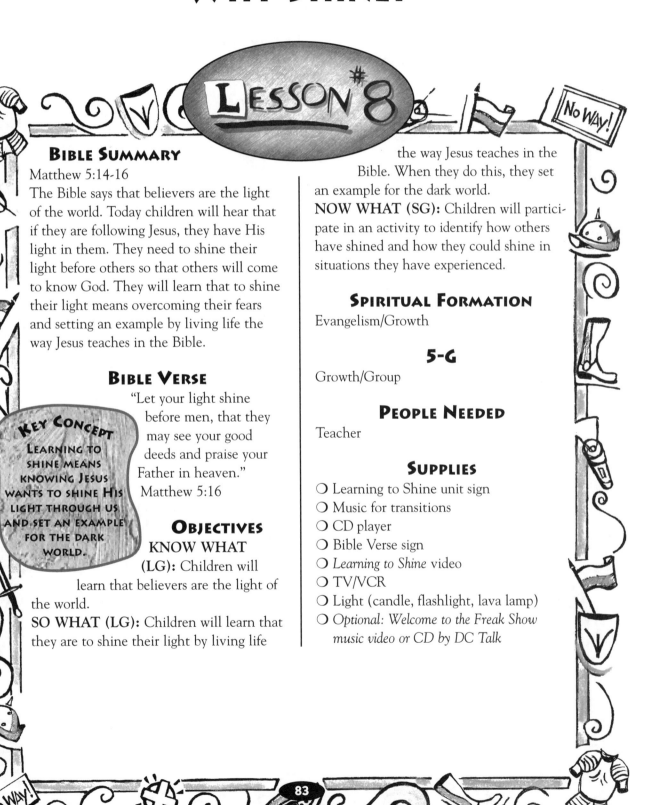

BIBLE SUMMARY

Matthew 5:14-16
The Bible says that believers are the light of the world. Today children will hear that if they are following Jesus, they have His light in them. They need to shine their light before others so that others will come to know God. They will learn that to shine their light means overcoming their fears and setting an example by living life the way Jesus teaches in the Bible.

BIBLE VERSE

"Let your light shine before men, that they may see your good deeds and praise your Father in heaven." Matthew 5:16

KEY CONCEPT
LEARNING TO SHINE MEANS KNOWING JESUS WANTS TO SHINE HIS LIGHT THROUGH US AND SET AN EXAMPLE FOR THE DARK WORLD.

OBJECTIVES
KNOW WHAT (LG): Children will learn that believers are the light of the world.
SO WHAT (LG): Children will learn that they are to shine their light by living life the way Jesus teaches in the Bible. When they do this, they set an example for the dark world.
NOW WHAT (SG): Children will participate in an activity to identify how others have shined and how they could shine in situations they have experienced.

SPIRITUAL FORMATION
Evangelism/Growth

5-G
Growth/Group

PEOPLE NEEDED
Teacher

SUPPLIES
○ Learning to Shine unit sign
○ Music for transitions
○ CD player
○ Bible Verse sign
○ *Learning to Shine* video
○ TV/VCR
○ Light (candle, flashlight, lava lamp)
○ *Optional: Welcome to the Freak Show music video or CD by DC Talk*

83

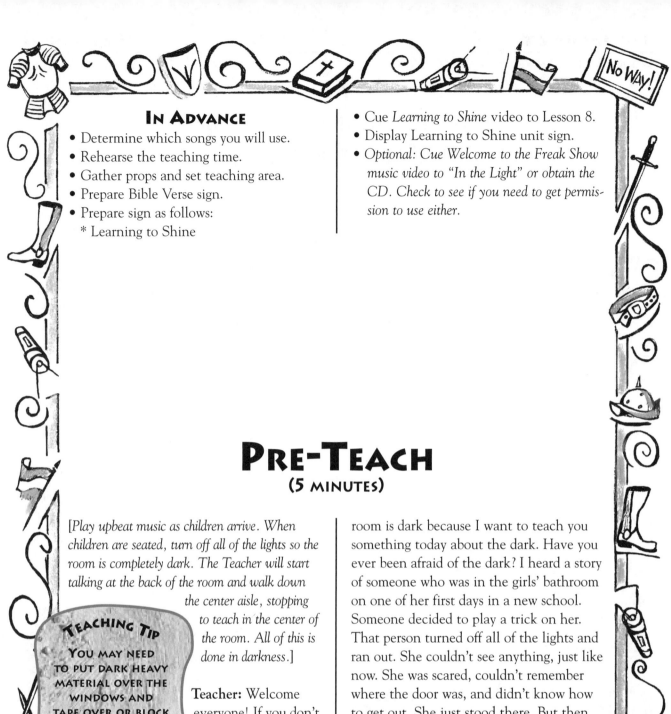

IN ADVANCE

- Determine which songs you will use.
- Rehearse the teaching time.
- Gather props and set teaching area.
- Prepare Bible Verse sign.
- Prepare sign as follows:
  * Learning to Shine

- Cue *Learning to Shine* video to Lesson 8.
- Display Learning to Shine unit sign.
- *Optional: Cue Welcome to the Freak Show music video to "In the Light" or obtain the CD. Check to see if you need to get permission to use either.*

PRE-TEACH
(5 MINUTES)

[*Play upbeat music as children arrive. When children are seated, turn off all of the lights so the room is completely dark. The Teacher will start talking at the back of the room and walk down the center aisle, stopping to teach in the center of the room. All of this is done in darkness.*]

Teacher: Welcome everyone! If you don't know me, my name is [*your name*]. You probably can't see me very well. The room is dark because I want to teach you something today about the dark. Have you ever been afraid of the dark? I heard a story of someone who was in the girls' bathroom on one of her first days in a new school. Someone decided to play a trick on her. That person turned off all of the lights and ran out. She couldn't see anything, just like now. She was scared, couldn't remember where the door was, and didn't know how to get out. She just stood there. But then she saw a little crack of light coming from under the door and she slowly followed it. It led her out of the dark bathroom and into the light.

> **TEACHING TIP**
> YOU MAY NEED TO PUT DARK HEAVY MATERIAL OVER THE WINDOWS AND TAPE OVER OR BLOCK OUT ANY CRACKS OF LIGHT UNDER DOORS OR LIGHTED SIGNS TO ASSURE THAT IT IS DARK.

TEACH
(15 MINUTES)

Teacher: In the Bible, God uses an illustration about light and darkness. The Bible says that most people live in darkness. They can't see where to go or how to get help because it's so dark. What makes the world dark? Sin and evil. We've been learning a lot about the battle between good and evil—between God and Satan. Another name Satan has is "The Prince of Darkness." Satan loves the dark. He causes the world to live in darkness and sin, and be blind to the fact that they need God. He makes them even blind to the fact that they're blind! Have you ever noticed that after you've been in the dark for a long time your eyes get adjusted to it and you forget that you're in darkness? That's what has happened to the world. People are in the dark and are blind to the fact that they live in sin and need God. Their lives are on a path that is separate from God and He is the only One who can offer hope, peace, and joy.

However, there is help for them. The Bible says that Jesus is . . . [*turn on all of the lights*] light. Jesus' light allows the world to see God and come to know Him. For others to see Jesus' light, however, it has to be shining. How do you think our dark world can see Jesus' light? [*Take a few answers.*] They can see it through those of us who are followers of Jesus. Each of you who has made the decision to become a Christ-follower has the light of Jesus inside of you. The Bible says that believers are the light of the world. The Bible also tells us what to do with our lights. It says this:

[*Show Bible Verse sign.*] "Let your light shine before men, that they may see your good deeds and praise your Father in heaven." Matthew 5:16

We are to let our light do what? (*shine*) Before whom does the verse say we need to shine our light? Before men—that means our friends and others we meet. It is our job to shine our light before others who don't know God so they can come to know Him. How do we make our lights shine? They shine when we make the everyday choices to live life the way Jesus teaches in the Bible. When we do what Jesus teaches us, we set an example for others who don't know God. We shine our light in the dark world.

Where we shine our light, darkness cannot be seen. We, as Christians, are given the power to stop the darkness. However, being a Christian in the real everyday world is a challenging thing to do. It is sometimes hard to shine our lights. That is because Satan tries to put obstacles in our way so that we won't shine Jesus' light. When we give in or trip on the obstacles that Satan puts in our way, we are choosing not to shine and instead hiding our light.

You will meet three kids—Nathan, Josh, and Liz. Two of them live in the darkness and one of them is a Christian. The Christian should be shining. Watch and see if you can identify the one who is supposed to shine their light.

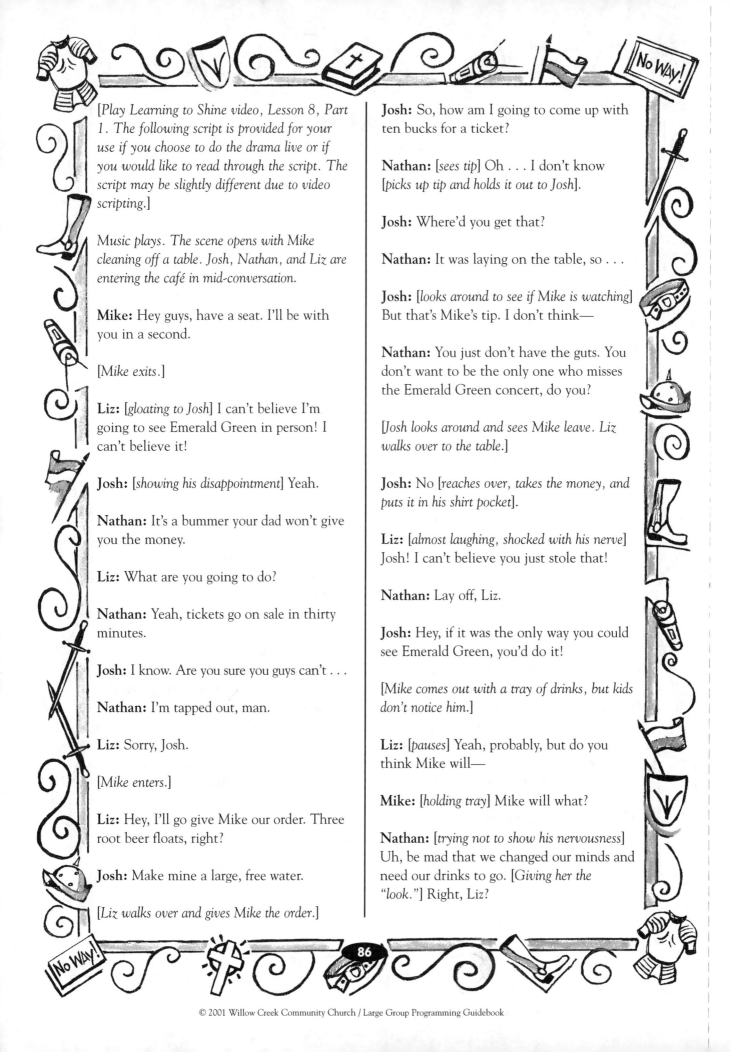

[*Play Learning to Shine video, Lesson 8, Part 1. The following script is provided for your use if you choose to do the drama live or if you would like to read through the script. The script may be slightly different due to video scripting.*]

Music plays. The scene opens with Mike cleaning off a table. Josh, Nathan, and Liz are entering the café in mid-conversation.

Mike: Hey guys, have a seat. I'll be with you in a second.

[*Mike exits.*]

Liz: [*gloating to Josh*] I can't believe I'm going to see Emerald Green in person! I can't believe it!

Josh: [*showing his disappointment*] Yeah.

Nathan: It's a bummer your dad won't give you the money.

Liz: What are you going to do?

Nathan: Yeah, tickets go on sale in thirty minutes.

Josh: I know. Are you sure you guys can't . . .

Nathan: I'm tapped out, man.

Liz: Sorry, Josh.

[*Mike enters.*]

Liz: Hey, I'll go give Mike our order. Three root beer floats, right?

Josh: Make mine a large, free water.

[*Liz walks over and gives Mike the order.*]

Josh: So, how am I going to come up with ten bucks for a ticket?

Nathan: [*sees tip*] Oh . . . I don't know [*picks up tip and holds it out to Josh*].

Josh: Where'd you get that?

Nathan: It was laying on the table, so . . .

Josh: [*looks around to see if Mike is watching*] But that's Mike's tip. I don't think—

Nathan: You just don't have the guts. You don't want to be the only one who misses the Emerald Green concert, do you?

[*Josh looks around and sees Mike leave. Liz walks over to the table.*]

Josh: No [*reaches over, takes the money, and puts it in his shirt pocket*].

Liz: [*almost laughing, shocked with his nerve*] Josh! I can't believe you just stole that!

Nathan: Lay off, Liz.

Josh: Hey, if it was the only way you could see Emerald Green, you'd do it!

[*Mike comes out with a tray of drinks, but kids don't notice him.*]

Liz: [*pauses*] Yeah, probably, but do you think Mike will—

Mike: [*holding tray*] Mike will what?

Nathan: [*trying not to show his nervousness*] Uh, be mad that we changed our minds and need our drinks to go. [*Giving her the "look."*] Right, Liz?

86

Liz: [*apologetically*] Right, sorry.

Mike: Not a problem. Just give me a few . . .

[*Mike turns to take tray back but they each grab a drink.*]

Josh: [*feeling guilty, doesn't want to get caught*] No, Mike, that's okay. We can just drink 'em real fast. Right, guys?

[*They all start gulping their drinks. Mike is watching them, trying to figure out why they are acting so strange.*]

Nathan: Oh, man! We'd better get going if we want a good spot in line.

[*They all gather up their stuff and begin to rush out. Mike just stands watching them.*]

[*Stop video.*]

Teacher: So who is the one that is supposed to shine the light? The Christian should be able to be identified by the way he or she chooses to live life. That person should be different from the rest of the world. You should be able to see that person's light shining. So who is the Christian? Is it Nathan? Is it Josh? Or is it Liz? You'll find out who the Christian is soon enough. But, I will say this much. It is hard to be a Christian in this dark world. It can be full of lonely risks and unpopular choices. And, even though Christians may sometimes think they're helping the dark world by going along with the world's choices, they're not. The only way Christians can really help is by learning to shine.

Optional: Play DC Talk's "In the Light" from the Welcome to the Freak Show music video. Another option is to play the song "In the Light" from the Welcome to the Freak Show CD.

[*Play Learning to Shine video, Lesson 8, Part 2.*]

Josh turns on his own lamp. He is in the "Light Chamber."

Josh: [*says soberly*] Yes, I'm the Christian. Hard to believe, isn't it? I know what you're thinking. How could someone who says he loves God ever act like that? You're right. [*Pauses*] But the truth is, I'm scared. I'm scared that I'm not going to be cool anymore. I'm scared that I'm going to lose all of my friends and I'll forever be one of those "religious freaks" they all make fun of. [*Pauses*] But I really do love God and I want to follow Him.

[*Turns off lamp.*]

[*Stop video.*]

Post-Teach
(10 minutes)

[*The room is again in darkness. The teacher walks to the front holding a candle or small light.*]

Teacher: Tell me 4th and 5th graders, out of everything in this room, what is the main thing you can see right now? (*the light*) Why is that? (*because everything else is dark*) This is how we can be—just like this light here. Our world is so dark and we have the opportunity to help them. **JESUS WANTS TO SHINE HIS LIGHT THROUGH US AND SET AN EXAMPLE FOR THE DARK WORLD.** He wants us to shine because He knows His light can help our dark world come to know Him.

How do we shine? By living our lives the way Jesus teaches in the Bible—making everyday choices to do what He says to do. As we saw in the drama, Satan tries to put obstacles in our way to keep us from shining. When Josh made the choice to steal, he made the choice NOT to shine. Why do you think Josh made the choice to steal? (*Allow kids to respond.*) Those are all obstacles to shining. And a big obstacle is fear. Many times I've felt like Josh—scared to make the unpopular decision, scared of what my friends might think about me, or scared that they'd reject me. But then I'm reminded of what the Bible says:

[*Show Bible Verse sign.*] "Let your light shine before men, that they may see your good deeds and praise your Father in heaven." Matthew 5:16

The Bible tells us to let our lights shine in the dark world. We are not to hide our love for God or how we're different. Rather, we are to shine. The Bible says when we do this—when we shine—our friends and others will see our lights shining in the darkness. They may then ask questions about our light, and maybe even decide they want to know Jesus and have His light inside of them too. That is a great thing and can happen all because we decided to shine. Let's learn to shine and take risks. Let's step out of our fears and shine for God, so we may know what God can do through us. Let's pray and ask God to teach us.

Prayer

Dear God,
Thank You for allowing us to be light to our friends so they can come to know You. Please help us to step out of our fear and learn to shine our light. Amen.

Teacher: Let's rewind and replay to see how it would look if our friend Josh was given a second chance to take the risk and shine.

[*Play Learning to Shine video, Lesson 8, Part 3.*]

Music plays. The scene opens with Mike cleaning off a table. Josh, Nathan, and Liz enter the café in mid-conversation.

Mike: Hey guys, have a seat. I'll be with you in a second.

[*Mike exits.*]

Liz: [*gloating to Josh*] I can't believe I'm going to see Emerald Green in person! I can't believe it!

Josh: [*showing his disappointment*] Yeah.

Nathan: It's a bummer your dad won't give you the money.

Liz: What are you going to do?

Nathan: Yeah, tickets go on sale in thirty minutes.

Josh: I know. Are you sure you guys can't . . .

Nathan: I'm tapped out, man.

Liz: Sorry, Josh.

[*Mike enters.*]

Liz: Hey, I'll go give Mike our order. Three root beer floats, right?

Josh: Make mine a large, free water.

[*Liz walks over and gives Mike the order.*]

Josh: So, how am I going to come up with ten bucks for a ticket?

Nathan: [*Nathan sees tip*] Oh . . . I don't know.

Josh: [*looks around to see if Mike is watching*] But that's Mike's tip. I don't think—

Nathan: You want to see Emerald Green don't you?

[*Josh looks around and sees Mike leave. Liz walks over to the table.*]

Josh: Yeah, I do, but . . .

Liz: So did you come up with any ideas on how to get the money?

Nathan: Yes!

Josh: [*firmly*] No.

Liz: I'm confused.

Nathan: Let's just say that I came up with an idea, but Josh hasn't got the guts to go for it.

[*Liz looks at Josh for an answer.*]

SHINE!

Josh: Nathan wants me to rip off Mike and I'm not doing it.

Liz: Josh, it's just a tip, he'll never miss it. Besides you have to come tonight. It won't be the same without you.

Nathan: She's right, man. The choice is yours. Go to the greatest concert ever or stay at home and play Scrabble® with the folks.

Josh: Then I guess I'll be playing Scrabble®.

[*Mike comes out with a tray of drinks, but the kids don't notice him.*]

Nathan: [*gets disgusted*] I don't get you man, you're weird. C'mon Liz, let's go. We don't want to miss a good spot in line.

Josh: [*trying to be positive*] Good luck, guys.

Nathan: [*blowing him off*] Yeah, whatever.

[*Nathan leaves.*]

Liz: [*lingers behind*] Look Josh . . . [*wants to say more, but doesn't know what to say*] If I have enough money, I'll bring you back a tee shirt.

Josh: Thanks.

[*Liz leaves and Mike enters.*]

Mike: Where'd they go?

Josh: To buy Emerald Green tickets.

Mike: Cool. Aren't you going?

Josh: [*showing his disappointment*] No. I didn't have the money.

Mike: [*starts picking stuff off of the table and cleaning up*] Too bad. Drink up.

[*Mike serves drinks to Josh. Mike starts to exit.*]

Josh: Mike?

Mike: [*turning to take tray and exit*] Yeah?

Josh: Don't forget this [*picks up tip and hands it to Mike*].

Mike: [*turns*] Thanks. My tips are always getting ripped off.

Josh: Yeah, I bet.

[*Stop video.*]

Teacher: One light, making a hard decision to follow God, even when what scares him the most comes true. But, he shined through the darkness and one of his friends noticed the difference. One light—shining through the darkness. This can change the world. Go out this week and do the same.

[*Dismiss to Small Groups. Play music as children exit.*]

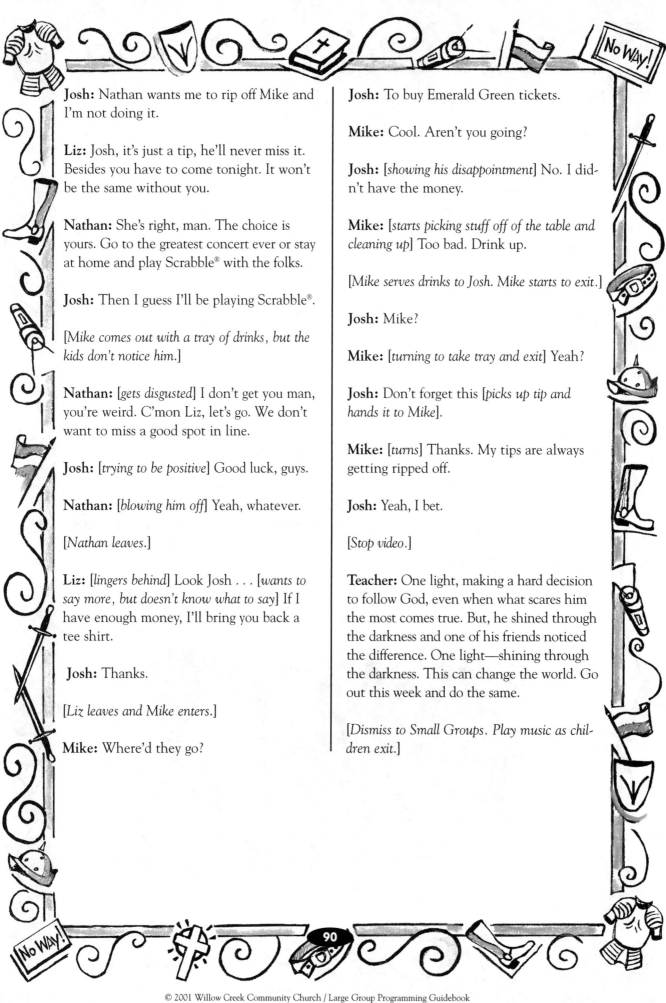

UNIT 2: LEARNING TO SHINE
FAITH INTO ACTION

LESSON #9

BIBLE SUMMARY
Matthew 5:16; James 2:17
The Bible teaches that we need to put what we believe into action. Our talk should be followed up by our walk. Children will hear how saying one thing and doing the opposite can be an obstacle to shining their light. They will learn that we need to shine by matching our faith and actions together so that our lost friends can come to know God.

UNIT BIBLE VERSE
"Let your light shine before men, that they may see your good deeds and praise your Father in heaven." Matthew 5:16

KEY CONCEPT
LEARNING TO SHINE MEANS PUTTING MY FAITH INTO ACTION.

LESSON BIBLE VERSE
"Faith by itself, if it is not accompanied by action, is dead." James 2:17

OBJECTIVES
KNOW WHAT (LG): Children will hear that the Bible teaches that our faith in God is shown through our actions.

SO WHAT (LG): Children will learn that when believers put their faith into action, they shine and others will be drawn towards God.

NOW WHAT (SG): Children will participate in an activity that helps them understand how to put their faith into action.

SPIRITUAL FORMATION
Faith/Self-discipline (words and actions)

5-G
Growth/Group

PEOPLE NEEDED
Teacher

SUPPLIES
- Learning to Shine unit sign (from Lesson 8)
- Music for transitions and singing
- CD player
- Unit Bible Verse sign (use the Bible Verse sign from Lesson 8)
- Lesson Bible Verse sign
- Shine Equation sign
- *Learning to Shine* video
- TV/VCR
- *Optional: Doing Life with God in the Picture CD*

91

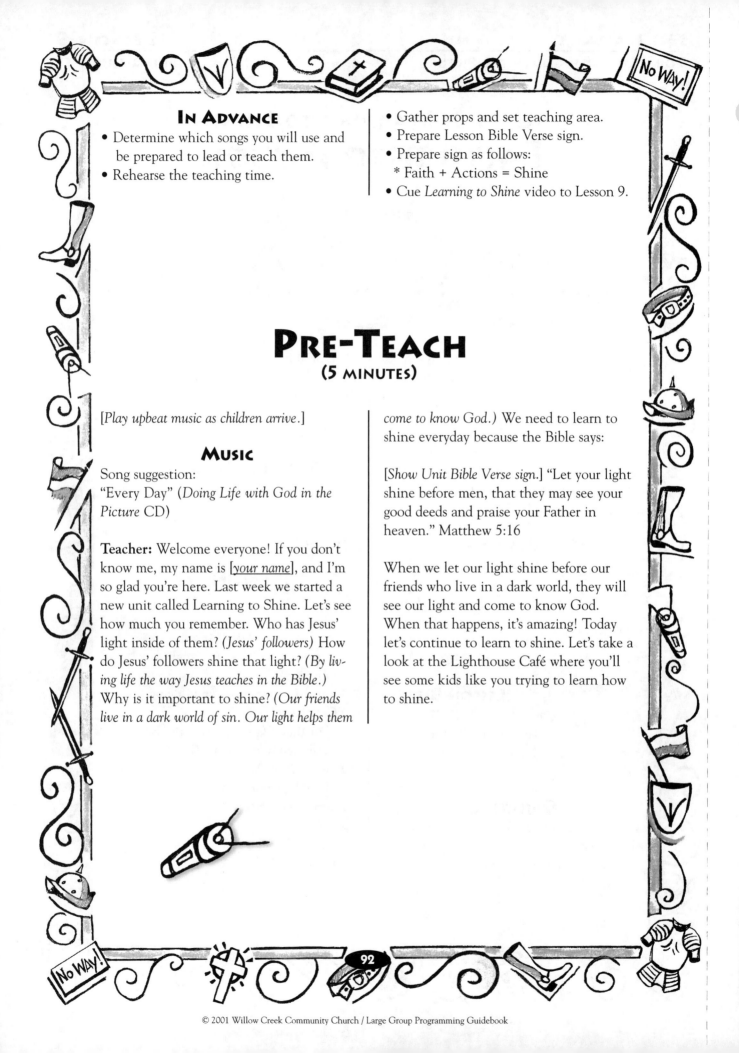

IN ADVANCE

- Determine which songs you will use and be prepared to lead or teach them.
- Rehearse the teaching time.

- Gather props and set teaching area.
- Prepare Lesson Bible Verse sign.
- Prepare sign as follows:
  * Faith + Actions = Shine
- Cue *Learning to Shine* video to Lesson 9.

PRE-TEACH
(5 MINUTES)

[*Play upbeat music as children arrive.*]

MUSIC

Song suggestion:
"Every Day" (*Doing Life with God in the Picture* CD)

Teacher: Welcome everyone! If you don't know me, my name is [*your name*], and I'm so glad you're here. Last week we started a new unit called Learning to Shine. Let's see how much you remember. Who has Jesus' light inside of them? (*Jesus' followers*) How do Jesus' followers shine that light? (*By living life the way Jesus teaches in the Bible.*) Why is it important to shine? (*Our friends live in a dark world of sin. Our light helps them come to know God.*) We need to learn to shine everyday because the Bible says:

[*Show Unit Bible Verse sign.*] "Let your light shine before men, that they may see your good deeds and praise your Father in heaven." Matthew 5:16

When we let our light shine before our friends who live in a dark world, they will see our light and come to know God. When that happens, it's amazing! Today let's continue to learn to shine. Let's take a look at the Lighthouse Café where you'll see some kids like you trying to learn how to shine.

TEACH
(20 MINUTES)

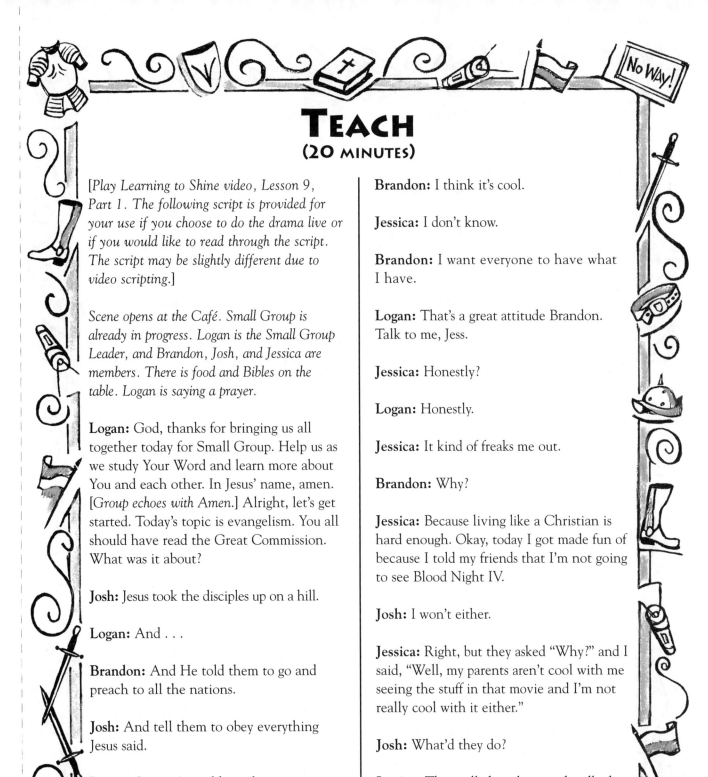

[*Play Learning to Shine video, Lesson 9, Part 1. The following script is provided for your use if you choose to do the drama live or if you would like to read through the script. The script may be slightly different due to video scripting.*]

Scene opens at the Café. Small Group is already in progress. Logan is the Small Group Leader, and Brandon, Josh, and Jessica are members. There is food and Bibles on the table. Logan is saying a prayer.

Logan: God, thanks for bringing us all together today for Small Group. Help us as we study Your Word and learn more about You and each other. In Jesus' name, amen. [*Group echoes with Amen.*] Alright, let's get started. Today's topic is evangelism. You all should have read the Great Commission. What was it about?

Josh: Jesus took the disciples up on a hill.

Logan: And . . .

Brandon: And He told them to go and preach to all the nations.

Josh: And tell them to obey everything Jesus said.

Logan: So, you've told me the story, now tell me what it means . . .

Brandon: To tell everyone we know about Jesus.

Logan: What do you think about that?

Brandon: I think it's cool.

Jessica: I don't know.

Brandon: I want everyone to have what I have.

Logan: That's a great attitude Brandon. Talk to me, Jess.

Jessica: Honestly?

Logan: Honestly.

Jessica: It kind of freaks me out.

Brandon: Why?

Jessica: Because living like a Christian is hard enough. Okay, today I got made fun of because I told my friends that I'm not going to see Blood Night IV.

Josh: I won't either.

Jessica: Right, but they asked "Why?" and I said, "Well, my parents aren't cool with me seeing the stuff in that movie and I'm not really cool with it either."

Josh: What'd they do?

Jessica: They called me loser and walked away laughing.

Brandon: That's cold.

Jessica: Yeah. But that was nothing. It was a movie. It's not like telling them that "I believe in Jesus and I think they should too." I'm sure I would lose them and that freaks me out.

Brandon: But don't your friends living in darkness for all of eternity without God freak you out too?

Jessica: Of course it does, but . . .

Brandon: But nothing. Look, I'm not trying to be mean, but if the Bible says, "Tell everyone about Jesus," then you just do it. It doesn't matter if it scares you. You have to get over it.

Logan: While that's true Brandon, it's a little extreme. Jess's feelings do matter and she's right. Telling people about Jesus is a risk and there's a good chance that you could lose some friends.

Josh: I did. [*Pauses then gets up to fill his drink.*] Last week I almost stole money from Mike because I wanted to look cool in front of Nathan and Liz.

Brandon: But you didn't steal it, right?

Josh: Right.

Jessica: Is that why Nathan won't talk to you anymore?

Josh: [*gets a little sad*] Yeah. But something good came out of it too.

Logan: What's that?

Josh: Well, Liz got curious about why I didn't steal and now we're having all these God-talks.

Logan: That's great man. You're living the mission. Good job. So Jess, any of this helping?

Jessica: Yeah. I want to be able to talk to my friends about God. So, I'll try.

Logan: That's all that God asks. Brandon, no problems for you on this right?

Brandon: Bring it on, I'm ready.

Logan: Okay, that's it for today. Let's meet this time next week. And Jess, tell Sara we missed her and catch her up on everything we did today. [*Jessica nods.*] Why don't all of us read the first couple chapters of James. It's about faith. Cool?

Group: Cool.

Logan: [*pulling flyers out of his bag*] Hey, anyone need any more flyers to the church outreach event? Oh. It's three weeks from today and from what I hear, it's going to be really cool. [*Starts to leave with Jessica.*] Jess, this may be a good way for you to start a God-talk with someone.

Jessica: [*taking some flyers*] I'll give it a shot.

[*Jessica and Logan leave, and Josh packs up his stuff. Brandon puts flyers in his backpack.*]

Josh: Brandon, you comin' or are you hangin' out?

Brandon: Hanging out. I have Social Studies to finish.

Josh: Okay, see you at school tomorrow.

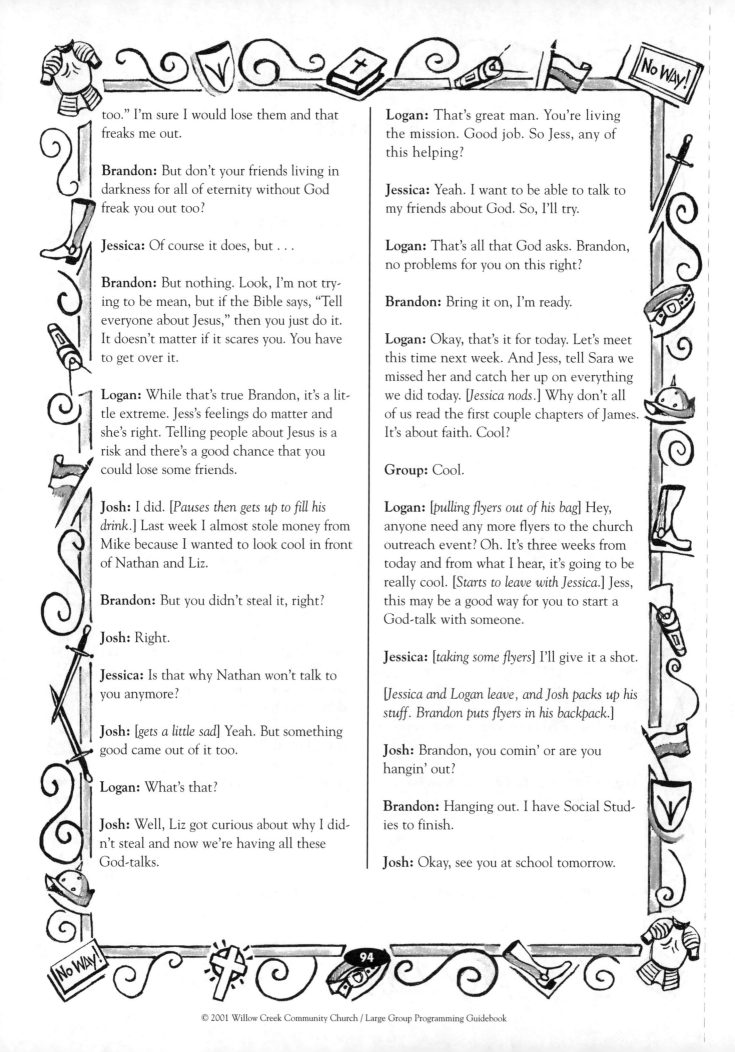

Brandon: Later.

[*Brandon begins to study when Colin, his friend from school walks in.*]

Colin: Brandon, what's up?

Brandon: What's up, my man? How was soccer practice?

Colin: It was alright. Coach didn't yell too much. I could have used you though. Jeff kept missing my passes. Where were you?

Brandon: Um . . . I had [*looks down at book*] some studying to do.

Colin: Oh hey, [*pulls flyer out of his back pocket*] get this. Some girl Sara in my math class gave this to me.

Brandon: [*getting nervous*] What is it?

Colin: An invitation to some church event thing, I don't know. I zoned out after about ten minutes of her Jesus speech.

Brandon: [*still nervous*] Uh . . . are you going to go?

Colin: I don't think so. I don't know anybody and this Sara girl is kind of hyper. I don't think I want to hang out with her.

Brandon: Yeah . . .

Colin: [*pauses then looks at Brandon*] What do you think about this Jesus stuff? [*Pauses just long enough to be vulnerable.*] Too lame, right?

Brandon: Um . . . [*looks at Colin, wants to be cool*] Yeah, totally lame.

Colin: Listen, I have to book. Do you have the notes from Science?

Brandon: [*nervously getting up to bring his cup to the counter*] Yeah, it's in my bag. You can grab it.

Colin: Thanks. [*A flyer drops out of the science notebook and Colin sees it.*] Dude, what's this? Is this yours?

Brandon: I can explain.

Colin: [*still looking through*] There's a whole bunch of these in here and a Bible. [*Gets mad.*] You're into the Jesus stuff, aren't you?

Brandon: [*stops to be honest and real*] Yeah. I would have told you.

Colin: Save it. I don't want to hear it. [*Shoves Bible and flyers on Brandon.*] You lied to me man. I'm out of here.

Brandon: Colin, I'm sorry. [*Blocks him from leaving.*] I just didn't want you to think I was a loser.

Colin: Well, [*gets in his face*] now I think you're a liar. [*Breaks away, but turns back before leaving.*] You were right though. Christians are lame.

[*Colin leaves mad and Brandon flops on the couch feeling regret and sadness.*]

[*Stop video.*]

Teacher: God says in the Bible that our

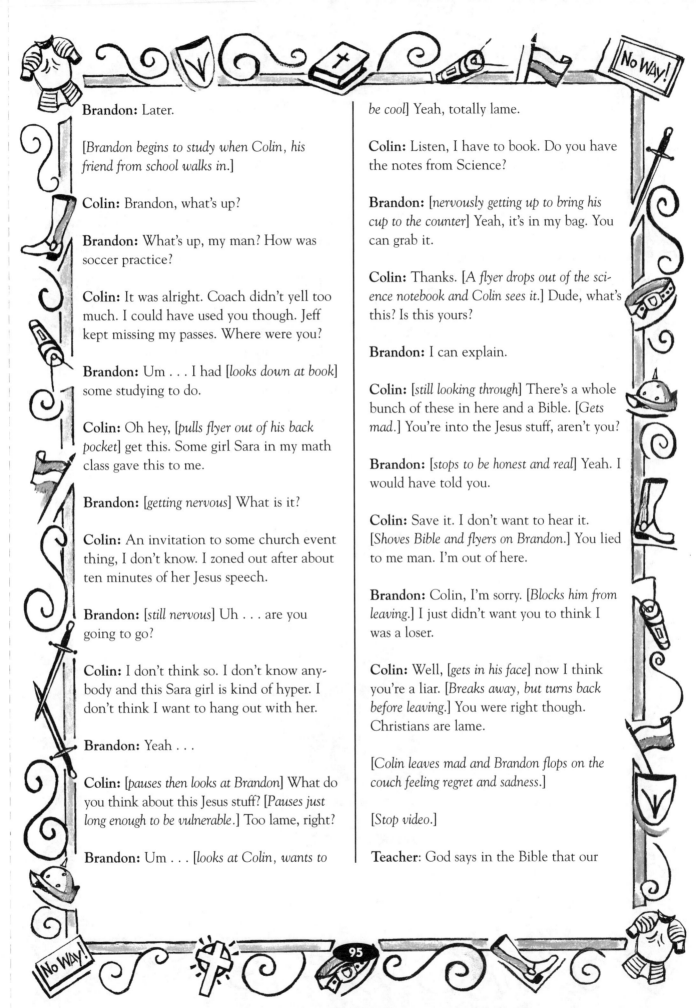

faith and actions must match. Our faith—what we say we believe—must be backed up by our actions. When we add our faith and actions together, then we shine.

[*Show Shine Equation sign.*] Faith + Action = Shine

The Bible says when we have one but not the other, then we don't shine. It is an obstacle to shining. Look at what the Bible says:

[*Show Lesson Bible Verse sign.*] "Faith by itself, if it is not accompanied by action, is dead." James 2:17

Those are strong words. We can't shine when we have only one, either faith or actions. Our walk must match our talk for us to shine in the lost world.

[*Cover up the word Action on the Shine Equation sign.*]

It is not enough to just believe in or have faith in God and what He says in the Bible. It's not enough to declare your belief in God on Sunday, but not follow Him with your actions everyday. When that happens, the equation doesn't add up. That's what happened with Brandon. He said he believed it was important to tell others about Jesus, but his actions didn't match up. He might be considered a "Sunday Christian." A Sunday Christian is someone who goes to church on Sunday or Saturday

night, and seems like a great Christian when they're there. But when Monday comes and they have to face the dark world and their lost friends, they hide their light and live like everybody else.

They say at church they believe what Jesus teaches, but outside of church their actions do not match the way Jesus taught us to live. Their walk doesn't match their talk. They may swear, make fun of other kids, disrespect their teachers, and even make fun of God. Sometimes like Brandon, they do the exact opposite of what they said they believed in Small Group. Their faith isn't backed up with actions.

There is another way some people live as well.

[Cover up the word Faith on the Shine Equation sign.]

Some people do lots of good actions, but don't have faith. They think that if they just do a lot of good things like giving money to the poor, volunteering for community work days, and rescuing homeless animals, those things will be enough. God says we must have faith in Him as well as good actions. If we don't, then the equation doesn't add up.

What does putting faith and action together look like in your life? If you believe that lying is wrong because God tells you that it is, then what do you do when you're goofing around with your friends and you accidentally spill grape juice all over the carpet and your mom asks what happened? *(don't lie)* If you believe that the Bible says stealing is wrong, do you

steal from the convenience store when friends are pressuring you to do so? *(No.)* If you believe that God says to follow Him and shine no matter what happens to you, your popularity, or your life, then what do you do? *(Follow Him and shine.)*

When we put our faith and action together, we shine. We need both for the equation to work. Learning to Shine means putting our faith into action, not just on Sunday, but everyday. Let's take a look at what Colin has to say after what happened earlier.

[Play Learning to Shine video, Lesson 9, Part 2. The following script is provided for your use if you choose to do the drama live or if you would like to read through the script. The script may be slightly different due to video scripting.]

Colin: *[turns on lamp in the Light Chamber, he is very mad]* I can't believe him. I can't believe he lied to me. You know these "Christians" are all the same. They talk a good squeaky-clean talk, but when it comes down to it, they live like everybody else. They're hypocrites *[pauses in his anger to reveal some vulnerability.]*

You know what? The truth is, and I would never tell anyone this, but I wouldn't have minded hearing about that church stuff. My life has been really rough lately. I don't know how to say it, but it's like something important is missing and I don't know what it is. *[Remembering Brandon]* Now I guess I never will, because if that *[pointing to couch area]* is how people who believe in Jesus act, then this Jesus is not for me.

[Stop video.]

POST-TEACH
(5 MINUTES)

Teacher: Let's not let our friends feel that way. Let's shine our lights by having our faith and actions match. Shine so that others can come to know God. Let's not let the obstacle of having faith without actions prevent us from shining. Our friends not only need to hear it, but they may be like Colin. We may be surprised that they actually want to hear about Jesus. If we don't shine in front of them, we may miss that opportunity to talk to them.

Let's live it out and shine. Take your faith, what you believe about God, and what He tells us in the Bible, and turn it into action. There are Colins out there who need you. It is never too late. Colin's life is not over. Tomorrow is another day for Brandon to try to shine in front of him. Will it take a lot of work and time for Colin to see that Brandon is for real? Yes. But is it too late? No. And that is the same for you too. If you've sat here today and realized that you don't live as an Everyday Christian, don't give up. Ask God for forgiveness. He loves us even when we mess up. And then know that tomorrow is another day. You can leave the past behind and become an Everyday Christian and shine right now. Let's pray.

PRAYER

Dear God,
Help us put our faith into actions. Help us be a light to our lost friends so they can come to know You. Amen.

MUSIC

Song suggestion:
"Learnin' To Shine" (*Doing Life with God in the Picture* CD)

Note: The lyrics on the CD jacket for this song are incorrect. Please see www.PromiselandOnline.com for correct lyrics.

[*Dismiss to Small Groups. Play music as children exit.*]

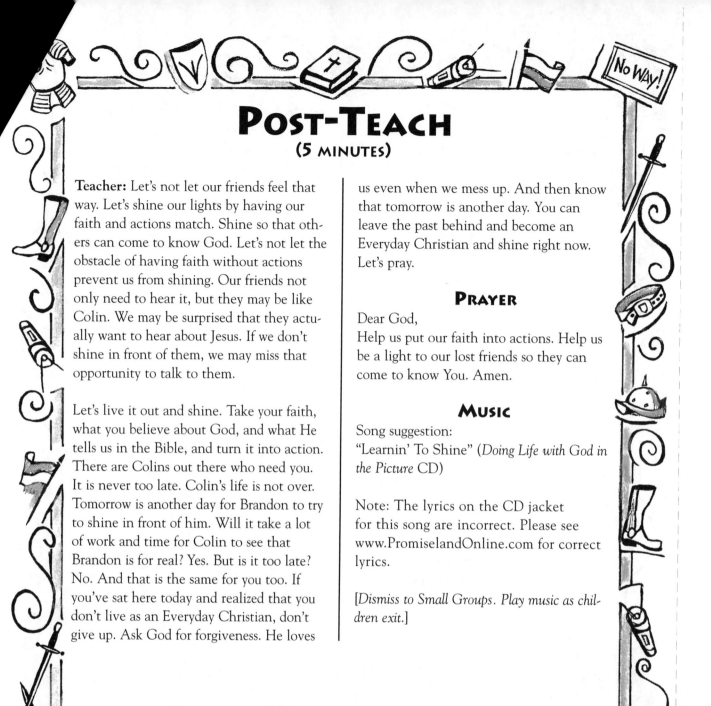

UNIT 2: LEARNING TO SHINE
CONFIDENCE

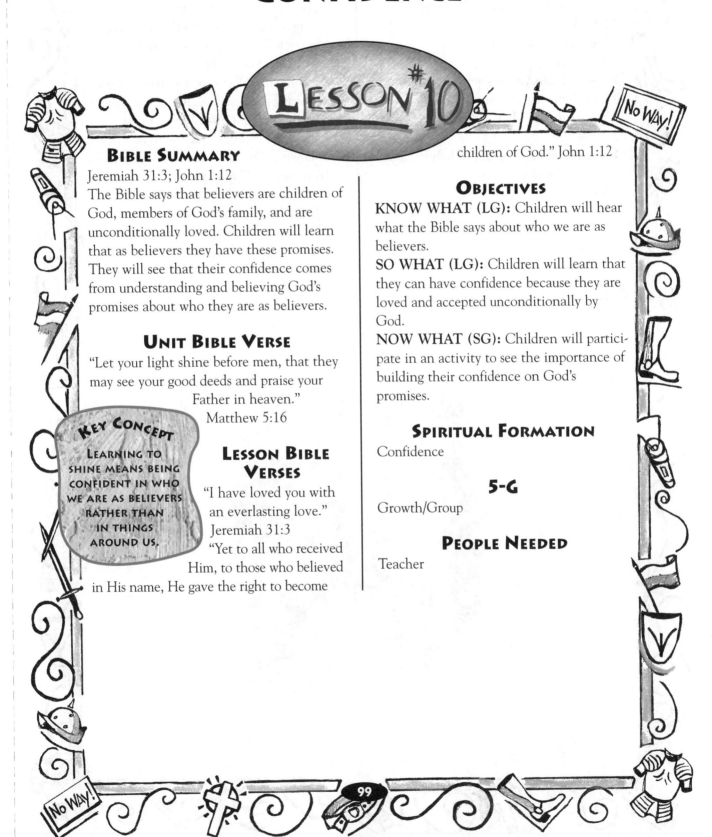

LESSON #10

BIBLE SUMMARY

Jeremiah 31:3; John 1:12
The Bible says that believers are children of God, members of God's family, and are unconditionally loved. Children will learn that as believers they have these promises. They will see that their confidence comes from understanding and believing God's promises about who they are as believers.

UNIT BIBLE VERSE

"Let your light shine before men, that they may see your good deeds and praise your Father in heaven."
Matthew 5:16

KEY CONCEPT

LEARNING TO SHINE MEANS BEING CONFIDENT IN WHO WE ARE AS BELIEVERS RATHER THAN IN THINGS AROUND US.

LESSON BIBLE VERSES

"I have loved you with an everlasting love."
Jeremiah 31:3
"Yet to all who received Him, to those who believed in His name, He gave the right to become children of God." John 1:12

OBJECTIVES

KNOW WHAT (LG): Children will hear what the Bible says about who we are as believers.
SO WHAT (LG): Children will learn that they can have confidence because they are loved and accepted unconditionally by God.
NOW WHAT (SG): Children will participate in an activity to see the importance of building their confidence on God's promises.

SPIRITUAL FORMATION

Confidence

5-G

Growth/Group

PEOPLE NEEDED

Teacher

SUPPLIES

- ○ Learning to Shine unit sign (from Lesson 8)
- ○ Music for transitions and singing
- ○ CD player
- ○ *Learning to Shine* video
- ○ TV/VCR
- ○ Lesson Bible Verses signs
- ○ Unit Bible Verse sign (use the Bible Verse sign from Lesson 8)
- ○ Table
- ○ Five blocks (shoe boxes or light-weight wooden blocks)
- ○ Two bricks
- ○ "Person" (made from a 2-liter plastic bottle)
- ○ Promise #1 sign
- ○ Promise #2 sign
- ○ *Optional: Doing Life with God in the Picture CD*

IN ADVANCE

- • Determine which songs you will use and be prepared to lead or teach them.
- • Rehearse the teaching time.
- • Using a plastic 2-liter bottle, photocopy the included figure, cut out, and attach to the front of the bottle.
- • Label the five blocks each with one of the following phrases: Dress Right, Look Right, Act Right, Right Stuff, Right Group.
- • Label the two bricks each with one of the following: You are loved unconditionally, You are a child of God.
- • Set the table at the front and place blocks, bricks, and "person" on top of it.
- • Prepare Lesson Bible Verses signs.
- • Prepare signs as follows:
  - * Promise #1: You are loved unconditionally. Jeremiah 31:3
  - * Promise #2: You are a child of God. John 1:12
- • Cue *Learning to Shine* video to Lesson 10.

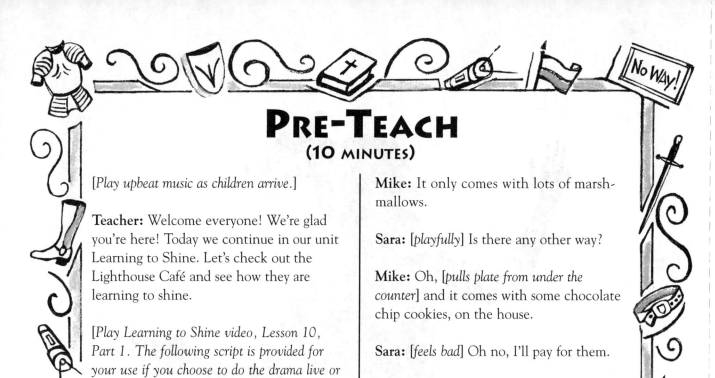

PRE-TEACH
(10 MINUTES)

[*Play upbeat music as children arrive.*]

Teacher: Welcome everyone! We're glad you're here! Today we continue in our unit Learning to Shine. Let's check out the Lighthouse Café and see how they are learning to shine.

[*Play Learning to Shine video, Lesson 10, Part 1. The following script is provided for your use if you choose to do the drama live or if you would like to read through the script. The script may be slightly different due to video scripting.*]

The first scene opens at the café. Rain and thunder can be heard. Mike is putting out bowls and buckets to catch the rain leaking through the roof. Sara runs into the café soaking wet. She is carrying a backpack and holding a bunch of wet flyers.

Sara: Whew! Could I be more wet?

Mike: [*laughs*] Doesn't look like it. Raining pretty hard out there, huh?

Sara: Yeah, and stupid me, I left my umbrella at home.

Mike: Hey, that's not stupid [*tosses a towel to her*]. When you live in this city, you can be up against a flood, blizzard, and tornado all in the same day. Can I get you something to warm you up?

Sara: Do you have hot chocolate? [*Hands towel back and sits on a stool.*]

Mike: It only comes with lots of marsh-mallows.

Sara: [*playfully*] Is there any other way?

Mike: Oh, [*pulls plate from under the counter*] and it comes with some chocolate chip cookies, on the house.

Sara: [*feels bad*] Oh no, I'll pay for them.

Mike: No, don't worry about it. My name's Mike by the way.

Sara: I'm Sara and thanks [*tastes a cookie*]. Mmm. Mrs. Field's® would be jealous.

Mike: [*pours hot chocolate and gives her a cup*] Secret recipe. Here you go . . . and I think I'll join you [*pours himself a cup*].

Sara: [*remembering*] Oh, duh, I almost forgot. My friend Jessica was here last week and left her Bible. I told her I'd pick it up for her.

Mike: Ah yes. I think I know where that is [*goes to get it*].

[*Two girls carrying umbrellas and shopping bags stop at the café entrance, each talking on a different cell phone.*]

Tori: Okay, we're here, so I'll talk to you later. Bye.

Sara: [*says to herself*] Oh no, not them. I've got to hide [*looks around, grabs her stuff, and runs to hide in the back*].

Mike: [*comes running out with the Bible*] Sara, I found [*knocks right into her, Sara falls, but gets up fast as if embarrassed*] . . . the book.

Sara: Thanks. [*Takes book then sees girls.*] Oh, hi!

[*The girls just stare at her and then look at Mike.*]

Mike: Hi girls! [*Looks at Sara nervously.*]

Girls: [*pretending to have a crush on him*] Hi Mike!

Mike: Good to see you in here again.

Ally: [*sarcastically*] Yeah, and look who else is back.

Mike: Can I get you guys some hot chocolate?

[*Sara takes a sip of hers.*]

Tori: Uh no, we're watching our weight.

Ally: But we'll take two bottled waters please.

Mike: Coming right up.

Tori: Speaking of water, Sara, you should try using a hair dryer some time.

Sara: Well I . . .

Ally: Yeah, it does wonders with getting that wet-dog-look out of your hair.

[*Lights go black.*]

Sara Voiceover: There are two groups of people in this world—the cool and the uncool. Those girls that just walked into the café are the coolest of the cool, most popular, and most beautiful girls in my school. They make me feel like I am the poster child for the uncool. I'm soaking wet and my hair is flatter than my stomach. I have so many zits that I tell people I have the chicken pox.

[*Pauses. Lights come up dimly on the girls at the couch. The girls are showing each other the trendy things they bought at the mall, reading magazines, and using their phones and electronic diaries. Mike brings them their waters.*]

Sara Voiceover: Look at them. They seem to have perfect bodies, perfect clothes, and perfect lives. The guys line up to take them to the spring dance and the girls fill out applications to just sit with them at lunch. I would give anything to be one of them. [*Referring to them.*] Ally is captain of the travel soccer team, and Tori gets all straight A's and started a fashion club at our school. Compared to them, I'm such a loser.

[*Lights go out on girls at the couch.*]

[*Stop video.*]

Teacher: Ever feel like Sara? Ever look around at all of the other people in the world and feel like you're just a loser compared to them? I bet we can all think of a time when we've felt that way. We've prob- ably all looked at what someone else has or looks like and felt worthless because we didn't have what they have or look like they look.

We often get messages in the world about what we have to have, be, and look like in order to be someone. The world says to girls, "You have to be thin, beautiful, popu- lar, all of your clothes have to come from popular, expensive stores, and you must look and be like a movie or pop star in order to be accepted and loved." The world says to boys, "You have to be strong, muscular, good at sports, funny, tough, and look like a movie or pop star in order to be accepted and loved." There is a lot of pressure in the world to be a certain way or have certain things in order to be significant.

104

TEACH
(15 MINUTES)

Teacher: How does this affect our lives? Let's look at it this way.

[*Pile each labeled block as you say each of the following phrases.*]

Let's pretend you are feeling good about yourself and confident because you dress right, look right, act right, have the right stuff, and are in the right group.

Dress Right

Look Right

Act Right

Right Stuff

Right Group

What happens when something doesn't go right? What happens if you get rejected from the group, make a mistake, or don't wear the cool clothes? What happens when you don't fit into the mold—are five pounds overweight, can't kick a soccer ball, or buy your clothes at a less popular store? Even if one of these things goes wrong, it will affect your confidence. You can feel like a loser and have no confidence about who you are. Your confidence will crumble.

[*Pull out one of the blocks so the pile falls over and the "person" falls off of the pile.*]

This is a picture of what it looks like to get your confidence from the things the dark world believes gives you confidence. You are constantly trying to keep your pile built up and intact so your confidence doesn't fall or crumble to the ground.

How does this impact your choices everyday? If owning the right stuff [*hold up block labeled "Right Stuff"*] makes you feel good about yourself and gives you confidence, how will you spend your money? [*Allow kids to think about this.*] You're probably going to choose to spend your money on making sure you have all the cool stuff.

If belonging to the right group [*hold up block labeled "Right Group"*] makes you feel good about yourself and gives you confidence, what will you do when the group wants you to do something you know is wrong? [*Allow kids to think about this.*] You're probably going to choose to go along with the group because staying in the group is so important to you.

The Bible teaches that there is a different place to get our confidence. The Bible says that we can get our confidence from the promises God gives us. His promises will never let us down. They are solid and will never change. One promise God gives us is this:

[*Show Promise #1 sign.*] Promise #1: You are loved unconditionally.

[*Place the brick labeled "You are loved unconditionally" on the table.*]

This brick will symbolize this promise. It is strong and sturdy which represents how strong God's promise is. God loves you unconditionally which means He loves you no matter what. The Bible says:

[*Show Lesson Bible Verse sign—Jeremiah 31:3.*] "I have loved you with an everlasting love." Jeremiah 31:3.

God created you inside of your mother. He knows every hair on your head and every mistake you've made. He knows what you look like in the morning and still He says, I love you. God doesn't have a mold you have to fit into to earn His love. He loves you no matter what. He loves you whether you are thin or overweight, have glasses or contacts, or play soccer or the tuba.

The second promise God gives us is we are His children.

[*Show Promise #2 sign.*] Promise #2: You are a child of God.

[*Place the brick labeled "You are a child of God" next to the first brick on the table.*]

If you have made a decision to believe in Jesus and follow Him, you are a child of

God. In the Bible, John 1:12 says:

[*Show Lesson Bible Verse sign—John 1:12.*] "Yet to all who received Him [Jesus], to those who believed in His name, He gave the right to become children of God." John 1:12

If you are a child of God, you are a member of God's family—which means you belong. So often we spend our days trying to fit into a certain group—the soccer team, the cool kids, or the older kids. This promise gives us confidence because we know that we already belong in God's family.

We can get confidence from these two promises: we are loved by God unconditionally and we are His children—we belong in His family.

[*Place the "person" on top of the two bricks.*]

If you get your confidence from God's promises, you will have the confidence to shine. Remember we learned the last two weeks that believers are the light of the world because they have Jesus' light inside of them. They shine their light by living life the way Jesus teaches in the Bible. Our friends live in a dark world of sin. Our light helps them come to know God. We need to learn to shine everyday because the Bible says:

[*Show Unit Bible Verse sign.*] "Let your light shine before men, that they may see your good deeds and praise your Father in heaven." Matthew 5:16

When you have confidence built on God's promises, you can shine. You no longer have to worry if your clothes are cool enough, if your hair is short enough, or what other people think of you. You just

have to remember what God says about you: You are loved and You belong. These things will never change.

When you have confidence built on what God says and your friends want you to do something you know is wrong, can you take the risk? Can you say "no" and shine, even though they may not like you or may not want to hang out with you anymore? Yes, because you can be confident you are still loved by God and still belong to His family. Nothing will change that.

If you have to choose between spending all of your money on a popular brand of jeans or share some of your money with the church and buy a less popular brand of jeans, can you take the risk? Can you share your money and shine, even though you may look different than the other kids? Yes, because you can be confident that you are still loved by God and still belong to His family.

It takes confidence to shine. To shine means we have to make hard and sometimes unpopular decisions. We have to say no to that movie even though everyone else is going to it. We have to refuse to cheat even if we're not going to get caught. We have to choose not to make fun of the new kid even though it would make us look cool and funny. Those are choices we have to make and they are choices that require confidence. Shining means taking risks and being different from the world. If we don't have confidence that comes from God's promises, then there is an obstacle to us shining.

[*Play Learning to Shine video, Lesson 10, Part 2.*]

Sara: [*turns on a light in the Light Chamber*] How can I possibly get them to go to church with me? [*Mocks herself.*] Hey, my church is having this big event. Here's a flyer, want to come? Yeah right, like they would ever come with me. I really do love God and I know God loves me no matter what. Maybe if I just walk up to them and invite them to come, maybe I would be surprised. Shining means taking risks, right?

[*Lights down on Light Chamber, up on café. Sara walks down to counter.*]

Mike: Sara, are you okay? They came down pretty hard on you [*whispering*].
Sara: Yeah, [*taking a deep breath*] I just have something I need to ask those girls.

Mike: Well, good luck.

Sara: [*walks over to couch where girls are looking at dresses they bought*] Hi, my church is having this cool event. Want to come?

[*Stop video.*]

POST-TEACH
(5 MINUTES)

Teacher: That is how I dream for you to be—confident in who you are as a believer by standing on what God says in His Word, and then making choices that will allow you to shine and help your friends come to know God. This lesson is so important for you, especially as you go on into junior high and high school. If you can get this, if you can truly get your confidence in what God says, then you can really be the person God wants you to be. It will change your whole life. You won't have to build your confidence any longer on the way you look, how different you are, or how other people view you, because you are confident that God loves you and you belong to Him. You can be free to shine.

PRAYER

Dear God,
Thank You for loving us unconditionally and making us Your children. Help us to build our confidence on these promises and shine our light for the dark world. Amen.

MUSIC

Song suggestion:
"Learnin' To Shine" (*Doing Life with God in the Picture* CD)

Note: The lyrics on the CD jacket for this song are incorrect. Please see www.PromiselandOnline.com for correct lyrics.

[*Dismiss to Small Groups. Play music as children exit.*]

UNIT 2: LEARNING TO SHINE
UNWHOLESOME TALK

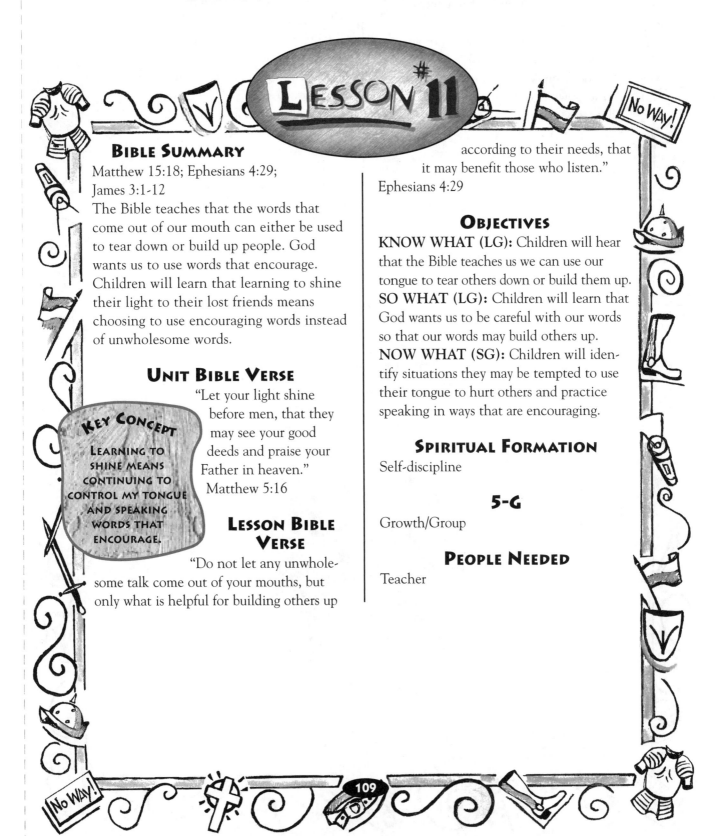

BIBLE SUMMARY

Matthew 15:18; Ephesians 4:29;
James 3:1-12
The Bible teaches that the words that come out of our mouth can either be used to tear down or build up people. God wants us to use words that encourage. Children will learn that learning to shine their light to their lost friends means choosing to use encouraging words instead of unwholesome words.

UNIT BIBLE VERSE

"Let your light shine before men, that they may see your good deeds and praise your Father in heaven."
Matthew 5:16

KEY CONCEPT

LEARNING TO SHINE MEANS CONTINUING TO CONTROL MY TONGUE AND SPEAKING WORDS THAT ENCOURAGE.

LESSON BIBLE VERSE

"Do not let any unwholesome talk come out of your mouths, but only what is helpful for building others up according to their needs, that it may benefit those who listen."
Ephesians 4:29

OBJECTIVES

KNOW WHAT (LG): Children will hear that the Bible teaches us we can use our tongue to tear others down or build them up.
SO WHAT (LG): Children will learn that God wants us to be careful with our words so that our words may build others up.
NOW WHAT (SG): Children will identify situations they may be tempted to use their tongue to hurt others and practice speaking in ways that are encouraging.

SPIRITUAL FORMATION

Self-discipline

5-G

Growth/Group

PEOPLE NEEDED

Teacher

SUPPLIES

○ Learning to Shine unit sign (from Lesson 8)
○ Music for transitions and singing
○ CD player
○ Unit Bible Verse sign (use the Bible Verse sign from Lesson 8)
○ Lesson Bible Verse sign
○ Tear-Down Words sign
○ Sarcasm sign
○ Gossip sign
○ Swearing/Bad Language sign
○ *Learning to Shine* video
○ TV/VCR

○ Optional: *Doing Life with God in the Picture CD*

IN ADVANCE

• Determine which songs you will use and be prepared to lead or teach them.
• Rehearse the teaching time.
• Gather props and set teaching area.
• Prepare Lesson Bible Verse sign.
• Prepare signs as follows:
  * Tear-Down Words
  * Sarcasm
  * Gossip
  * Swearing/Bad Language
• Cue *Learning to Shine* video to Lesson 11.

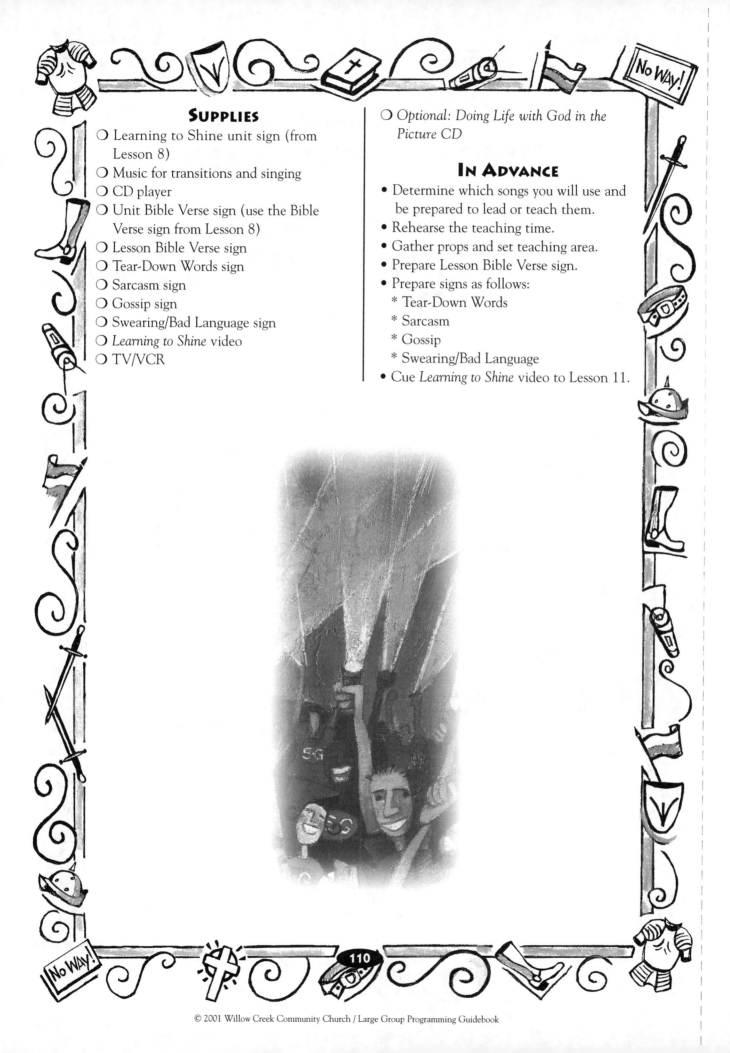

Pre-Teach
(5 minutes)

[Play upbeat music as children arrive.]

Teacher: Welcome everyone! Today we are continuing our unit Learning to Shine. We have learned over the past few weeks that believers have the light of Jesus inside of them and are the light of the world. God tells us, as His followers, what we are to do with our light. The Bible says:

[Show Unit Bible Verse sign.] "Let your light shine before men, that they may see your good deeds and praise your Father in heaven." Matthew 5:16

How do we, as Jesus' followers, shine that light? (By living life the way Jesus teaches in the Bible.) Why is it important to shine?

(Our friends live in a dark world of sin. Our light helps them come to know God.)

We have been learning that sometimes we face obstacles that keep us from shining. The first week we learned that we need to overcome the obstacle of fear. The second week we learned that we need to overcome the obstacle of having our actions not match our faith. We must put our faith into action by becoming Everyday Christians. Finally, last week we learned that building our confidence on things other than God's promises can be an obstacle to shining. Knowing God loves us and we belong in His family can give us the confidence we need to shine.

111

TEACH
(20 MINUTES)

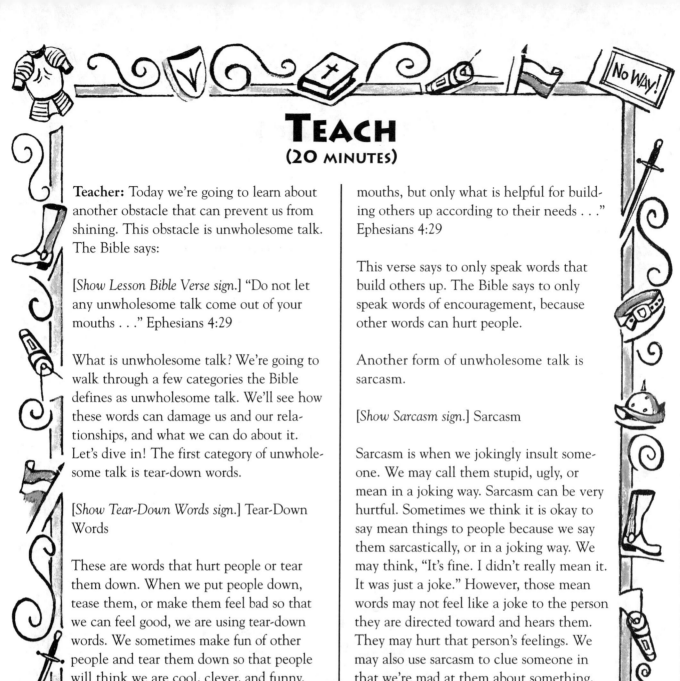

Teacher: Today we're going to learn about another obstacle that can prevent us from shining. This obstacle is unwholesome talk. The Bible says:

[*Show Lesson Bible Verse sign.*] "Do not let any unwholesome talk come out of your mouths . . ." Ephesians 4:29

What is unwholesome talk? We're going to walk through a few categories the Bible defines as unwholesome talk. We'll see how these words can damage us and our relationships, and what we can do about it. Let's dive in! The first category of unwholesome talk is tear-down words.

[*Show Tear-Down Words sign.*] Tear-Down Words

These are words that hurt people or tear them down. When we put people down, tease them, or make them feel bad so that we can feel good, we are using tear-down words. We sometimes make fun of other people and tear them down so that people will think we are cool, clever, and funny. Sometimes we tear our teachers down when they ask us a question and we purposely answer the question wrong so that our friends will think we're cool and funny. The Bible says that when we tear someone down like that, we speak in an unwholesome way. The Bible verse goes on to say:

[*Show Lesson Bible Verse sign.*] "Do not let any unwholesome talk come out of your

mouths, but only what is helpful for building others up according to their needs . . ." Ephesians 4:29

This verse says to only speak words that build others up. The Bible says to only speak words of encouragement, because other words can hurt people.

Another form of unwholesome talk is sarcasm.

[*Show Sarcasm sign.*] Sarcasm

Sarcasm is when we jokingly insult someone. We may call them stupid, ugly, or mean in a joking way. Sarcasm can be very hurtful. Sometimes we think it is okay to say mean things to people because we say them sarcastically, or in a joking way. We may think, "It's fine. I didn't really mean it. It was just a joke." However, those mean words may not feel like a joke to the person they are directed toward and hears them. They may hurt that person's feelings. We may also use sarcasm to clue someone in that we're mad at them about something, but we're too scared to say it. So, instead we say it sarcastically.

These forms of unwholesome talk can be very damaging to us and our relationships. These can be obstacles to us shining our light. When we use unwholesome talk, we are not shining or helping people come to know God. That is why God commands us not to speak in an unwholesome way. Take a look at this drama where two Christian friends at the Lighthouse Café experience conflict. Watch for the real reason why Brandon gets upset. See how tear-down words and sarcasm take a little conflict and rip apart a friendship.

[*Play Learning to Shine video, Lesson 11, Part 1. The following script is provided for your use if you choose to do the drama live or if you would like to read through the script. The script may be slightly different due to video scripting.*]

Scene opens with Brandon at the table talking on a cell phone.

Brandon: No way. She likes him?! I can't believe that! [*Sees Sara running into the café.*]

Oh, she's finally coming. I have to go. Bye.

[*Sara comes running in with her arms full of supplies.*]

Sara: Hey Brandon, sorry I'm late. I was talking to Jessica on the phone and just lost track of time.

Brandon: [*sarcastically*] That's okay, I only left soccer practice early so I could sit and wait twenty minutes for you to come.

Sara: Well, I'm here now. Let's do this project thing.

Brandon: [*starts looking through her supplies*] Where's the foam board?

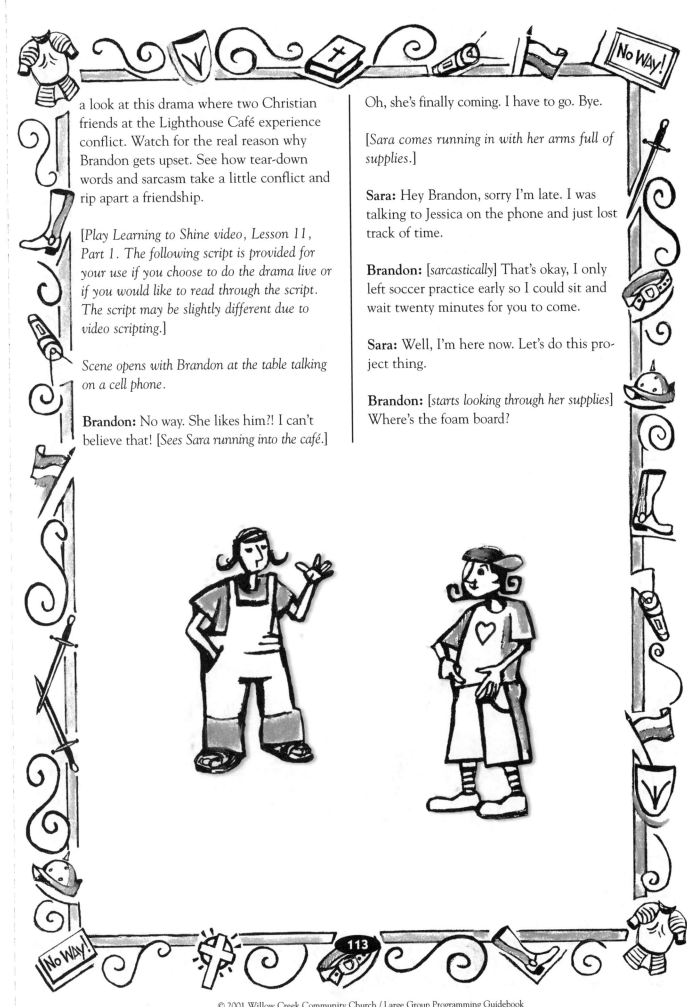

Sara: What foam board?

Brandon: The board we're going to build our entire Social Studies project on.

Sara: Oh, I'm sorry, I totally spaced it.

Brandon: [*sighs*] Just get it tonight. We have two days to finish this project. We're running out of time.

Sara: Okay. [*Muttering to herself.*] Someone woke up on the wrong side of the bed this morning.

Brandon: [*muttering sarcastically back*] Well at least I woke up on time. Just let me see the article we found on the Internet. I want to take notes on it.

Sara: Yeah, it's right . . . [*looks through backpack*] umm . . .

Brandon: Let me guess, "you spaced it."

Sara: I think I left it on the printer.

Brandon: [*gets up angrily*] That's great, just great.

Sara: I'm sorry.

Brandon: This is the second time we have met to work on this project and you've been late and now you've forgotten stuff.

Sara: Don't freak out Brandon. It's just a Social Studies project.

Brandon: I need a good grade on this and you don't seem to care.

Sara: Look, I'll bring everything tomorrow. I promise.

114

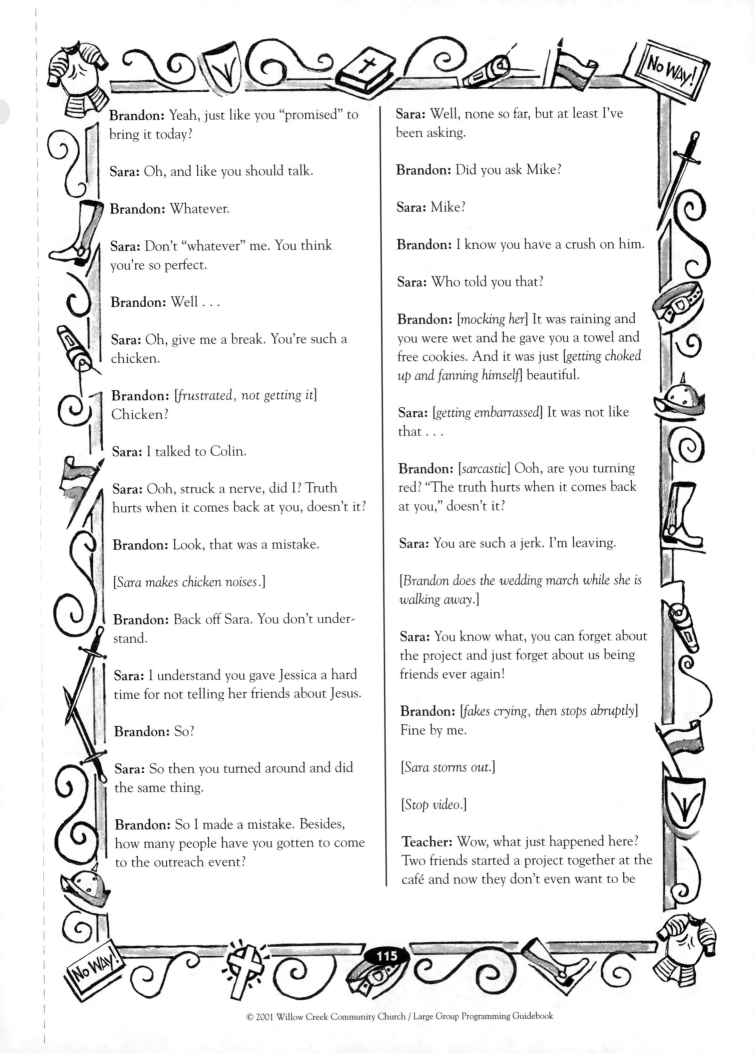

Brandon: Yeah, just like you "promised" to bring it today?

Sara: Oh, and like you should talk.

Brandon: Whatever.

Sara: Don't "whatever" me. You think you're so perfect.

Brandon: Well . . .

Sara: Oh, give me a break. You're such a chicken.

Brandon: [*frustrated, not getting it*] Chicken?

Sara: I talked to Colin.

Sara: Ooh, struck a nerve, did I? Truth hurts when it comes back at you, doesn't it?

Brandon: Look, that was a mistake.

[*Sara makes chicken noises.*]

Brandon: Back off Sara. You don't understand.

Sara: I understand you gave Jessica a hard time for not telling her friends about Jesus.

Brandon: So?

Sara: So then you turned around and did the same thing.

Brandon: So I made a mistake. Besides, how many people have you gotten to come to the outreach event?

Sara: Well, none so far, but at least I've been asking.

Brandon: Did you ask Mike?

Sara: Mike?

Brandon: I know you have a crush on him.

Sara: Who told you that?

Brandon: [*mocking her*] It was raining and you were wet and he gave you a towel and free cookies. And it was just [*getting choked up and fanning himself*] beautiful.

Sara: [*getting embarrassed*] It was not like that . . .

Brandon: [*sarcastic*] Ooh, are you turning red? "The truth hurts when it comes back at you," doesn't it?

Sara: You are such a jerk. I'm leaving.

[*Brandon does the wedding march while she is walking away.*]

Sara: You know what, you can forget about the project and just forget about us being friends ever again!

Brandon: [*fakes crying, then stops abruptly*] Fine by me.

[*Sara storms out.*]

[*Stop video.*]

Teacher: Wow, what just happened here? Two friends started a project together at the café and now they don't even want to be

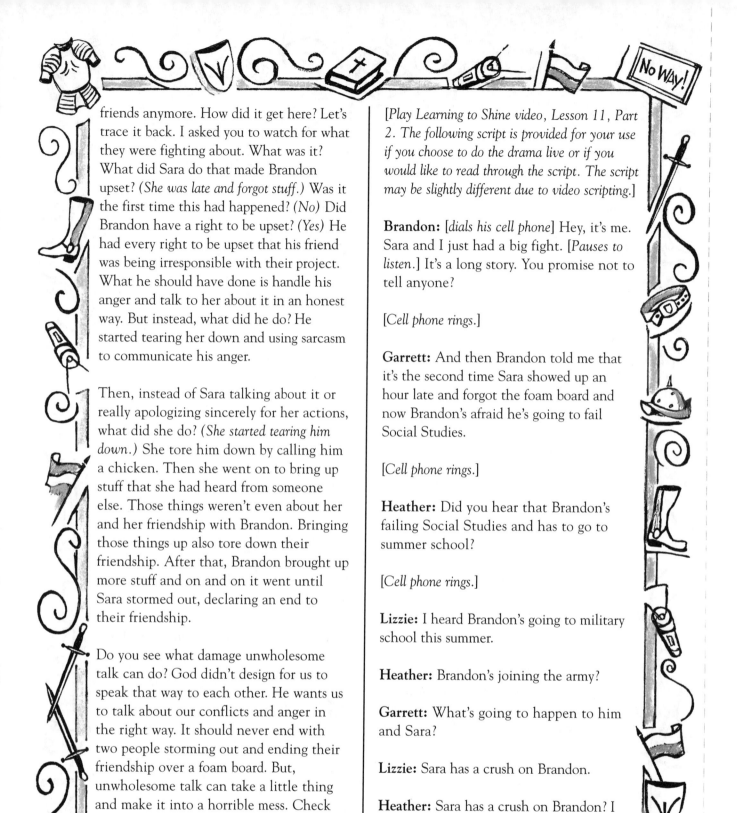

friends anymore. How did it get here? Let's trace it back. I asked you to watch for what they were fighting about. What was it? What did Sara do that made Brandon upset? (*She was late and forgot stuff.*) Was it the first time this had happened? (*No*) Did Brandon have a right to be upset? (*Yes*) He had every right to be upset that his friend was being irresponsible with their project. What he should have done is handle his anger and talk to her about it in an honest way. But instead, what did he do? He started tearing her down and using sarcasm to communicate his anger.

Then, instead of Sara talking about it or really apologizing sincerely for her actions, what did she do? (*She started tearing him down.*) She tore him down by calling him a chicken. Then she went on to bring up stuff that she had heard from someone else. Those things weren't even about her and her friendship with Brandon. Bringing those things up also tore down their friendship. After that, Brandon brought up more stuff and on and on it went until Sara stormed out, declaring an end to their friendship.

Do you see what damage unwholesome talk can do? God didn't design for us to speak that way to each other. He wants us to talk about our conflicts and anger in the right way. It should never end with two people storming out and ending their friendship over a foam board. But, unwholesome talk can take a little thing and make it into a horrible mess. Check out what can happen when gossip gets added into an already bad situation.

[Play Learning to Shine video, Lesson 11, Part 2. The following script is provided for your use if you choose to do the drama live or if you would like to read through the script. The script may be slightly different due to video scripting.]

Brandon: [*dials his cell phone*] Hey, it's me. Sara and I just had a big fight. [*Pauses to listen.*] It's a long story. You promise not to tell anyone?

[Cell phone rings.]

Garrett: And then Brandon told me that it's the second time Sara showed up an hour late and forgot the foam board and now Brandon's afraid he's going to fail Social Studies.

[Cell phone rings.]

Heather: Did you hear that Brandon's failing Social Studies and has to go to summer school?

[Cell phone rings.]

Lizzie: I heard Brandon's going to military school this summer.

Heather: Brandon's joining the army?

Garrett: What's going to happen to him and Sara?

Lizzie: Sara has a crush on Brandon.

Heather: Sara has a crush on Brandon? I thought Sara had a crush on Mike.

Garrett: I thought Sara had a crush on me!

Girls: Dreamer.

Heather: Did you hear that Brandon sang the wedding song to Sara?

Garrett: No way!

Lizzie: No way! Did you hear that Brandon proposed to Sara?

Garrett: Yeah, in the rain with a foam board.

Heather: Mike showed up with a towel and chocolate chip cookies.

Lizzie: But Sara got mad and called him a turkey.

Garrett: So Mike said "Fine by me" and left crying.

Heather: Mike said, "marry me" and was crying?

Lizzie: Did you hear that Sara's going to marry Mike?

Garrett: I thought Sara was going to marry me?

[*Stop video.*]

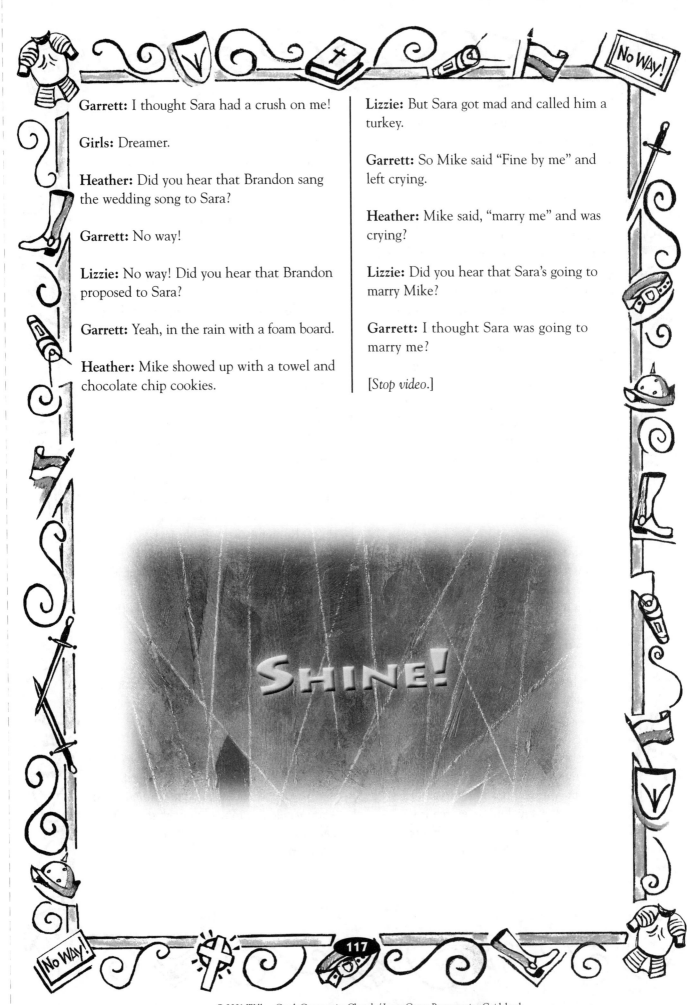

SHINE!

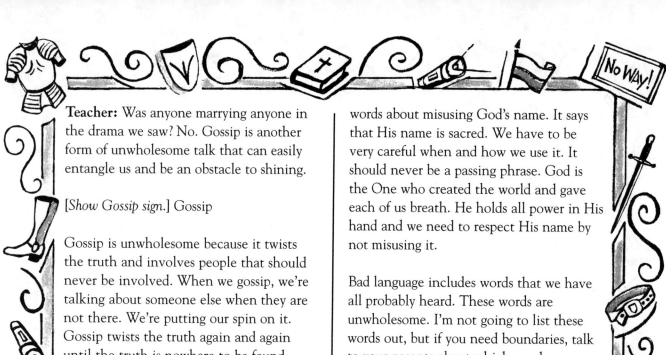

Teacher: Was anyone marrying anyone in the drama we saw? No. Gossip is another form of unwholesome talk that can easily entangle us and be an obstacle to shining.

[*Show Gossip sign.*] Gossip

Gossip is unwholesome because it twists the truth and involves people that should never be involved. When we gossip, we're talking about someone else when they are not there. We're putting our spin on it. Gossip twists the truth again and again until the truth is nowhere to be found. When we make a habit of gossiping, we don't become trustworthy friends. We share secrets with people who shouldn't know them. Gossip does not help us shine. It hurts our reputation and damages the truth of what really happened.

[*Show Swearing/Bad Language sign.*] Swearing/Bad Language

The last category of unwholesome talk is swearing/bad language. This is an especially difficult obstacle to overcome because we live in a world where we are bombarded with these words all of the time. They get stuck in our brains and come out sometimes when we get really angry, before we even know what we're saying. Sometimes we swear, which means to misuse God's name, just because we don't think about it. The phrase "Oh my God" is used almost as often as the words "the" or "and" in the world right now. I bet there are some of you in this room who say that phrase all of the time and probably don't even realize you're saying it because it becomes such a part of your language. The Bible has very strong words about misusing God's name. It says that His name is sacred. We have to be very careful when and how we use it. It should never be a passing phrase. God is the One who created the world and gave each of us breath. He holds all power in His hand and we need to respect His name by not misusing it.

Bad language includes words that we have all probably heard. These words are unwholesome. I'm not going to list these words out, but if you need boundaries, talk to your parents about which words are wholesome and unwholesome. A lot of times we say these words because we're really angry and they seem satisfying to say to express our anger. However, these are words that God doesn't want us to use. They are words that are used often in the dark world. God wants us to be different. He wants us to shine by using wholesome words, ones that encourage others who hear them. Remember the Bible says:

[*Show Lesson Bible Verse sign.*] "Do not let any unwholesome talk come out of your mouths, but only what is helpful for building others up according to their needs, that it may benefit those who listen." Ephesians 4:29

Let's see if Brandon and Sara ever worked their conflict out and got their tongues under control.

[*Play Learning to Shine video, Lesson 11, Part 3. The following script is provided for your use if you choose to do the drama live or if you would like to read through the script. The script may be slightly different due to video scripting.*]

118

Brandon and Sara are together.

Brandon: This whole thing got blown way out of proportion.

Sara: Way out.

Brandon: Our words got out of control.

Sara: And messed with our friendship.

Brandon: Yeah, don't do that.

Sara: Yeah, don't. Brandon had every right to be mad at me.

Brandon: Yeah, and I shouldn't have gotten so ticked off.

Sara: And I shouldn't have called you a chicken.

Sara: Anyway, we worked it out.

Brandon: And now we're good.

Sara: Yeah, it's all good.

[*Cell phone rings.*]

Brandon: Hello? [*Pauses.*] What? Sara, why didn't you tell me you and Garrett are getting married?

[*Stop video.*]

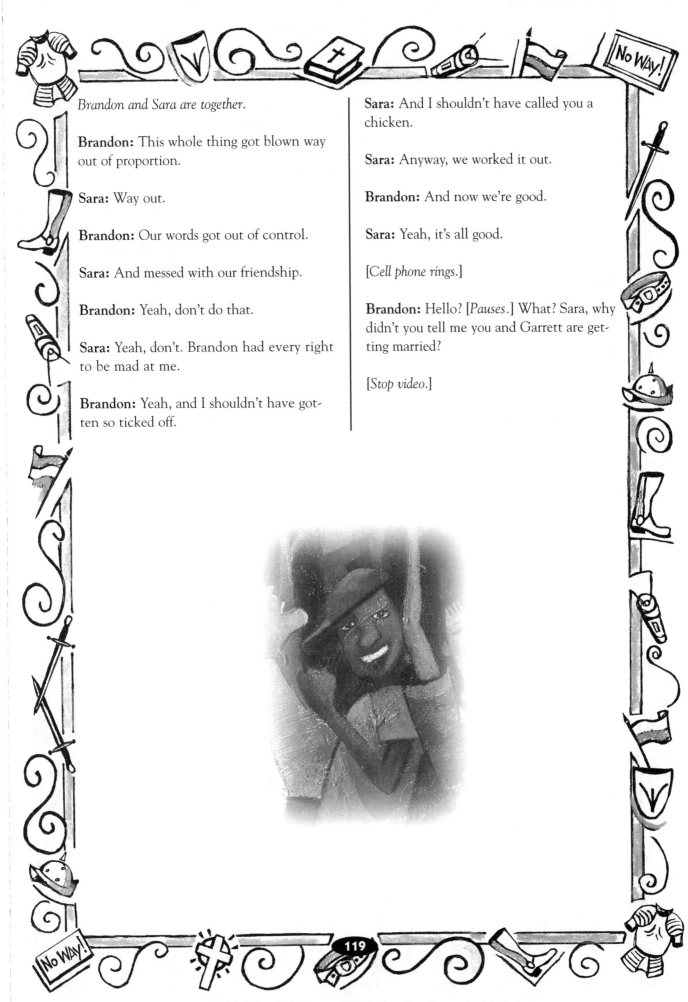

POST-TEACH
(5 MINUTES)

Teacher: If we are going to learn to shine, we are going to need to control our tongues. Stick out your tongues, everybody.

[Have everyone stick out their tongues and repeat phrases in the following teaching where indicated.]

We need to get control of our tongues. We need to learn how to think before we speak. Say these phrases with me with your tongues out: "I need to think before I speak."

[Have kids say it with their tongue out. Say it with them as well.]

Good. Okay, now let's say this together: "I only need to speak words that encourage."

[Say it together.]

"No sarcasm."

[Say it together.]

"No gossip."

[Say it together.]

"No swearing."

[Say it together.]

"No bad language."

[Say it together.]

These phrases are reminders to help us control our tongues. The way we use our words can help us shine or stop us from shining. Let's learn how to zip it sometimes and instead say encouraging words. **LEARNING TO SHINE MEANS CONTINUING TO CONTROL MY TONGUE AND SPEAKING WORDS THAT ENCOURAGE.** Let's stick out our tongues one more time and say, "I'll learn to zip it!"

[Have kids say it with their tongues out.]

Good. Let's pray and ask God to help us.

PRAYER

Dear God,
Please help us control our tongues and learn how to speak encouraging words to one another. Help us shine our light through the words we use so our lost friends will come to know You. Amen.

MUSIC

Song suggestion:
"Learnin' To Shine" (*Doing Life with God in the Picture* CD)

Note: The lyrics on the CD jacket for this song are incorrect. Please see www.PromiselandOnline.com for correct lyrics.

[Dismiss to Small Groups. Play music as children exit.]

120

Unit 2: Learning to Shine
Joy No Matter What

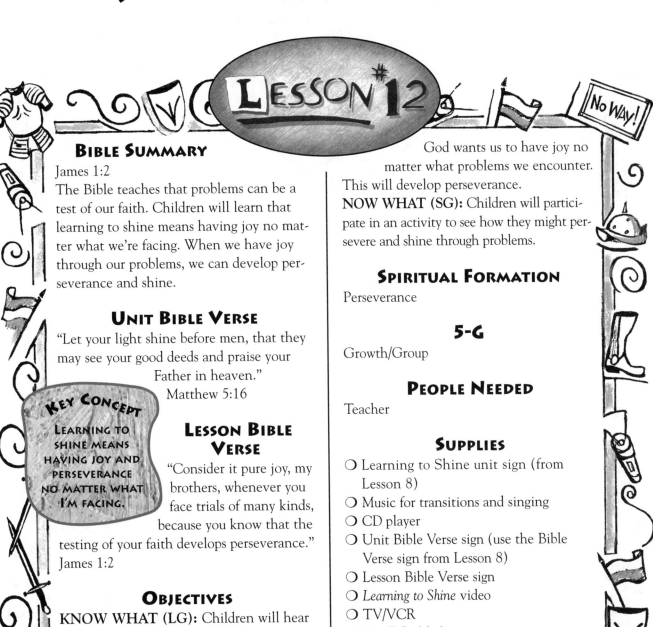

Lesson #12

Bible Summary

James 1:2
The Bible teaches that problems can be a test of our faith. Children will learn that learning to shine means having joy no matter what we're facing. When we have joy through our problems, we can develop perseverance and shine.

Unit Bible Verse

"Let your light shine before men, that they may see your good deeds and praise your Father in heaven."
Matthew 5:16

Key Concept
LEARNING TO SHINE MEANS HAVING JOY AND PERSEVERANCE NO MATTER WHAT I'M FACING.

Lesson Bible Verse

"Consider it pure joy, my brothers, whenever you face trials of many kinds, because you know that the testing of your faith develops perseverance."
James 1:2

Objectives

KNOW WHAT (LG): Children will hear that the Bible teaches that problems can be a test of our faith.
SO WHAT (LG): Children will learn that God wants us to have joy no matter what problems we encounter. This will develop perseverance.
NOW WHAT (SG): Children will participate in an activity to see how they might persevere and shine through problems.

Spiritual Formation

Perseverance

5-G

Growth/Group

People Needed

Teacher

Supplies

- ❍ Learning to Shine unit sign (from Lesson 8)
- ❍ Music for transitions and singing
- ❍ CD player
- ❍ Unit Bible Verse sign (use the Bible Verse sign from Lesson 8)
- ❍ Lesson Bible Verse sign
- ❍ *Learning to Shine* video
- ❍ TV/VCR
- ❍ Small flashlight
- ❍ *Optional: Doing Life with God in the Picture CD*

121

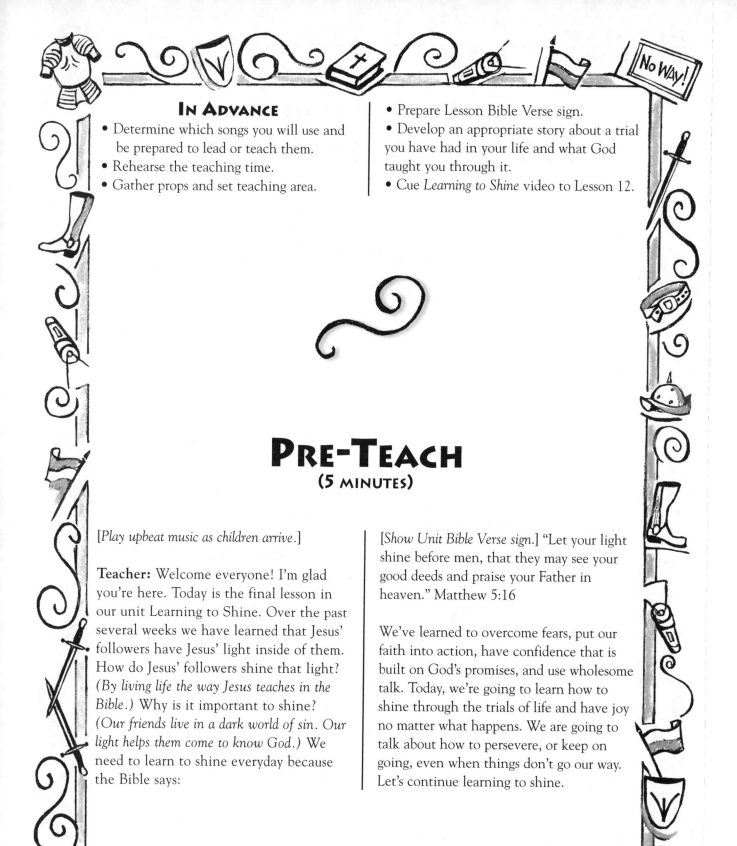

In Advance

- Determine which songs you will use and be prepared to lead or teach them.
- Rehearse the teaching time.
- Gather props and set teaching area.

- Prepare Lesson Bible Verse sign.
- Develop an appropriate story about a trial you have had in your life and what God taught you through it.
- Cue *Learning to Shine* video to Lesson 12.

Pre-Teach
(5 minutes)

[Play upbeat music as children arrive.]

Teacher: Welcome everyone! I'm glad you're here. Today is the final lesson in our unit Learning to Shine. Over the past several weeks we have learned that Jesus' followers have Jesus' light inside of them. How do Jesus' followers shine that light? *(By living life the way Jesus teaches in the Bible.)* Why is it important to shine? *(Our friends live in a dark world of sin. Our light helps them come to know God.)* We need to learn to shine everyday because the Bible says:

[Show Unit Bible Verse sign.] "Let your light shine before men, that they may see your good deeds and praise your Father in heaven." Matthew 5:16

We've learned to overcome fears, put our faith into action, have confidence that is built on God's promises, and use wholesome talk. Today, we're going to learn how to shine through the trials of life and have joy no matter what happens. We are going to talk about how to persevere, or keep on going, even when things don't go our way. Let's continue learning to shine.

TEACH
(20 MINUTES)

[Play Learning to Shine video, Lesson 12, Part 1. The following script is provided for your use if you choose to do the drama live or if you would like to read through the script. The script may be slightly different due to video scripting.]

The first scene opens with Sara and Jessica at the couch making a sign for the outreach event. Mike brings in cookies and drinks.

Mike: Here you are ladies—two lemonades and chocolate chip cookies. [*Puts them down and sees poster.*] What are you working on?

Jessica: A banner for the outreach tonight.

Sara: Yep, just putting on the finishing touches. Hand me that glitter glue.

Jessica: Will it dry fast enough?

Mike: What's an outreach?

Sara: It's this thing . . .

Jessica: You know, an event . . .

Sara: For our church . . .

Jessica: It's really cool, we have music . . .

Sara: And food . . .

Jessica: And we talk about God and what He means to us.

Mike: [*not sure*] Okay . . .

Sara: We've been planning it for weeks.

Jessica: Yeah, trying to invite as many of our friends to come check it out.

Sara: You should come.

Jessica: Yeah, what do you think? [*Holds up the banner*]

Mike: Looks great. I'll think about it.

Sara: Really? Here's a flyer. It has directions and stuff.

Mike: [*looking at flyer*] Oh, it's tonight?

Sara: We'd love for you to come.

Jessica: Yeah, that'd be great.

Mike: I'll see if I can get someone to cover the café [*walks back to the counter*].

[Brandon passes Mike on the way in.]

Mike: Hey Brandon, what's up?

Brandon: [*distracted*] Not much [*goes over to girls on the couch*].

Jessica: Brandon, what do you think? [*Shows him the banner.*]

Brandon: Forget about it.

Sara: Forget about what?

Brandon: I was just over at the church

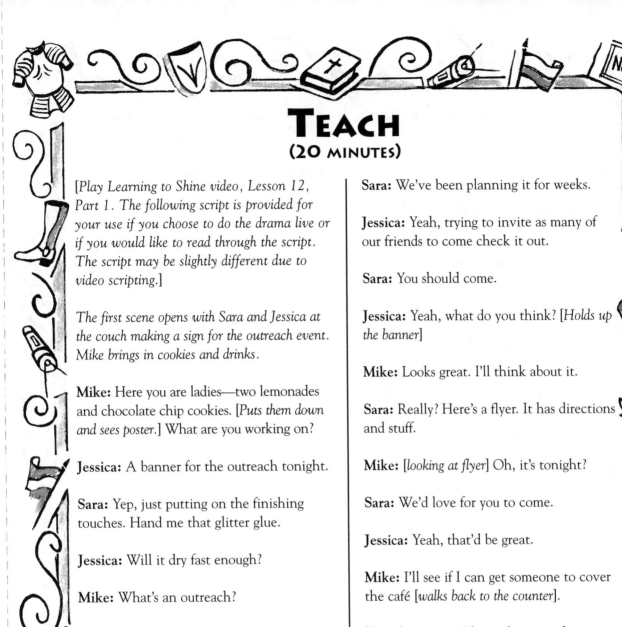

dropping off balloons with my mom. But they wouldn't let us in.

Sara: What?

Jessica: What are you talking about?

Brandon: Somehow the copy machine overheated last night and it caught on fire.

Jessica: No way.

Sara: Was anybody in there?

Brandon: Just the janitor who smelled the smoke and called the fire department. By the time they got there, the whole basement was destroyed.

Jessica: Is the rest of the church okay?

Brandon: Yeah, but there was so much smoke that they've closed the building until they can clean it out.

Jessica: Closed the building?!

Sara: Can't we just go clean it up?

Brandon: No, it's going to take weeks and they're going to get some professionals to do it.

Sara: What about tonight?

Brandon: I guess we're going to have to cancel it.

[*Silence, they all sit down.*]

Sara: This is crazy! How does a copier catch on fire? It doesn't make sense.

[*Jessica gets up and starts pacing.*]

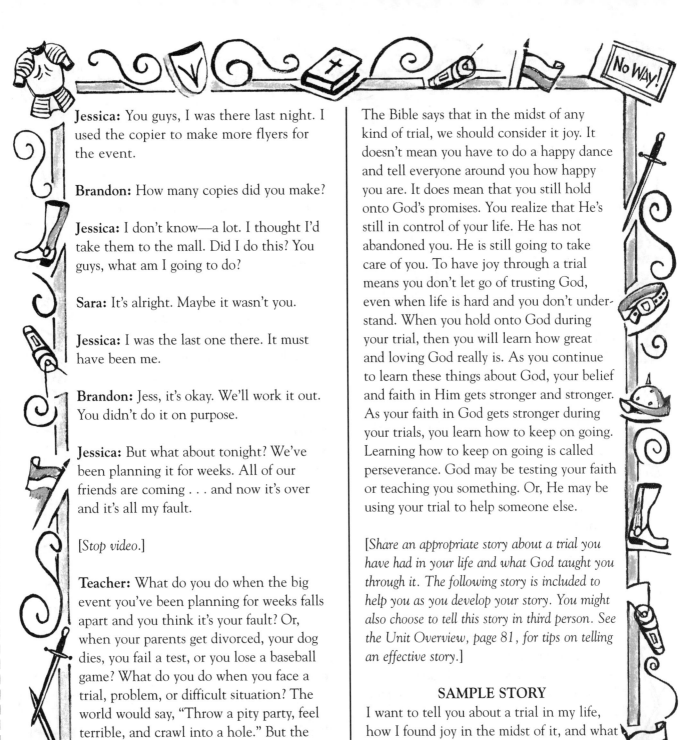

Jessica: You guys, I was there last night. I used the copier to make more flyers for the event.

Brandon: How many copies did you make?

Jessica: I don't know—a lot. I thought I'd take them to the mall. Did I do this? You guys, what am I going to do?

Sara: It's alright. Maybe it wasn't you.

Jessica: I was the last one there. It must have been me.

Brandon: Jess, it's okay. We'll work it out. You didn't do it on purpose.

Jessica: But what about tonight? We've been planning it for weeks. All of our friends are coming . . . and now it's over and it's all my fault.

[*Stop video.*]

Teacher: What do you do when the big event you've been planning for weeks falls apart and you think it's your fault? Or, when your parents get divorced, your dog dies, you fail a test, or you lose a baseball game? What do you do when you face a trial, problem, or difficult situation? The world would say, "Throw a pity party, feel terrible, and crawl into a hole." But the Bible has a different way than the world. The Bible says:

[*Show Lesson Bible Verse sign.*] "Consider it pure joy, my brothers, whenever you face trials of many kinds, because you know that the testing of your faith develops perseverance." James 1:2

The Bible says that in the midst of any kind of trial, we should consider it joy. It doesn't mean you have to do a happy dance and tell everyone around you how happy you are. It does mean that you still hold onto God's promises. You realize that He's still in control of your life. He has not abandoned you. He is still going to take care of you. To have joy through a trial means you don't let go of trusting God, even when life is hard and you don't understand. When you hold onto God during your trial, then you will learn how great and loving God really is. As you continue to learn these things about God, your belief and faith in Him gets stronger and stronger. As your faith in God gets stronger during your trials, you learn how to keep on going. Learning how to keep on going is called perseverance. God may be testing your faith or teaching you something. Or, He may be using your trial to help someone else.

[*Share an appropriate story about a trial you have had in your life and what God taught you through it. The following story is included to help you as you develop your story. You might also choose to tell this story in third person. See the Unit Overview, page 81, for tips on telling an effective story.*]

SAMPLE STORY

I want to tell you about a trial in my life, how I found joy in the midst of it, and what God did through my trial. It's hard to talk about, but I want to share it with you so that maybe it can help you.

Last summer, in June, I went to my doctor for a sore throat and while doing a checkup, she felt something near my stomach. After x-rays and seeing another doctor,

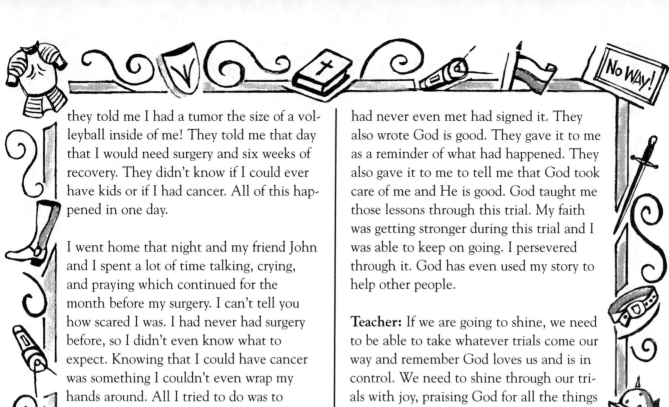

they told me I had a tumor the size of a volleyball inside of me! They told me that day that I would need surgery and six weeks of recovery. They didn't know if I could ever have kids or if I had cancer. All of this happened in one day.

I went home that night and my friend John and I spent a lot of time talking, crying, and praying which continued for the month before my surgery. I can't tell you how scared I was. I had never had surgery before, so I didn't even know what to expect. Knowing that I could have cancer was something I couldn't even wrap my hands around. All I tried to do was to remember that God was in control, He promised to take care of me, and prayer works. A lot of people were praying on July 10th when I went to have the surgery. It was pretty difficult because there were complications and I had to stay five days in the hospital. As it turns out, there was no cancer. Six weeks later I was back to normal besides having a scar.

That was the biggest trial of my life. I want to tell you what God did for me during that time. The last year or so before the surgery, I was struggling with thinking that no one besides my family really cared about me. While I was in the hospital and after I got out, I was flooded with flowers, cards, toys, and visits. I was blown away by one card in particular. It said, "You are loved more than you'll ever know." It was amazing! People I barely knew were calling me, writing me, and encouraging me not to lose faith. They told me they were praying and I was loved. My favorite gift, one that sits in my living room is a volleyball. Some people I didn't know very well all signed it—some people I

had never even met had signed it. They also wrote God is good. They gave it to me as a reminder of what had happened. They also gave it to me to tell me that God took care of me and He is good. God taught me those lessons through this trial. My faith was getting stronger during this trial and I was able to keep on going. I persevered through it. God has even used my story to help other people.

Teacher: If we are going to shine, we need to be able to take whatever trials come our way and remember God loves us and is in control. We need to shine through our trials with joy, praising God for all the things He has done for us, and for all the things that He is. God's promises never change even when our life circumstances do. We can be sad, feel hurt, and be confused. However, we can still have joy as our faith develops and we persevere.

I want to take you back to the Lighthouse Café where our friends are going through their own trial. Put yourself in their shoes. They have all of their non-Christian friends coming to this big event and now it's ruined. On top of that, Jessica thinks it's her fault. Will they find joy through their trial? Let's watch and see.

[*Play Learning to Shine video, Lesson 12, Part 2.*]

Sara: What are we going to do?

Brandon: I don't know. Maybe we do it another night, but my mom's outside waiting in the car.

Mike: [*he's been listening*] Hey, I don't know

if it'll help, but you can have it here tonight if you want.

Sara: At the café?

Brandon: [*figuring it out*] I don't know if there's enough room.

Mike: You can set up your band over there.

Sara: That's not a bad idea.

Brandon: I don't know. How are we going to tell everyone?

Sara: Listen, this is what we're going to do [*taking charge*]. I'll make signs to put up on the church doors directing everyone here. Brandon, you go get the decorations out of the car and call the band to have them come here.

Mike: I can help you with food or whatever you need.

Sara: Thanks Mike.

Mike: I'm glad I could help.

Sara: Oh, I should call Logan and tell him what we're doing.

Jessica: No Sara, I'll do it. I think I want to call Logan. He's our Small Group Leader, and I think I need to tell him what happened.

Sara: Okay Jess [*on her way out*]. Hey Brandon, do you think your mom can take the signs over to the church?

Jessica: Mike, may I use your phone?

Mike: Sure, here.

Jessica: [*Jessica dials.*] Hello, Logan?

[*Music plays. Kids reenter to set up.*]

Jessica: Hey, people are coming.

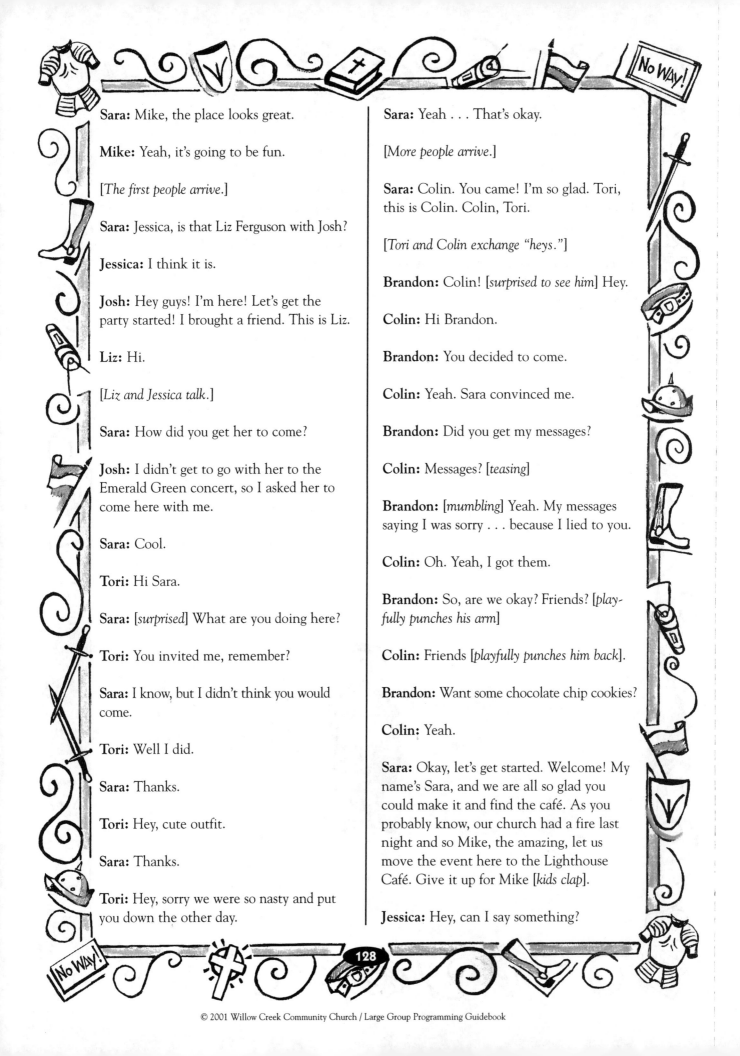

Sara: Mike, the place looks great.

Mike: Yeah, it's going to be fun.

[*The first people arrive.*]

Sara: Jessica, is that Liz Ferguson with Josh?

Jessica: I think it is.

Josh: Hey guys! I'm here! Let's get the party started! I brought a friend. This is Liz.

Liz: Hi.

[*Liz and Jessica talk.*]

Sara: How did you get her to come?

Josh: I didn't get to go with her to the Emerald Green concert, so I asked her to come here with me.

Sara: Cool.

Tori: Hi Sara.

Sara: [*surprised*] What are you doing here?

Tori: You invited me, remember?

Sara: I know, but I didn't think you would come.

Tori: Well I did.

Sara: Thanks.

Tori: Hey, cute outfit.

Sara: Thanks.

Tori: Hey, sorry we were so nasty and put you down the other day.

Sara: Yeah . . . That's okay.

[*More people arrive.*]

Sara: Colin. You came! I'm so glad. Tori, this is Colin. Colin, Tori.

[*Tori and Colin exchange "heys."*]

Brandon: Colin! [*surprised to see him*] Hey.

Colin: Hi Brandon.

Brandon: You decided to come.

Colin: Yeah. Sara convinced me.

Brandon: Did you get my messages?

Colin: Messages? [*teasing*]

Brandon: [*mumbling*] Yeah. My messages saying I was sorry . . . because I lied to you.

Colin: Oh. Yeah, I got them.

Brandon: So, are we okay? Friends? [*playfully punches his arm*]

Colin: Friends [*playfully punches him back*].

Brandon: Want some chocolate chip cookies?

Colin: Yeah.

Sara: Okay, let's get started. Welcome! My name's Sara, and we are all so glad you could make it and find the café. As you probably know, our church had a fire last night and so Mike, the amazing, let us move the event here to the Lighthouse Café. Give it up for Mike [*kids clap*].

Jessica: Hey, can I say something?

Sara: Sure. Everyone, this is Jessica.

Jessica: Hey everyone. I just have to say that this could have been the worst day of my life. This event almost didn't happen because of me.

Sara: [*interupts*] No, come on.

Jessica: [*finding her words*] But I'm really thankful that God put people in my life like Sara who organized everything and Brandon who was there to help and Mike [*says to him*] you gave us this place! I also want to say thanks to everyone for coming and let's have fun tonight!

[*Stop video.*]

Teacher: That is joy no matter what. Jessica faced a difficult situation, but she remembered the big picture, found joy, and persevered. To persevere means to not give up. We need to not give up shining our lights, no matter what happens to us. We need to still be Everyday Christians who shine with confidence and speak whole-some words. When you continue to shine, it affects the people around you. People come to know God. Colin and Tori, who don't know God, may want to know more about God because of their friends. Sometimes you will know who's affected by your light and sometimes, you will have no idea the impact you have had on someone.

[*Play Learning to Shine video, Lesson 12, Part 3.*]

Mike: These kids are thanking me because I let them use the café for their event, but I should be thanking them. They've been changing my life. It really started when Josh handed me my tip money when he could have stolen it to buy his concert tickets. I couldn't believe he did that! And then Sara, just when these girls were ripping on her, turns around and invites them to her church. I would never have done that. That took guts. And then tonight. Wow, they've got something—something different—something I want for me.

[*Stop video.*]

POST-TEACH
(5 MINUTES)

Teacher: For those of you that have been here each week in this unit, you've seen Mike. Did you think that he would be the one most affected by the light of that group? That's what is so cool about God. He is working on all sorts of levels—some you will know and others you may not know until you get to heaven. If you shine and persevere no matter what, you can be sure that God will use you to change the world.

[*Have Small Group Leaders give a small flashlight to each child in their group.*]

I want to give you a visual picture of what your perseverance and shining can do.

[*Turn off all of the lights. Hold up your small flashlight.*]

I have one light and I am going to turn my light on because I shined the light of Jesus and became friends with you.

[*Walk over to one child.*]

Because I shined my light, you were changed. You decided to become a Christian and shine your light.

[*Touch the child's flashlight with your flashlight.*]

I then do the same to you [*pick another child and touch his/her flashlight*]. Now three of us are shining. Here's what I want you to do. You two pick two more people and touch their lights. When someone whose light is on touches your flashlight, turn your flashlight on and touch two more people's flashlights. Go ahead and start.

[*As they are doing this, encourage them by saying the following until all lights are lit.*]

See what can happen when you shine your one light in the dark world? God uses you to change people, then they help other people, and so on until everyone in this room has been changed and they are shining their lights.

This is why you and I need to persevere. No matter what happens in your life, no matter what the circumstances are, persevere so you can change the world. Remember why we shine—it's a dark world and our friends can come to know God through us. Take everything you've learned here and go out and shine! Let's praise God for all of the things He's been teaching us.

PRAYER

Dear God,
Thank You for teaching us to shine. Help us everyday to persevere no matter what and shine our light in the dark world. Amen.

MUSIC

Song suggestion:
"Learnin' To Shine" (*Doing Life with God in the Picture* CD)

Note: The lyrics on the CD jacket for this song are incorrect. Please see www.PromiselandOnline.com for correct lyrics.

[*Dismiss to Small Groups. Play music as children exit.*]

UNIT 2: LEARNING TO SHINE
5-G REVIEW AND SMALL GROUP CELEBRATION

LESSON #13

BIBLE SUMMARY

John 15:12

The Bible teaches that God wants us to be fully devoted followers of Christ and love one another. Children will hear a review of the 5-Gs: Grace, Growth, Group, Gifts, and Good Stewardship, and learn that these are five marks of someone growing in his or her relationship with Christ. In Small Group, kids will have an opportunity to love and care for one another by participating in a Small Group celebration.

KEY CONCEPT

DOING LIFE WITH GOD IN THE PICTURE MEANS BEING PART OF A COMMUNITY OF OTHER BELIEVERS.

BIBLE VERSE

"Love each other."
John 15:12

OBJECTIVES

KNOW WHAT (LG): Children will hear a review of the 5-Gs.

SO WHAT (LG): Children will learn that God has an overall plan for us. He wants us to be fully devoted followers of Christ.

NOW WHAT (SG): Children will review the 5-Gs and participate in a Small Group celebration where they will celebrate with their Small Groups all that God has done throughout this year.

SPIRITUAL FORMATION

Celebration

5-G

Grace/Growth/Group/Gifts/Good Stewardship

PEOPLE NEEDED

Teacher

SUPPLIES

- ❍ Music for transitions and singing
- ❍ CD player
- ❍ Large flashlight
- ❍ Globe
- ❍ Bible
- ❍ Tape measure
- ❍ Ball of string
- ❍ Two stuffed animals
- ❍ Wrapped present
- ❍ Puzzle piece used in Lessons 6-8 of the *5-G Impact* Winter Quarter curriculum
- ❍ Offering plate
- ❍ Five easels
- ❍ GRACE sign
- ❍ GROWTH sign
- ❍ GROUP sign
- ❍ GIFTS sign
- ❍ GOOD STEWARDSHIP sign

131

❍ Optional: *Doing Life with God in the Picture CD*
❍ Optional: *The Give-and-Smile Hunter Video from the 5-G Impact Winter Quarter curriculum*
　❍ Optional: *TV/VCR*

IN ADVANCE

• Determine which songs you will use and be prepared to lead or teach them.
• Rehearse the teaching time.
• Gather a puzzle piece used in Unit 2 of the Winter Quarter curriculum. If you have not saved any pieces from that unit, create a new puzzle piece by cutting out a design from foamcore.
• Prepare 5-G signs as follows:

* GRACE
* GROWTH
* GROUP
* GIFTS
* GOOD STEWARDSHIP

• Set up five stations around the room as indicated in the following. Place an easel at each station. A 5-G sign will be placed on the easel and props will be placed at the station.
Station 1: GRACE sign, globe, flashlight
Station 2: GROWTH sign, Bible, tape measure
Station 3: GROUP sign, ball of string, two stuffed animals
Station 4: GIFTS sign, wrapped present, puzzle piece
Station 5: GOOD STEWARDSHIP sign, offering plate
• *Optional: Cue The Give-and-Smile Hunter video, found in the Winter Quarter 5-G Impact Curriculum kit, to a clip desired.*

> **TEACHING TIP**
> IF YOU HAVE NOT USED THE WINTER QUARTER CURRICULUM, A SUGGESTION IS TO USE THE LARGE GROUP TIME FOR SINGING AND WORSHIP ONLY. PREPARATION, THEREFORE, WILL ONLY INVOLVE SELECTING MUSIC AND SETTING UP YOUR LARGE GROUP ROOM FOR WORSHIP AND SINGING.

PRE-TEACH
(5 MINUTES)

[*Play upbeat music as children arrive.*]

Teacher: Welcome everyone! If you don't know me, my name is [*your name*]. We have learned so much this year. We want to remember all that we have learned. As you look around the room, you can see a sign at each station.

[*Point to each sign.*]

We call these the 5-Gs: GRACE, GROWTH, GROUP, GIFTS, and GOOD STEWARDSHIP. These are the five marks of a fully devoted follower of Christ—someone who is growing in his or her friendship with Jesus and becoming more like Him. If you look around the room, you'll see a bunch of props. All of these props will remind us of the important things we have been learning all year about the 5-Gs.

TEACH
(10 MINUTES)

Station 1:
[*Walk to Station 1 and hold up the globe.*]

Teacher: What does this globe remind you of? (*Our world.*) We learned that our world is lost and separated from God by sin. The people in the world need to hear that God loves them and Jesus took the punishment for their sins. This is the message of Grace and God wants us to share Grace with our friends and family.

[*Hold up and shine the flashlight.*]

This dark and lost world is filled with people who don't know God and need to come to know Him. We, as believers, need to shine our lights so others can come to know God and begin to learn about GRACE. When you see a flashlight, remember God's grace for you and shine your light to others so they can know His love and grace as well. GRACE is the first G.

Station 2:
[*Walk to Station 2 and hold up the Bible and tape measure.*]

The Bible and tape measure remind you to follow God's truth and wisdom in the Bible, live God's way, and grow more like Jesus.

[*Open the Bible.*]

This Bible reminds us of all of the lessons that were based on the Bible—all of God's truths and how He wants us to live.

[*Pull some tape out from the tape measure.*]

This tape measure reminds us that the more we choose to read and study the Bible, the more we will GROW to be like Jesus. When you see a Bible and a tape measure, remember that when you read, study, and do what the Bible tells you, you can know how to live life best. You will grow in your understanding of who Jesus is and how to live life with Him. GROWTH is the second G.

Station 3:
[*Walk to Station 3 and hold up the ball of string. Choose four kids to come up from the audience and stand in a circle. Ask them to throw the string to one another so that each kid eventually is holding on to a piece of string.*]

This string reminds us of the many activities we did in our Small Groups. When we all held onto the string, like these kids are doing, we saw that the more we got to know each other, the more connected we became. Our community grew.

[*Have the kids return to their seats. Take out the two stuffed animals and pretend that they are having an argument.*]

These two stuffed animals remind us that sometimes community can break down. We need to go straight to each other and work out the conflict so we can continue to do life together with God. When you see a ball of string or a stuffed animal, remember how important doing life together with God is and how your Small Group can help you get closer to God. GROUP is the third G.

Station 4:

[*Walk to Station 4 and hold up the wrapped present and puzzle piece.*]

What do these two things remind you of from this year? (*The spiritual gifts we learned.*)

When you see a gift, remember that God has given unique gifts to each of us who are His followers. We have learned some of the spiritual gifts this year, like the gift of teaching, helps, and craftsmanship.

This puzzle piece reminds us that we need to spend time discovering the spiritual gifts God has given each of us and how we can use those gifts to serve the Church. Remember, if we are not discovering and using our gifts, there will be missing pieces in the Church. As you get older, continue to explore different ministries around our church to see what spiritual gifts you have. When you see a puzzle piece or gift, remember how important the spiritual gifts are that God has given you for serving the Church. GIFTS is the fourth G.

Station 5:

[*Walk to Station 5 and hold up the offering plate.*]

Optional: Play a clip from the Give-and Smile Hunter Video.

What does this remind you to do? (*Tithe, use good stewardship, give to the church, join the Giving Adventure.*)

When we see an offering plate, remember that God wants each of us who follow Him to give 10 percent of our money back to Him to use to help the church. The Bible calls this our tithe. We learned there are many places God uses our tithes to help the church and others. Giving our tithes is called Stewardship, being wise in what we do with what God has given us. It is definitely a Giving Adventure! When you see an offering plate, remember the importance of giving the tithe and how it helps the Church and others. GOOD STEWARDSHIP is the fifth and last G.

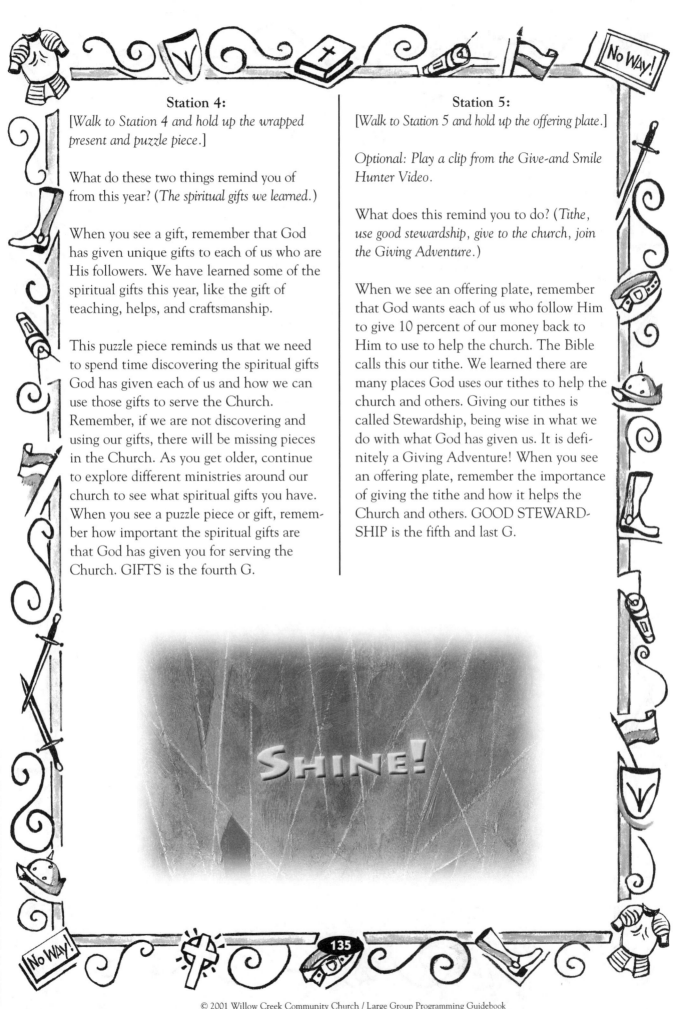

SHINE!

135

POST-TEACH
(5 MINUTES)

[*Point to each of the 5-G signs: Grace, Growth, Group, Gifts, and Good Stewardship.*]

Teacher: These are the 5-Gs and what we have been learning all year. These are marks of a fully devoted follower of Christ. Putting these into practice is how we do life with God in the picture. Living life with God in the picture is something to celebrate! Let's celebrate together with music and worship.

MUSIC

Song suggestions:
"Doin' Life Together" (*Doing Life with God in the Picture* CD)

"Learnin' To Shine" (*Doing Life with God in the Picture* CD)

Note: The lyrics on the CD jacket for this song are incorrect. Please see www.Promise-landOnline.com for correct lyrics.

PRAYER

Dear God,
Thank You for teaching us how to do life together with You. Thank You for loving us and creating each of us. Help us to continue putting the 5-Gs into practice.
Amen.

[*Dismiss to Small Groups. Play music as children exit.*]